"You know this is a million dollar deal you're messin' wit?" A six-foot-tall Rastafarian named Rohan stood on the terrace of his plush beach home. In the distance, palm trees and a never-ending blanket of sparkling blue beckoned the weary traveler, promising luxury and relaxation. The perfect getaway, the perfect escape.

"I know what I'm doing." The burly American sat in a chair on the terrace, thinking and re-thinking the plan that had been discussed. It would work, he knew it would. In six months he'd be safe in Negril, away from Baltimore, away from the accusations and speculation that had plagued him for the last ten years. He'd start all over again, leaving his sordid past behind him. Building a whole new life wouldn't be easy, he admitted, but at least he wouldn't be alone. He'd be married by the time the deal closed, and he and his wife would move to Negril and live happily ever after. That was the plan. That was his plan.

LOVE ME CAREFULLY

A. C. ARTHUR

Genesis Press, Inc.

Indigo Love Stories

An imprint of Genesis Press, Inc.
Publishing Company

Genesis Press, Inc.
P.O. Box 101
Columbus, MS 39703

ISBN: 1-58571-177-2
Manufactured in the United States of America

First Edition

Visit us at www.genesis-press.com
or call at 1-888-Indigo-1

DEDICATION

To Minister Harvey and Annette Moore and Deacon Ernest and Marlene Arthur for setting the example of what a good marriage should be.

ACKNOWLEDGMENTS

For the man that bumped into me on Howard and Clay Streets fourteen years ago…you had enough space to move around, but I'm glad you didn't.

To André, Asia and Amaya, my triple dose of inspiration. Thanks for all the input, your spontaneous promotion and yes, the days you leave me alone long enough to write. Mommy loves you!

Thanks so much to Angelique for seeing the potential and keeping me on my toes!

PROLOGUE

December
Negril, Jamaica

"You know this is a million dollar deal you're messin' wit?" A six-foot-tall Rastafarian named Rohan stood on the terrace of his plush beach home. In the distance, palm trees and a never-ending blanket of sparkling blue beckoned the weary traveler, promising luxury and relaxation. The perfect getaway, the perfect escape.

"I know what I'm doing." The burly American sat in a chair on the terrace, thinking and re-thinking the plan that had been discussed. It would work, he knew it would. In six months he'd be safe in Negril, away from Baltimore, away from the accusations and speculation that had plagued him for the last ten years. He'd start all over again, leaving his sordid past behind him. Building a whole new life wouldn't be easy, he admitted, but at least he wouldn't be alone. He'd be married by the time the deal closed, and he and his wife would move to Negril and live happily ever after. That was the plan. That was his plan.

"Dat's a lot of ganja to move." His Jamaican accent thick and profound, the tall man lit a cigarette and took a puff.

"I don't have to move it. All I have to do is make sure it's delivered safely to Jones and he can take it from there." Dismissing Rohan's concerns with a flick of his wrist, the burly man sat back in the chair. "You just make sure Jones is where he's supposed to be, when he's supposed to be there."

"He'll be d'ere. Don't you worry."

"I'm not worried at all."

CHAPTER ONE

February
Baltimore, Maryland

Terrell Pierce had worked all night, his mind reeling with computer code and logistics. This had been his routine for the past couple of months. SISCO Engineering was a huge job that he was lucky to land as an independent contractor. By Christmas the re-design of SISCO's entire system would provide him with more than enough money to have him comfortably in his own home.

That went along perfectly with his timeline. His life had been planned and scheduled since the day he turned sixteen. He knew exactly what he wanted and wasn't about to stop until he had it all. The college degrees, the perfect job, the six figure salary, all that had come easily enough with dedication and determination—of which he had plenty to spare. Now he was moving towards the next phase of his dream.

He needed a family to round out his perfect scenario. He wanted the whole nine yards—successful career, a wife, kids, house and pets. That was where Tanya came in. She was beautiful, educated and classy. She would be perfect standing beside him as he continued his climb to the top. As soon as things slowed down a bit at work, he would propose and, hopefully, by this time next year they would already be on their way to starting a family.

Life was good.

Pressing the appropriate code, he gained entrance to the high-priced condo he leased. As if on cue, his stomach growled. He dropped his suitcase and headed for the kitchen. But then he heard something. His feet stopped, his ears perking up like those of a hound hearing a fox call.

Plush charcoal gray carpet lined the living room and dining room floors, so his steps were muffled.

The moaning he'd heard coming from his bedroom was not.

He moved quickly then, propelled by adrenaline. When he approached the door the moaning subsided. For one brief minute he thought he might have imagined it.

"Oh baby, I'm about to cum!" a male voice groaned.

His hand was on the knob, his imagination never having been that good. Shock didn't begin to describe what he was feeling the second he stepped into that room.

In the middle of his bed—in the middle of his king-sized cherry wood Signature bed—some guy's ass was moving in and out of some woman with the vigor of a champion stallion.

The female's feet bobbed on the man's shoulders and Terrell couldn't quite see her face.

"Oh yeah, come on, baby. Cum for mama!"

But he knew the voice—knew it very well.

Consumed with their activities, neither person heard him approach. He cleared his throat once, then again for good measure. They stopped mid-stroke.

He wouldn't overreact, wouldn't turn this scene into some drama-filled fight that his neighbors would hear and disapprove of, even though his frantically beating heart was trying to lead him in that direction.

"What the hell?" the man yelled.

"Terrell!" Tanya screeched.

With clenched teeth Terrell stood at the end of the bed, waiting to receive an explanation, which he doubted he'd understand. "Am I interrupting?" He stuffed his hands into his pockets to keep from dragging her from the bed.

The man jumped up, surprise and embarrassment apparent in his eyes. "I thought you said you lived alone." He looked at Tanya as he reached for his pants.

Tanya sat up on the bed, not the least bit bothered by her nakedness. "I can't believe you found your way in here. It's been so long since I've seen you in the bedroom." She crossed her legs Indian style, her palms on her bare thighs.

Terrell took in the display; after all, he was a man. But it was like looking at a stranger. Her usually neat and perfectly styled hair was in disarray, she wore no makeup, and her eyes were dark, excited. This was not the woman he'd known for the past nine months. The thought should have made him feel at least a little better about the situation, but really didn't.

He clamped his teeth down so tight he thought for sure he'd get lockjaw. He refused to talk to her until they were alone. The man was hastily getting his clothes on, looking from Terrell to Tanya, yelling expletives as though one or both of them should have been doing something other than staring at each other. In retrospect, Terrell figured the man was probably right. This had to be the worst busted lover scene in history. It was too calm, too quiet, but then that was the kind of man Terrell was.

"You don't even care, do you?" Tanya asked after her lover had finally gone.

Terrell took a deep breath. "Do I care that you're cheating on me, or do I care that you were tasteless enough to do it in our bed?"

She gave a wilted chuckle. "It would be more like you to be concerned about the bed than what I was doing in it," she spat.

He turned his back to her, then moved to stand near his dresser, his hands still stuffed in his pockets. Inside he was roiling with anger, and his shoulders stiffened as he replayed the visions of them together. Still, he didn't yell, didn't demand an explanation.

"Aren't you even going to ask me why?" she yelled from behind him.

"Is it going to matter?" he spoke quietly. In his book infidelity was a definite negative. At this very moment he was witnessing his dream begin to crumble, and, for once in his life, he was powerless to stop it. He'd chosen her carefully, made sure she met every one of his criteria before asking her to move in with him. It was a sure thing with her, they were a sure thing; he'd already picked out the engagement ring.

Tanya jumped off the bed, pulled on his shoulder until he turned around. "This is it, this is the problem right here! This is why I've resorted to someone else. But a lot of good it's done me. You can't even muster enough emotion to fight to understand why this happened."

Terrell took a step back because her pulling on his shoulder had brought him dangerously close to shaking the hell out of her. She seemed to want a different reaction from him, yet he knew if he unleashed his fury things would go too far, he wouldn't be able to control himself. Distance was definitely needed. "Are you saying this is my fault?"

"You're damned right it's your fault. If you'd pay attention to something other than your computers and your money you would have seen this coming. You would have tried to do something to stop it."

He couldn't believe she had the audacity to try to blame her betrayal on him. "I am not going to take the blame because you couldn't keep your legs closed. That was your stupidity." He did raise his voice then, because the pain of still seeing her naked and writhing beneath that other man was all too real. "I gave you everything, anything you wanted and this is how you repay me. I'm working all night long to make things better for us while you're screwing some dude in our bed. How exactly is that my fault, Tanya?"

"I didn't ask for any and everything, Terrell. I only wanted to be with you. But you were so busy trying to own every damned dollar in the world that you couldn't see that. We didn't need anything else except each other." A lone tear slipped down her face streaking the smooth honey toned skin. "I needed you, not your money," she whispered.

"Well, now you'll have neither." There was nothing else to be said. If he couldn't depend on her loyalty, they had nothing. He would not listen to her excuses, would not give them a second thought. She was wrong, and now it was over.

He pinched the bridge of his nose, knowing a headache was inevitable, and moved towards the bathroom. Pausing at his dresser, he retrieved boxers and a t-shirt. "I'm going to take a shower. You need to be packed and gone by the time I finish."

Leah Graham refused to celebrate Valentine's Day, but she had agreed to go out with Leon on the night before Valentine's, tonight. She was already seated at the restaurant when he called her cell phone to say he was running a little late.

She had gone out with Leon Reynolds, a cool guy she'd met at a wedding show, at least half a dozen times, and they seemed to get along pretty well. Leon was the marketing director for Onyx Apparel, a black-owned and operated business specializing in business and business casual attire for the urban marketplace. He owned half the company, partnering with his brother, Calvin, who actually did most of the designing.

They'd met in Cleveland. He was vending the company's first evening wear line at the same convention. It just so happened that they both worked and resided in Baltimore.

Lately, Leon was hinting at taking their relationship to another level. Leah was hesitant.

To her, sex meant commitment. And commitment led to moving in together. And moving in together led to marriage. And Leah was never, ever, getting married.

When she was eight she had envisioned what her wedding would be like. She'd wear a long flowing white gown, with a glittering tiara and a seven-foot veil. She'd walk down the aisle of the church and meet her husband-to-be, who would be clad in a white tuxedo with tails, and a smile meant only for her. She'd take his hand and they'd recite their vows to each other. They'd go on a fabulous honeymoon to Hawaii and come back to Baltimore to set up house. They'd both have full-time jobs but would be home together at night. She'd have two kids and they would live happily ever after.

Yeah, right.

On her ninth birthday Leah's mother announced that she was divorcing her father. The word *devastated* did not describe how Leah felt. The thought of her father not being in the same house with her was a hard blow to take. Just days after her birthday all her father's things were gone, and so was he. A few months later she received a letter from him telling her that he was moving to Alaska to open his own business. Leah had cried for days.

By Leah's eleventh birthday her mother had married again. A year later she'd had another baby. By the time Leah graduated from high school, her mother had married two more times and had two more children, thus proving to Leah that marriage wasn't the lifetime commitment she had first thought it to be.

As she grew up, however, she never lost her interest in weddings, their grandeur, the playing out of the ultimate fairy tale. She loved planning them, loved feeling like an artist unveiling a new painting, a director standing proud at his movie's debut. She'd become a wedding planner even though the institution of marriage held little personal appeal to her.

Leah sat back in her chair, sipped from her glass of white wine, and thought about Leon. She wasn't angry that he was late. Actually, she'd hoped he was calling to say he couldn't make it. No such luck, though. She took another sip.

Leon wanted to have sex. She knew that, had known that the last two times she'd been with him. But she wasn't there yet—didn't even know if she'd ever get there. Hell, kissing him had become a chore.

Damn. What was she going to do? She took another sip. She couldn't play coy—she'd never mastered the games some women played. She liked to be up front and brutally honest with the men she was dating, especially since she had no intention of being with any of them forever.

Looking up from her glass she saw Leon walking toward the table. All six feet, four inches of his ebony beauty approached in that cool swagger that let everybody know he was the bomb!

Damn.

"Hey beautiful," he whispered, bending so that his lips could brush hers.

Leah tried to calm her rampant thoughts. "Hello."

"Did you order?" he asked while taking his seat.

She nodded. "Yes, the waiter came over right after I spoke to you."

"Good. I want to get you home as soon as possible."

Tell me something I don't know. He licked his thick lips, not looking a bit like LL, she thought dismally. His eyes glistened with promises she didn't want to acknowledge, and his large hands reached for hers. "We could have had dinner at my place," she said, glad they hadn't. At least this way she could give him a goodnight kiss and go into her apartment alone.

"I wanted to take you out. We'll be alone soon enough." He winked at her.

No, he wanted to be in control. Leon thrived on control, and normally that was fine with her. She ran her business like a tight ship, but in her relationships, as few as there were, she was used to letting the guy take the lead—at least until she was finished with him. Then it became her show.

Leon liked to make the plans, liked to come up with the surprises, and for right now, she was simply a willing participant. She dated for entertainment purposes only. There would be no grand love affair happening in her life, so there was never a power struggle. He could do what he wanted as long as she allowed it. Tonight, however, she wondered how long it would be before Leon would use his control to try to bed her.

The food came and she grabbed the waiter's jacket sleeve. "Another drink, please." This was going to be a long night.

"Who's next?" Extravagantly painted three-inch nails tapped on the marble counter, waiting for a reply.

"Mary's next on your list," Rosie told the skinny young woman who stood in front of her, chewing gum like a cow. "And stop chewin' with your mouth open. It ain't ladylike," she fussed.

Keesha frowned at the older woman sitting behind the desk. "I never made any claims about being a lady."

"And nobody'll ever mistake you for one, either." Rosie rolled her eyes. "Come on, Mary, you're next."

A tall, heavy-set woman got up from the leather couch in the waiting room and walked over to the counter. Keesha stood on her tiptoes and raked her fake nails through the woman's hair. "What are you gettin' done today, girl?"

"I want something sexy. My man's taking me out later tonight, and I want to look good." Mary put her hands into her hair, trying to demonstrate a style. "You know, something like a little up, and then a little something soft around my face."

Mary had a big face, with bubble eyes and large lips. Keesha was going to have to do a lot of work to make a soft, sexy hairdo for her. "I know what you mean, honey." Keesha made the gum pop again as the lie slid effortlessly from her lips. But she'd do her best for the sixty-five dollars she was going to charge Mary. "Come on back."

The two females walked to the back of the shop, where shampoo girls waited for their next client. Mary sat down and Chantel tied a cape around her neck before lowering her head into the sink and switching on the warm water.

The bell on the door chimed, signaling the entrance of yet another woman on a mission to be beautified.

Finished with her clients for the day, Rosie was still sitting up front playing receptionist. She didn't mind the task because it gave her a chance to get off her feet until Donald came to pick her up.

"Hey Rosie, y'all got any cancellations?" Monica, a regular at Innovations, came in on a fresh gust of cold air from outside.

"Now Monica, you know it's Friday *and* it's Valentine's Day. The other girls are booked solid and I'm finished for the day." Monica was stuck-up, and a pain in her wide behind, so Rosie didn't even entertain the idea of putting her in her chair.

"Come on, I know Nikki can probably squeeze me in." Standing on her tiptoes, Monica tried to spot Nikki's chair in the back. To her chagrin, Nikki was styling a client and had another client sitting in the chair across from her, waiting.

"Uh un, she got two back there and three waiting and she's going out tonight. She ain't takin' no walk-ins. Why didn't you make an appointment?"

"I forgot. I thought I was going to be out of town but then things changed. Can't I just wait and see if she'll take me?"

"You can wait, but I don't think she will."

"I'll ask her when she comes up," Monica said hopefully.

"Suit yourself," Rosie told her.

Nikki wasn't going to take her. Rosie knew that for a fact. Nikki was going out with Brock Fuller tonight. She'd sashayed and primped and chased that man for a full month until he'd finally asked her out and, now that she had her second date with him, she wasn't about to miss it. Nope, Monica would be sitting there looking stupid for a few hours before she'd finally give up and go home with her hair looking just as it had when she'd come in.

As the hours passed, ladies came in and out of Innovations, dropping lots of money on their way out. Rosie carefully counted all that money and placed it in the moneybag in the bottom drawer. When she saw Donald later, she'd give him tonight's earnings, along with the receipts.

Rosie had worked at Innovations since its opening five years ago, but she'd only started dating Donald, the owner of the shop, five months ago. Donald was a good man. His wife had died three years earlier from lung cancer and he had concentrated solely on the business after that. But when the shop finally started turning a good profit, he'd relaxed a bit. His two daughters were grown and married with children now, so, after his wife's passing, he was alone.

A few days before Halloween he'd come into the shop and asked Rosie if she'd go to a Halloween party with him. She'd agreed and, in time, they'd become an item.

Although Rosie hadn't dated in more than twenty-five years, Donald was a good friend, and it hadn't seemed so awkward when they started dating. Now Rosie had become accustomed to being with him. And just in the last month they'd started sleeping together. She discovered that she had missed that intimacy.

Sitting at the receptionist's desk gave her the opportunity to keep an eye on what was going on outside the front door. In the last few weeks there'd been a lot of strange cars parked in their parking lot, and men they didn't know driving them. All sorts of rumors were floating around, some of which involved the beauty shop.

An hour before closing time, a long black limo pulled in front of the shop window. The two ladies that were still waiting to get their hair done stared out the window, wondering who would emerge from the vehicle. Rosie stopped massaging lotion into her hands and fixed her eyes on the limo.

The driver of the limo got out of the car first with a vase full of red roses. As he made his way to the front door, the ladies in the shop began to chatter.

"Oooh wee! Somebody's gettin' flowers," Monica said from her seat closest to the door.

"Damn! It's a lot of them, too. That's about three hundred dollars worth, I figure," Ms. Ruth assessed.

The girls in the back all stopped doing hair to see who the flowers were for.

"Nikki, you think they're from your sugar daddy?" Keesha asked, referring to Brock Fuller, who was about fifteen years older than Nikki.

"No, my 'sugar daddy,' as you put it, wouldn't be so predictable as to bring me flowers on my job." Nikki rolled her eyes at Keesha, but kept her eye on the door just in case.

"Well, I know it ain't mine. Ricky's too cheap to pay my way into the movies, let alone buy me some roses." Keesha rolled her eyes at the thought of the boyfriend she'd been planning to dump for the last six months.

"Ms. Rosetta Pierce?" the driver asked as he made his way through the door and over to the desk where Rosie sat.

Eyes bulged and jaws dropped as the girls wondered who had sent Ms. Rosie flowers.

"Oh my, that's me." Rosie's newly moisturized hand went to her beating heart.

"Read the card, ma'am." The driver pointed to the little white card sticking out of the side of the flowers.

"Oh, okay." With shaking fingers, she removed the card from its envelope.

Scribbled in black ink, the words stood out on the cardboard paper: *Will you marry me? Nod once for yes and twice for no.* Rosie shut her eyes, afraid she'd read it wrong. But when she opened her eyes again, the words were still there. Her heart hammering in her chest, she had to struggle to remain calm. All eyes were on her, and she wasn't about to act a fool for an audience.

It was Donald, she knew. And he was proposing to her. Here at the shop on Valentine's Day, he was asking her to marry him. Rosie had lost her husband, Paul, twenty-five years ago to a car accident. And she'd raised her only son, Terrell, by herself until he'd gone away to college. Up until last October she hadn't given another man a thought. And re-marrying had been the farthest thing from her mind.

But then Donald had come into her life. A friend and confidant had turned into a lover. And she cherished him. She loved him.

Now he wanted to marry her. Her heart was so full she thought it would surely burst.

"What does it say?" Monica yipped.

"Who's it from, Ms. Rosie?" As was her nosy nature, Keesha approached the front desk.

Rosie knew her answer and lifted her head to see out to the limo. But the driver and Monica were standing in front of her, blocking her view. If she couldn't see the car, then the person in the car couldn't see her, and he wouldn't know her answer.

One thick honey brown arm stretched out to move the driver aside, while, with the other, she elbowed Monica out of the way. Standing in front of the window with the name Innovations spelled out in swirling letters, Rosie nodded her head one time and waited for the car door to open.

Within seconds the door to the limo opened and Donald eased his way out of the back seat. He wore a black suit, crisp white shirt and bright red tie. A long black wool overcoat hung on his large frame, protecting him from the cold winter night. His hair was cut close, and his goatee glistened with gray. His full mouth was spread into a large smile.

Ignoring the gasps and murmurs behind her, Rosie gave her complete attention to the man making his way through the door. The bell chimed when it opened, but Rosie didn't hear it. Holding his arms out for her, Donald welcomed his bride-to-be.

Rosie threw her big arms around Donald's thick neck and hugged him tight. His arms, too, were fat and short, but made their way almost completely around Rosie's large waist. Somebody started to clap, and then applause filled the room as Donald kissed Rosie right there in the middle of the shop.

Plopping down on the couch, Leah gathered her blanket close and snuggled deep into the cushions of the sofa. It was Valentine's Day, and she was spending it alone. Rather, she was spending it with a steamy romance novel, eating Cheez-Its and sipping Pepsi. She'd carefully nipped her would-be Valentine in the bud last night.

Leon hadn't been happy, but she'd kissed him one more time for good measure, rubbed his chest a little more softly than usual, then told him she wasn't ready to sleep with him. He'd looked at her strangely, and for a moment she'd thought he was going to protest. But then his thick lips spread into a wide grin and he'd brushed his fingers over her cheek. "Your time is running out, Leah."

What the hell is that supposed to mean?

She said goodnight again and closed the door, locking it securely. "No, Leon, your time's running out."

Some would call her a tease, but she considered it taking her time, looking before she leapt.

The phone rang just as she was opening her book. With a deep sigh, she leaned over to pick up the receiver.

"Hello?"

"Hi, baby." Her mother's voice echoed through the line. "I knew you'd be home. What you doing?"

Her voice crisp and to the point, Leah answered, "Nothing."

"Girl, I'm about ready to put this man out, you hear me?"

Oh Lord, here we go again. Marsha Baker was on husband number five, Darryl Baker, who owned several barber shops around the city. Leah thought Darryl was a nice man, even though he was almost sixty. Her mother had married him last year after having an affair with him for two years and finally convincing him to divorce his wife.

"What's wrong now, Mama?" It was a shame she couldn't muster any sympathy for her own mother. Wasn't that pitiful? No, she told herself, it was honest. Her mother went through husbands like a cheap pair of shoes, and Leah was long past the point of trying to figure out why.

"You know he ain't even came in here with my Valentine's gift yet?" Marsha screeched into the phone.

"Mama, the night's not over yet. And besides, I told you this was a stupid holiday anyway." Rolling her eyes toward the ceiling, Leah slammed her book on the table. She'd be on the phone with her mother at least another forty-five minutes, discussing why Darryl was a bum and how soon she was going to put him out and move on.

Settling herself, Leah prepared for the tedious conversation. It was just more evidence for never getting married.

CHAPTER TWO

Rosie and Donald spent the entire weekend together at a little bed and breakfast on the Eastern Shore. And on Tuesday morning Rosie was glowing like a light bulb when she walked into Innovations.

"Good morning, Ms. Rosie." Keesha was sitting in Rosie's chair talking on the phone when she came in.

"Good morning." Rosie took off her coat and hung it on the coat rack near the door. Moving toward her station, she signaled for the girl to get out of her chair. "My clients will be coming in soon. It don't look good with you sitting there on the phone."

"I'll be done in a minute." Keesha continued with her conversation, one long skinny leg propped up on the counter as she giggled into the receiver.

"You're done now, girlie." Rosie snatched the phone out of her hand and slammed it into its holder. "Now get out of my chair before I hurt you." Rosie stood over the girl, waiting for her to move. She knew she would. For as sassy and mouthy as Keesha was, she knew that when Rosie meant business, she meant business.

"Alright, you don't have to get all uptight. What's the matter, you didn't get any over the weekend?" Keesha smiled coyly as she made her way out of the chair.

"That ain't none of your business. Now move, I gotta see when Leah's coming in again." Rosie flipped through the appointment book, looking for the name.

Rosie had been doing Leah Graham's hair since she was in high school. Leah was a good girl, punctual, professional and pretty as a picture. On more than one occasion she'd wished Leah could turn her son's head. But they both seemed so hell-bent on their careers they didn't have time to find the right person.

Leah was a wedding planner who ran her own shop down in Mount Vernon. When Cheryl Pinder had gotten married last summer, Leah had planned her wedding and reception and it had been beautiful. That was the kind of wedding Rosie pictured for herself.

Per Donald's instructions, she was to plan the wedding however she wanted, and she wanted it to be perfect. She'd married Paul Pierce in her mother's living room with twenty-five of her closest family members assembled, flocking around the floral-patterned furniture as her father led her down the staircase to meet the man she planned to spend the rest of her life with. Potted plants had lined the living room, while two-dozen daisies had been perched high atop the mantelpiece behind the minister. The ceremony had lasted all of fifteen minutes before it became a regular family gathering with cousins and uncles and aunts filling and re-filling their plates, then sitting around talking about old times.

They hadn't had a honeymoon because Paul was leaving for the army two weeks later. So Rosie had moved into their one bedroom apartment and set up house by herself. She'd worked at the Hecht Company eight hours a day and come home at night to the quiet little apartment. Then she'd found out she was pregnant.

"Hey, did y'all hear what went down last night?" Nikki came out of the bathroom talking, and approached Rosie and Keesha's station with a catlike saunter.

Rosie paused, looked over at the young girl. Nikki and Keesha were Leah's age—all of them young enough to be her daughters, most of the time acting just like they were. "What happened?" she asked.

Nikki rested her big breasts on the back of the chair while surveying her nails. "Some dumb ass drug dealers got into a fight out in the parking lot. By the time the police got here, one person had been stabbed."

"Is that why I saw all that yellow tape out there this morning?" Keesha queried.

Nikki nodded. "Yup. I heard it was a mess. The cops will probably be snooping around here this morning."

Rosie half listened to them, her mind still on her pending nuptials. She'd put her hands in her lap the moment the girls came near enough to see. She planned to tell them about her engagement but wanted the timing to be perfect. Still, she chimed in. "Good, maybe those trespassers will get the hint once they see the police and stop hanging around here. Some of my customers are starting to complain. They're afraid to take late appointments because they don't want to be out there at night."

"All they need is a good ol' can of Mace, like I carry in my bag," Keesha quipped.

Nikki sucked her teeth. "Girl, please, Mace ain't no match for a gun."

"Anyway, Ms. Rosie, why are you looking for Leah?"

Lifting her hands and placing them flat on the desk Rosie smiled. "I'd like her to plan my wedding."

"Your wedding!" Keesha screamed first. "Ms. Rosie, you gettin' hitched?" She'd been walking back to her booth when Rosie's words stopped her cold. Now she all but ran back to where the woman stood.

Nikki moved in closer, scooping Ms. Rosie's left hand from the desk. With her free hand she covered her eyes as if blinded by the glare. "Damn, that's a pretty piece of ice! Who are you marrying?" she asked while still surveying the jewel. Then, as if the revelation finally hit her, she looked at Rosie. "Uh-uh, wait a minute. I know Mr. Donald didn't ask you to marry him."

When Rosie didn't answer, only smiled, both girls broke into screeches and screams.

"Oh my God! That is so cute." Keesha leaned against Rosie's high-backed chair and put her arms around her. "I'm so happy for you and Mr. Donald. Y'all make a cute couple.

And he's got good taste in jewelry," she added, after her own perusal of the engagement ring.

"That limo and those roses, that's what that was all about? He proposed on Valentine's Day! That is so romantic!" Nikki clapped her hands together in excitement. But as quickly as it had come, Nikki's elation faded slightly. "Are you sure about this, Ms. Rosie? I mean, Mr. Donald's cool and everything, but you know what they've been saying."

They had all heard the rumors, but Rosie would put a stop to them right now. "Chile, that's nonsense and a bunch of foolishness. That stuff happened a long time ago, before me and him even started seeing each other." Rosie huffed and went about taking her combs and other accessories out of her drawer. "Donald's not like that now."

Both Keesha and Nikki knew when to keep their mouths shut. In fact, Nikki felt like a total idiot now for even bringing it up. "Well, Leah will definitely plan you a slammin' wedding."

Rosie grinned, relieved that they weren't going to have a long drawn-out conversation about Donald's past. "That's what I know. She's coming in at eleven today. I've got to hurry up and call Terrell."

"Where's he been hidin'?" Nikki asked. "Him and that fake girl-friend of his still together?"

Keesha laughed. "Girl, the last time she was in here I couldn't believe all that weave she had. Poor bald horsey."

Nikki slapped her five as they both giggled.

"That's not funny," Rosie chirped, trying to hide her own grin as she dialed her son's number. "Hush, the phone's ringing," she whispered to them.

The phone rang three times before someone picked it up. It was a woman.

"Ah, hello? This is Rosie Pierce, I'm Terrell's mother. Is he there?" The female seemed angry as she called Terrell to the phone.

"Hello?" Terrell all but yelled into her ear.

"Well, hello to you too," Rosie answered.

"Mama?"

"Yes, it's your mama, not that you'd recognize my voice, since I haven't heard from you in so long." It had been at least two weeks since she'd spoken to him, and she missed him terribly.

Terrell's tone changed dramatically. "I could never forget my mama's voice. How are you? Is something wrong?"

"No, nothing's wrong and I'm doing just fine. How are you? Did I interrupt something? You and your young lady sound a little upset."

Terrell and Tanya had been in the middle of tidying up their last connections. She'd left some things behind the other day, he suspected purposely, and today she'd come by to get them. Her attempts to talk to him, to explain where they'd gone wrong, were lost on him, and he wasted no time telling her this. She'd retaliated by accusing him of seeing someone else, and had answered the phone in anticipation of talking to the new woman in his life. "Nah, just tying up loose ends, Mama. So what's been going on with you?"

"Actually, a lot has been going on. I wanted to talk to you about something." Rosie didn't know how to begin. She hadn't told Terrell about dating Donald, mostly because her son never asked about her love life, and probably believed she didn't have one.

"What's the matter? You need some money? I can come by the shop on my way to work." Whatever his mother needed, he'd give her. She'd given him so much.

"No, no, it's nothing like that. I, um, I just wanted to tell you what's been going on with me."

"Are you sick?" Terrell panicked.

"No, baby, I'm not sick. I'm getting married." Rosie waited for his response, but didn't get one. "Terrell? You still there?"

"I'm here, Mama." He was quiet again, trying to digest her words.

"Well, you see, I met this nice man. Actually, I've known him for about five years now. He owns the beauty shop, and his wife died about three years ago. We've been good friends for a while now. He's a really good man."

"And he just up and asked you to marry him?" Terrell tried to be calm, but his hands felt numb, and he could feel himself beginning to sweat. His mother, getting married. He couldn't see it. He didn't want to see it, especially now.

"Our friendship sort of turned into something more about five months ago and Friday he proposed." Her son's silence confirmed that he wasn't as excited about the impending nuptials as she was. Terrell had always tried to hide his feelings, but she could tell he wasn't thrilled to hear her news. "I love him, Terrell."

"I'm sure you do. But does he love you?" As far as Terrell was concerned, there was no man who could possibly love his mother the way his father had. No other man could marry her. She was his mother and his father's wife. It didn't matter that his father had been dead and gone for twenty-five years now.

"Yes, he does, Terrell. I think it's time you two meet." And she wanted the chance to talk to him face to face, to explain to him that this was what she really needed.

With a long, disgusted sigh Terrell asked, "When's the wedding?"

"May 15th."

"May? You're not wasting any time, are you? Is he dying or something?"

"Terrell! I'm gonna pretend I didn't hear you say that. I'd like my only child to give me away. So if you can find time in your busy schedule, I'd appreciate you coming to see your mother."

"Yes, ma'am," was all he could manage to say. "I'll see what I can do."

"Good. Donald thinks an engagement party would be a good idea. When can you get away? I'd like to plan it for a weekend that's good for you, since I expect you to be there."

"Oh, his name's Donald?"

"Terrell, I asked you a question." Rosie's patience was wearing thin. She'd known that Terrell wasn't going to be pleased with her announcement but, by God, he would respect her and her wishes. She would accept nothing less.

"I don't know. I guess this weekend is as good as any," he sighed. He didn't have any other plans this weekend, since he was now unattached. "Or is that too soon for you and Donald?"

"That's cutting it close, but I'm sure we could throw together a nice little gathering."

"Fine. I'll come by the house Saturday evening."

"Thank you, baby." Rosie's heart ached for her child. He sounded so distant, so lonely. She wanted so much for him. Not just happiness, 'cause, Lord knows, happiness depended on things happening and could last just for the moment. She was happy the moment she married Paul. She was happy the moment she found out she was pregnant with Terrell. But the day that police officer knocked on her door and told her that her husband had been killed, her happiness disappeared.

For days she'd wondered how she'd make it without Paul. But she had Terrell, and she knew she had to get it together for her child. And as the years had gone on, she'd found happiness at other times. When Terrell graduated from high school with honors. When Terrell was accepted at Howard. These things had made her happy. But then Terrell had left for college and she'd been alone. And happiness was gone again.

She didn't want that for Terrell, happiness that would come and go as it pleased. She wanted her son to be complete. She wanted him to love and to be loved. He was a successful computer programmer; he made good money, and he had a lot of nice things. But he didn't have anyone to love, anyone to take care of him when he got sick. That's what she wanted for him. But she didn't know how to show him that's what he needed.

"Mama loves you, Terrell," she said to him finally. Because in the end, that was all she could say.

"I love you too, Mama."

Donald slammed his thick hand against the steering wheel. "Your boys are bringing too much heat around my shop, Cable." His voice echoed through the interior of his truck.

The man sitting in the seat beside him shook his head. "Man, I don't know what's going on with them. It's some territory war going on down there. I can't seem to get a handle on it."

"Well, you'd better get a handle on it, and quick. This thing's winding down and I don't need any screw-ups. And we definitely don't need those dumb ass city cops on our tail." At the mention of the police, Donald searched his surroundings. They were parked in a crowded underground lot at one of the downtown office buildings. That was the last place he expected any officers to be, but with his luck he couldn't be sure.

"If this deal goes bad, it's going to ruin a lot of lives, Cable. We can't mess this up," Donald said seriously.

"Nothing's going to go bad. I've got everything under control."

Donald looked at his companion again and decided he had no choice but to believe him. But he had a lot riding on this deal—his future literally depended on it.

Leah was having a difficult morning. The Ortega wedding was scheduled for the next Saturday. The caterer had changed the menu and the bride's veil had been ripped. She spent her first two hours in the office attempting to calm down a hysterical Hispanic woman and her mother who were ready to go down to the cleaners and beat the Korean owner senseless for tearing the two hundred dollar veil.

Then she spent forty-five minutes on the phone with the caterer, informing him of his contractual obligations and that any changes were in direct violation of the agreement. This was the first quiet moment she'd had all morning, and she wanted to savor it. Leaning back in her chair, she rubbed her eyes with the back of her hands.

Melinda, her assistant, peeped her head into the office. "Your hair appointment is at eleven, Leah."

"Oh Lord, please give me strength," Leah sighed. She needed her hair done badly. Her new growth was showing and her split ends were driving her mad. And just yesterday she had broken a nail while making the favors for next week's wedding. "I need to go somewhere and get a massage." Rising from the chair Leah began putting papers she'd scattered across her desk back into the Ortega file.

"I know what you mean. But look at the bright side. We don't have another wedding for almost two months." Melinda crossed over to Leah's desk and picked up her calendar.

"Are you sure?" Leah shuffled papers around, looking for her keys. She always misplaced her keys. It was a terrible habit of hers. Though she could remain organized and on point with all her clients, when it came to her own keys, she could never seem to remember where she put them.

"Yup, April first, Blake wedding. Invitations went out on Friday, hall is paid in full, photographer is booked and florist has been commissioned. April 29th, Avarez wedding. Guest list is finalized, invitations are addressed and in the file cabinet waiting to be mailed. Hall's not paid for, but her uncle owns it, so that shouldn't be an issue."

"Yeah, right. Family's what you have to worry the most about. Call Maria on Monday and ask her what's going on. I want that paid in full before the first of March. She's got the money, and I don't want any last minute changes in location because she spent the weekend in Atlantic City instead of paying off the hall." Pulling open her desk drawers, she continued the search.

"Alrighty." Melinda closed the book and wrote herself a note on a sticky pad.

Leah glanced about the room in search of some clue as to where her keys had gone.

"Ah, Leah?" Melinda called her.

Leah turned to look at her receptionist and followed her gaze. There were her keys, crunched in the folds of the chair Leah had been sitting in.

"Girl, I'm gonna lose my mind trying to find these keys one day." Scooping them up, she came around the desk and crossed to the coat stand.

"You need a clapper."

"A what?" Sliding her arm into her black wool coat, she spared Melinda another glance.

"You know, a clapper." Melinda clapped her hands. "That way when you can't find your keys you just clap your hands and they'll beep. Then you'll know where they are."

"Yeah, well, buy me one for my birthday." Leah went to the door. "I'll be back about one. Hold down the fort."

"I always do," Melinda yelled at her boss's retreating back.

"That's what I pay you the big bucks for," Leah added before closing the front door behind her.

She shouldn't have taken the scenic route; she should have gotten on the highway as she had originally planned. The streetlights weren't in sync, so every time she stopped for one light, the light a block ahead was turning green. Leah's nerves were wearing thin by the time she turned into the parking lot in front of Innovations.

Her best friend Nikki had worked there since they opened. And Ms. Rosie, her stylist, had gotten a job there as well. She heard the shop was doing well, so she was happy for both of them. Half the parking lot was full of run-down cars that people were trying to sell. It looked like a junkyard or a used car lot, depending on the weather.

There were three ladies in the waiting area when she walked in. She took her coat off and hung it up. Going over to the counter, she waited for Ms. Rosie to finish her telephone conversation before speaking.

"Morning, Ms. Rosie."

"Hey Leah, I been waitin' for you."

Leah looked at the older woman. She looked different today. It wasn't her hair; that was in the same wrapped style she always wore it in. It wasn't her nails; they were clipped and neatly painted as usual. But something was definitely different about her.

"Really? Am I late?" Leah looked down at her watch.

"No. You're right on time. I need to ask you something before you get shampooed."

"Oh, okay." Leah relaxed. She hated being late, and that traffic had been a mess. "What's up?"

"I'm getting married." Rosie extended her hand, showing off the two-karat diamond Donald had given her.

"Oh, damn, that's a big rock, Ms. Rosie." Leah took the woman's hand, examining the ring. "It's a good cut, too. He spent a pretty penny on that."

"I know he did." Rosie blushed.

"So when's the big day? I know I'm on the guest list." Leah released Rosie's hand and watched as the woman continued to beam. That was what was different, Leah thought, Rosie was tickled pink about her engagement.

"May 15th, and not only are you on the guest list, but I want you to plan the wedding."

"What?" Leah was shocked. She'd been planning weddings for years now but had never planned one for anybody close to her. That was probably because Nikki was no closer to getting married than she was.

"I know that's your business and Cheryl Pinder's wedding was fabulous. Her mother goes to my church. You know, First Baptist, where they got married. So anyway, I was there and I loved it. I asked her mother afterwards if she had done all that herself, and she told me that Cheryl had hired you. So now I want to hire you because I want my wedding to be just as fabulous as hers." Rosie smiled. "No, I want mine to be better." She laughed.

Both happy about the word of mouth referral and Rosie's good news, Leah found it hard not to smile with her. "Well, I'm, ah…I'm flattered. I'd love to plan your wedding for you. Let me look at my calendar and make sure I don't have any conflicts." Pulling her black organizer out of her bag, she flipped to the month of May. "I have only one booking for the end of May, and they haven't paid their deposit yet, so it looks like I'm free."

"Good. Now, Donald said that whatever I wanted was fine with him, so you just let me know what your fee is and I'll take care of it."

"Why don't we schedule a time to sit down and talk about what it is you want. Then we can discuss figures."

"Okay. I'm planning a little engagement party at the house Saturday. Why don't you come by and meet Donald."

"Yeah, that sounds good. About what time?" Rosie told her the time and Leah scribbled it into her organizer.

"Hey girl, I see you finally made it. Rosie's been pacing around here waiting for you." Nikki came up to the desk just as Leah was putting her book back into her bag.

"Yup, just taking care of business with my new client here." Leah smiled at Rosie.

"Oh, you asked her?" Nikki said.

"And she agreed. I want you to bring her past the house on Saturday for the party."

"Who said I was coming?" Nikki joked with Rosie.

"Oh, you're coming, if I have to come out to Yale Heights and bring you there myself."

"That's right, I am. Because I know you're cooking those slammin' hot wings and potato salad. I'll be the first one there." Nikki laughed, her raisin-colored lips shining.

"She's always eatin'." Rosie rolled her eyes.

"I don't know where she puts it," Leah commented as they all walked to the back of the shop where the stations were. Nikki was only five foot three inches, a perfect size ten. She had a big booty and even bigger breasts. Today she wore tattered jeans that hung low on her hips and a pre-shrunk shirt that exposed her gold-toned midsection. A beaded jean jacket, equally as tattered as her pants, completed the ensemble.

"It don't matter, baby. It all gets to the right places," Nikki grinned. "Now get in Rosie's chair and get something done to that mop on your head."

CHAPTER THREE

An envelope on his credenza held the house key he'd given Tanya. Terrell sighed; she was really out of his life. He still wasn't sure how that made him feel. Would he miss her? Would she try to get back with him? A part of him felt that he was losing a good thing, but the greater part figured he was cutting his losses. If Tanya could cheat on him so easily when they weren't even married, just imagine what she'd do when they fully committed to each other.

It was probably all for the best. He'd simply have to start his search again. His dream hadn't changed just because he'd misjudged one woman. He knew there was a woman for him out there somewhere, a woman who would complete him, who could complement him and his future. He simply had to find her, the missing piece to the puzzle, and things would be on the right track again.

He thought of Tanya again, of what had initially attracted him to her. She was definitely fine. Five feet, seven inches, light skinned, with long tinted hair and slanted eyes like an Asian and a body that wouldn't quit. Those physical features alone should have warned him. Beautiful women tended to come with a lot of drama, and she'd proven that fact. After almost a year of dating, it was over.

His eyes scanned the empty spots in the closet where her clothes used to hang, the long stretch of the mahogany dresser left vacant by the removal of her perfumes and other toiletries and he felt a wave of distress. Cursing, he left the bedroom. He was tired of wasting time. He was thirty-three years old; it was time to settle down.

Walking through the apartment his mind moved to how he'd come to be at this point in his life. He'd graduated tops in his class back in Baltimore and gone on to graduate *cum laude* in his class at Howard.

Now he was writing his own contracts and picking and choosing which companies he'd work with.

His savings account had plenty of zeroes in it, and had afforded him the luxury of living in an upscale condo on Baltimore's waterfront and membership to its full-service gym. There he'd met a few guys and they'd started hanging out. Then the women had noticed him. He was no stranger to women, but wasn't really accustomed to the overt passes he now experienced, since during his teenage years he had been known as a nerd. At six one, about one eighty, with honey brown skin and more than average intelligence, he considered himself a good catch.

Compared to the guys he hung out with—buff, two-twenty, flashy dressers with smooth lines—Terrell was the strong, silent type. He wore wire-rimmed glasses and often had a tendency to talk only about work.

Then he had met Tanya.

She'd bowled him over with her stunning good looks and her air of class. And the sex wasn't too bad either. He'd thought he had the perfect package. One of his friends had mentioned that she looked high maintenance before Terrell had gathered the nerve to approach her, so on their first date, he'd picked her up in a limo and taken her to a ritzy restaurant. From that moment on he'd wined and dined her, buying her expensive gifts and flowers, lavishing her with everything a woman could ever want. But apparently that hadn't been enough.

So now he sat on his couch, alone in his apartment, wondering when he'd gotten off track. When had he lost sight of the type of woman he really needed in his life? He reached into his back pocket and pulled out his wallet. Behind his library card was a tattered piece of paper. On that paper were the criteria to becoming Terrell Pierce's wife. He'd made the list when he was fifteen. He smiled at the memory and read the words he'd believed were a sure thing.

Number one—cute. She didn't have to be a raving beauty. During his childhood he was convinced that his thick glasses and braced teeth would only grow worse, so having a beautiful wife was unlikely. He'd figured as long as she was pleasing to look at, that would be good enough.

Number two—short. His father had been barely six feet, and Terrell had been the smallest child in his class. Now that he'd grown up, topping his dad's height, it made him smile to think what a short woman would look like beside him.

Number three—job. His mother had always been home with him before his father died. He'd thought his wife shouldn't work. That way she'd have more time to raise the kids and run the household. Besides, he was going to be successful, so he'd make enough money to take care of his family. That goal had been realized. A six-figure salary was nothing to complain about. It was more than enough to support a wife and kids.

Number four—cook. She had to cook. Terrell loved to eat. He could cook a little himself, but he still wanted a woman who could throw down.

And *number five—love.* The woman he married had to love him unconditionally. He hadn't been the best looking boy on the block, and he had been skinny. Figuring he probably wouldn't change much in the years to come, he had added this final requirement. While his looks had improved, the need for unconditional love was still crucial.

Although he was grown now and not as idealistic as that child had been, he still wanted a good woman by his side, and held out hope that he'd find her one day. But for now, that would have to go on the back burner. His mother needed him.

It had always been just the two of them. Now, with her nuptial announcement, that was changing. He put his little piece of paper back into his wallet, determined not to think about his own love life for the time being. Tired of thinking about his life, period, he leaned over and pressed the message light on his answering machine.

"Hi, Terrell, this is Mama. I wanted to remind you about the party on Saturday. I'm looking forward to seeing you. Love you. Bye."

His mother's voice echoed through his apartment. He missed her. The last few weeks at work had been pretty hectic, but he knew that was no excuse. He needed to see her. She'd tell him what went wrong with Tanya and how to start the search again. His mother was like that, always giving him the best advice, always looking out for his best interests.

With a start, he figured it was probably time he started doing the same for her. She'd announced she was getting married, but Terrell had no idea to whom. Sure, she'd told him the man's name—and come to think of it, she'd only told him his first name—and that was all he knew about him. When had she started dating? Throughout the years since his father's death they'd remained pretty close, confiding in each other as much as humanly possible, yet he didn't know she'd found a man worthy of settling down with.

So, he pushed aside his own troubled love life and focused on his mother and her matrimonial plans. Right now the condo held too many memories for him to stomach, and deciding to spend the weekend at his mother's house, he packed some clothes in a duffle bag, grabbed his suit off the door—Mama would make him go to church on Sunday, of that he was sure—locked up the condo and climbed into his Mercedes.

In the car he turned on the radio. When he heard the first notes of Toni Braxton's "Another Sad Love Song," he quickly switched the station.

Rosie clucked around the kitchen moving from the stove to the refrigerator to the table and back to the stove again. She had macaroni boiling for the seafood salad; potatoes sitting in a strainer in the sink waiting to be mixed with the secret ingredients of her potato salad; chicken wings marinating in hot peppers and Tabasco; and iced tea chilling in the refrigerator. She loved to cook, so when Donald offered to have the party catered, she'd squawked about wasting money and set out to prepare it all herself.

They were having twenty of their closest friends and relatives at her house tonight. Last night she'd cleaned the living room and dining room furiously. The upstairs she could do later this morning. That way it would be fresh when the guests arrived.

Her spirits were high as she sailed through the little kitchen humming and singing. Terrell had come in last night. He'd come home. She couldn't believe he'd decided to stay overnight. He lived only about twenty minutes from her, yet he'd brought his clothes and gone to his old room as if he'd never left. He had grown a little beard since the last time she'd seen him, and picked up a little weight. Both looked good on him. He'd become a really handsome man who reminded her a lot of his father. She hadn't realized how much she'd missed her only child until he'd grabbed her for a big bear hug.

She was waiting for him to get up now so they could have some time alone to talk. Donald was going to come over a few hours before the party so that he and Terrell could meet before the other guests arrived. However, she sensed something was bothering Terrell, and wanted the chance to talk to him alone first.

"Mornin', Mama." Still rubbing sleep out of his eyes, Terrell stepped into the kitchen, interrupting Rosie's thoughts.

"Mornin', baby. Sit down and I'll get you something to eat." Moving the chicken from the table to the counter, Rosie made room for her son to sit down.

"Nah, I'll just have some coffee." Taking a seat, Terrell noticed all the things his mother had going. "You sure you're cooking enough?"

"You know I like to have more than enough," Rosie chuckled. She filled a mug with hot coffee from the carafe and placed it in front of him.

"Boy, it's good to be home." Terrell stretched his legs and reared back in the chair, which he knew had to be about twenty years old. The design was so seventies, he noted, high metal backs and teal and white leatherette seats. The Formica tabletop matched the chairs, with a swirling teal design on a backdrop of white, accented with specks of glitter.

"Yeah, I miss seeing you sittin' there watching me cook. You used to do your homework right there in that very chair every night while I fixed your dinner." Rosie remembered it as if it were yesterday.

"And every time I tried to sneak a cookie when your back was turned you'd scold me something terrible," he grinned. "Never did figure out how you could see me with your back turned." Taking a quick sip of the hot coffee, he closed his eyes to the memory.

"Mama's got eyes in the back of her head, I told you." Rosie moved the large strainer filled with potatoes over to the table, then went to the refrigerator to retrieve the mayonnaise, relish and eggs she'd boiled earlier. Coming back to the table, she sat across from her son.

"So tell me what's been going on with you." Opening the jars, she scooped one ingredient after another into the bottom of an empty pan.

"Not as much as what's been going on with you," he quipped.

"Probably not, but I asked you first," she responded with definitive authority.

Agreeing with a shrug, Terrell figured he'd go first, but he had questions for his mother, and he expected answers. "I just broke up with my girlfriend."

"Really? What happened?" She remembered the female who'd answered his phone and the tension she'd sensed that day.

Expelling a deep breath, Terrell propped his elbows up on the table and slid his glasses further up on his nose. He didn't want to talk about his problems; well, he did, but not just yet. He wanted to hear about her first, about the man in her life. But she was still the mother, so he decided to obey her request. "I don't know. I guess I was good enough to spend my money on her, let her live in my house for free and pay most of her bills, but I wasn't good enough to be loyal to or honest with. She was cheating, said I wasn't paying enough attention to her. I wasn't giving her what she really needed." Folding his hands beneath his chin, he figured that summed up his relationship with Tanya pretty accurately.

"Well, were you?" Rosie poured the potatoes into the pan and began to stir. "Giving her what she needed, I mean?"

"I gave her everything. I paid all her bills, I gave her money to buy clothes, she didn't even really have to work. I took good care of her." He shrugged. "What else could she have possibly wanted?"

Rosie shook her head, stared at him in disbelief. "Son, please tell me you aren't shallow enough to think that material things are enough to keep a woman satisfied. Not a good woman, anyway."

"What?" Terrell looked at his mother in question. "I was showing her that I could take care of her, that she would never have to worry about things like that because I would handle it all. That's what a man's supposed to do, right?"

Rosie sucked her teeth while her fingers mixed the potato salad. "Yes, a man's supposed to take care of his woman, but that doesn't only mean seeing to her every material need. Women have emotional needs, Terrell, and if you were so busy working and paying all the bills, then you probably were too busy to see hers."

"So she decided to cheat on me, and I should accept that as my fault?" He looked incredulous at that notion.

Rosie rolled her eyes. "Now, I'm definitely not saying that. She should have tried talking to you first. Cheating was wrong, and it sounds like both of you needed to do a little growing up." Rosie paused, thought a moment. "But you know, this might be a good sign. Maybe she wasn't the right woman for you. Maybe the right woman is just waiting around the corner for you to sweep her off her feet."

Terrell smirked. "Yeah, right. I'm beginning to doubt that."

"What are you talking about? You're a good looking man, you've got a good head on your shoulders and just as soon as you learn that life isn't all about accomplishments, you'll be a good catch for any woman. Any real woman, mind you."

He grinned into his coffee cup before taking a sip. "You're biased."

"I'm still a woman, and I got good eyes. You look fine, and you've got a good head on your shoulders. I see them girls down at the shop running after every flashy car and good dresser they see. And then when I leave the shop I see those same flashy cars and good dressers running after every woman they see. So sometimes you gotta re-evaluate what it is you want in a mate." Rosie stood so she could get a better handle on the spoon to properly mix the salad.

"Is that what you did? Re-evaluate what you wanted in a mate?"

Rosie stopped stirring the mixture to look at her son. So much like his daddy, looking at her with those pensive dark eyes, barely holding on to his anger. "I haven't had a mate in a long time, Terrell," she told him.

"I know. That's what amazes me most about this sudden jump to matrimony. You never seemed to care that you didn't have a man before. What changed?"

"When your daddy died, I was so devastated I thought I would die right along with him. But I had you to take care of. So I dedicated myself to doing just that, taking care of you. I didn't have time to sit still long enough to figure out what I needed. But when you went away to school I was here, in this house, alone. I went to work and I came home and that's it. I didn't have a lot of friends to go out with 'cause they were all married and had their own lives to live." Sprinkling salt and pepper into the pan, she spared her son a glance before she continued. "I figured I'd better make a life of my own before I got too old to enjoy it. So I took those classes at the beauty school and I went to work at the shop. All those young people and energy got me going again. Those girls down there became my friends, well, more like my daughters, but it felt good all the same. Then when Donald asked me out I didn't see anything wrong with it, he was nice enough. But slowly things began to change, and I found myself really wanting to be with him."

"And now you find yourself really wanting to marry him?" Terrell watched his mother's big arms working the mixture together, knowing exactly how the finished product would taste. He had to admit his mother looked pretty damn happy. Which made his position in this matter even more disconcerting.

"Now I find myself in love with a good man and tired of being alone," she said simply.

"What about Daddy?" Pushing his glasses up on his nose, he sat back in the chair and waited for her reply.

"Terrell, your daddy's been dead and gone a long time now." Her heart ached for the little boy that used to sit in his room and cry because all the other boys on the block had their fathers and he didn't. But he was a grown man now, and she couldn't hold him in her arms and tell him that things would be all right. She could, but she doubted that would make him feel any better.

"So you just forgot about him?" Hurt welled up inside of him, along with another foreign emotion.

"I will never forget your daddy. Paul was my first love and the father of my only child. He will always have a place in my heart, but it's been a long time now that he's been gone. And I have to move on." Wiping her hands on her dishcloth, she moved to stand behind her son and wrapped her arms around his neck, pulling him close to her bosom. "I loved your daddy, too, Terrell. But he would want me to be happy, don't you think?"

Terrell let his head rest against his mother. Her arms around him felt so good, so safe. For a moment, only a moment, things were the way they used to be, when it was just the two of them.

"I'll wait until I meet him before I decide if he's good enough for you," he said finally.

"He's good enough, I promise you." Rosie kissed his forehead. "I will always love you most, Terrell."

"I love you most, too, Mama." And at that moment he identified the emotion that had simmered within him over the last five days. Fear. He was afraid that this marriage—his mother's union with this man—would take her away from him. And then he'd have no one. His father was gone, and now his mother would be gone too.

Her touch and her words of love had dispelled that notion. His mother had always been there for him, and probably always would be. She looked really happy, so despite his own personal selfishness, if this man was the reason for that, he'd gladly give the union his blessing.

Terrell had just finished moving the furniture in the living room around to afford as much open space as possible. Considering his mother still possessed the biggest, heaviest furniture around, that wasn't an easy feat.

He heard the front door open, then voices in the hall. Wiping his hands on his jeans, he turned towards the entryway, knowing he was about to meet his mother's fiancé.

The man that walked into the room beside his mother was stocky, a Gerald Levert look-alike in expensive clothes. His mother seemed to adore him.

Terrell moved closer, his arm extended. "Terrell Pierce."

The older man clasped his hand and they exchanged the male street handshake and half hug. "Donald Douglas. It's good to finally meet you."

Douglas. The name rang a bell. "I've heard a lot about you, too, Mr. Douglas." Even saying the name sparked a familiar cord in Terrell's mind.

"Call me Donald. After all, we're about to be family."

Donald kept a protective arm around Rosie and Terrell watched his mother inch closer to him. "Yeah, I guess we are," he mumbled, unsure of how comfortable he was with another man touching his mother.

Donald noted the way the younger man watched him, and figured they needed to talk alone so that he could reassure this young fellow that he meant his mother no harm.

"Baby, why don't you go ahead and finish cooking that good food while Terrell and I get to know each other."

Rosie looked from one man to the other. "Okay, that's probably a good idea."

When they were alone, Donald looked around. "You need some help in here?" He took off his leather jacket and tossed it on the chair.

Terrell took a step back. "I think I've made as much space as I can, but I don't want to hear Mama's mouth later."

Donald laughed. "Yeah, if it's not just right she's liable to go off on both of us."

Terrell joined him in laughing as they lifted the ottoman and moved it into the hallway. "I'll take good care of her if that's what you're worried about," Donald said when it appeared Terrell wasn't going to broach the subject.

Terrell wiped the beads of sweat from his forehead with the back of his hand. "And by take good care of her you mean…?" Rosie said he owned the shop, but was that enough for them to live comfortably? Could his mother finally retire on this man's income alone?

Donald took deep, steady breaths, feeling every year of his age with each step he took carrying that heavy furniture. "We are both alone. We both need somebody. Rosie's good for me, and I've got to believe that I'm good for her. I won't hurt her."

Terrell frowned. Was he the only one who thought financial stability was the key to a good life? "And while you're being good for her, who's paying the bills?"

Donald chuckled. "Son, the last thing you've got to worry about is my finances. I'm secure for the rest of my life, and once I marry your mother, she will be too."

Terrell narrowed his eyes. "She's been working all her life. It's time she took a break."

"I hear you loud and clear on that one, and plan to sit her pretty little self down as soon as we tie the knot. It's all going to work out just fine. You'll see." Donald's thick lips spread into a warm grin.

Reluctantly, Terrell smiled too, willing himself to relax. Donald seemed sincere enough but there was something else nagging him about the man. He'd ask him a few more questions, talk to him until this disconcerting feeling went away—after all, they were about to be family.

Black slacks and a black blazer were both business and casual, Leah thought. A red blouse provided the splash of color she needed to perfectly balance the outfit. Sliding her feet into her black boots, she wondered what type of wedding Ms. Rosie would want.

Her job was to give couples the ultimate fantasy. Whatever they envisioned for that special day, it was her job to create it. Most men didn't really have any special ideas or requests for the ceremony. But the brides, the brides always had requests and demands and silly little whims that Leah sometimes found irritating and inconsequential.

Leah figured Ms. Rosie to be old-fashioned and set in her ways. A traditional church ceremony with lots of flowers, she thought. An evening reception with candles and jazz; a small hall, something cozy and intimate; probably one hundred to one hundred and fifty guests; warm colors—maybe ivory or rose, something like that. Her mind was exploding with ideas as she put the finishing touches on her makeup. Ms. Rosie had created a halo of curls around her face, so she didn't have much preparation in the hair department.

One last side-glance in the mirror showed that she looked satisfactory. The red blouse brightened her face, and the black suit hung on her slim frame perfectly. Her hands smoothed down the lapels of her jacket, and she picked at a piece of lint.

Grimacing, she noticed that her nails needed to be done. She hadn't had time to get them done yesterday because Melinda had called her with an emergency. Maria Avarez had called in a tizzy; her uncle had rented the hall out to someone else on the same date as her wedding. As Leah had told Melinda just yesterday morning, family were always the ones to start trouble.

Another call from her mother proved that theory as well. Marsha was contemplating another divorce. Every time her husband didn't do exactly what she wanted she was ready to kick him to the curb. Leah had listened to the recitation with barely contained fury. She hated how her mother jumped from relationship to relationship so easily. She wanted to tell her to just be by herself for a while.

Leah had vowed to always be by herself. She never wanted to commit to a serious relationship. Dates were fine, but anything beyond that was out of the question. On the rare occasions she allowed herself to have sex, she remained detached and distant. It wasn't because she didn't like it; she didn't really know if she liked it or not; she was always so busy making sure that her innermost feelings were well hidden that she never allowed herself to enjoy it.

There were four steps in a relationship for her. The first was dating, which was basically cool, dinner and a movie and then home. The second was the fifth date, which was sort of a milestone because if you went out with a guy more than four times then you must really like him. The third was sex. Once you allowed yourself to sleep with the man it meant that you liked him enough to explore the possibility of commitment. The fourth step, the one she'd vowed never to consider, was marriage.

Two times in her whole thirty years Leah had made it to the third step, after which she had quickly retreated and ended the relationship. The memory caused her to shiver as she slid her arms into her leather coat. "Never again," she muttered to herself. She scooped up her purse and grabbed her keys from the table near the door.

"Terrell, have you seen Donald?"

Terrell nodded his head in the direction of his mother's fiancé. "He's over there with the rest of his beauty shop clan."

"Oh, I see him." Rosie started to walk away, then changed her mind and turned back to her son. "You could mingle a little, son, talk to some people. There's no need for you to stand in this corner sulking all night."

After their talk earlier, Terrell felt that Donald definitely had feelings for his mother, yet he hadn't shaken the feeling that he knew Donald, or his name, from somewhere.

"I'm not sulking. I don't know these people." Hunching his shoulders, Terrell leaned back against the sturdy cherrywood china cabinet. He really wasn't in the mood for a party. He'd been thinking a lot about what his mother had said about Tanya, wondering if he had been wrong in his approach with her. All around the room were beauty shop girls, who reminded him of how pampered and primped Tanya was. In the beginning he'd admired that about her; now it seemed to sicken him. Scantily clad women with too much makeup on eyed him as he stood in his corner, and others he figured he was somehow related to whispered as they pigged out on his mother's food. He wanted desperately to go to his room, to log on to his computer and submerge himself in endless lines of code. That would keep him from thinking about his own dismal love life and his mother's blossoming one.

"If you walked around the room I'm sure you'd get to meet them. Besides, Aunt Pearl is right over there. Go on and speak to her."

"Mama," Terrell frowned. "Aunt Pearl is a moocher. The last time I saw her she borrowed a hundred dollars to go to Atlantic City. I haven't seen a penny of that money yet."

"If you really need it, I can give you the money back. Besides, that was almost a year ago," Rosie argued.

Terrell finished his drink and sighed. "The money's not the issue. I just don't feel like being bothered." As he said the words he looked at the disappointment on his mother's face and felt like a colossal ass. "But it's not about me tonight. So if it'll make you happy, I'll mingle."

Rosie smiled and smoothed her hand over his cheek. "That would make me very happy, baby."

Leah had just walked through the door when Nikki spotted her and grabbed hold of her arm. "You look nice." Looking her up and down, Nikki assessed her friend's choice of clothes. "You could unbutton that jacket and show some of that cleavage, though," she commented.

"This is not the club. And besides, I don't have much cleavage to show." Self-consciously, Leah looked down at her less-than-adequate breasts and frowned.

"Yeah, you're right," Nikki laughed. "At least unbutton that jacket. You look so uptight in all that black."

Leah noted Nikki's outfit and cringed with envy. Nikki's curves were amply displayed in the tight low-ride jeans that buttoned just below her navel and clung to her legs until they reached her knee, where they swung out freely in the returning seventies style. Her blouse was some filmy white material that hugged her heavy breasts and molded against her torso while the sleeves swirled loosely at her wrists. Large dangly earrings hung from her ears and framed her cherub-like face.

Leah fought the urge to give in to her longtime jealously of her best friend's good looks. Instead, she took the defensive route. "You could cover up a little more. It is February, you know," she told her wryly.

"Girl, please, this *is* covered up. I decided that it would be an older crowd here and the last thing I wanted was to cause some poor old man to have a heart attack." Twirling a long thick auburn curl between her fingers, Nikki's eyes roamed across the room.

"So where's the happy couple?" Leah searched for Rosie. She wanted to make an appearance at the party, to show her support for Ms. Rosie, even though she really wasn't in the mood. Leon had called her cell while she was in the car, wanting to see her tonight. She was more than glad to have an excuse to avoid him, yet he persisted and, finally, she'd promised to at least call him when she was leaving the party to see if hooking up were possible. She really needed to give this relationship with him some serious thought. It just didn't seem like fun anymore. Lately it seemed more like work.

The small row house was filled with people and food. Women and men sat in every imaginable spot in the house, from the couch to the dining room chairs to the footstool in the hallway and even the steps leading to the upstairs. In their hands they held plastic plates heaped with what she imagined was home-cooked soul food. Leah spotted Rosie talking to a tall, sort of attractive gentleman who looked less than pleased to be there. Leah felt for him; she wanted to go home too.

"I'm gonna go over and speak to Ms. Rosie," she told Nikki.

"Where is she?" Nikki had been watching a young man herself, but not the same young man that Leah had seen with Rosie. No, this man was tall, dark-skinned and positively scrumptious.

Placing the palm of her hand firmly into Nikki's nest of curls, Leah turned her friend's head in Rosie's direction. "If you'd stop drooling over Mr. Wonderful for just a second, you would see there are other people in this room."

"Yeah, yeah, yeah. Those other people don't look half as good as Mr. Wonderful does." Rolling her eyes, Nikki returned her attention to the man they had correctly dubbed Mr. Wonderful. "Just wait a minute, and I'll go over with you."

Leah looked at her friend, who stood with her eyes transfixed on the man who had just returned her smile. Nikki's face lit up, and Leah knew it was hopeless to try to reach her now. "That's okay. You stay here and keep watch, I'll be right back."

"Mmmhmm," Nikki mumbled as Leah walked away from her.

Terrell had taken a few steps toward his Aunt Pearl when a woman with a mop of curls on her head appeared in his path. Before he could move out of her way, they collided.

She knew the guy had seen her coming and figured he would move to the side to allow her to pass. Obviously, she had assumed wrong. Reining in her temper, she righted herself and mumbled, "Excuse me."

"No, excuse me. I thought we had enough room to move around each other." Terrell looked down at her.

If you had attempted to move we probably would have had enough space, Leah thought to herself before realizing that this was the guy Rosie had been speaking to a few moments ago. His deep voice resonated in her ears, and she felt as if they were the only two people in the room. He seemed taller now that she stood face to face with him. Long, slender fingers still gripped her arm where he had grabbed her to keep her from hitting the floor.

Dark brown eyes stared down at her through thin, gold-rimmed glasses. A tingling began deep down in her stomach. The aroma of food must be getting to me, she thought. She needed to talk to Rosie, then she'd get something to eat, then she'd leave.

"If you'll excuse me again, I'd like to talk to Ms. Rosie before someone else gets to her." Leah made a futile attempt to break free of his grasp. Despite his deceptive looks, he was quite strong.

Terrell noticed the questioning in the hazel eyes that stared at him. Following their gaze to where his fingers lay on her arm, he slowly moved his hand away. He instantly regretted that action. The moment he'd bumped into her he'd felt something. A surge so deep and so potent he couldn't quite explain. "I'm sorry, I just didn't want you to fall." He liked touching her, liked it immensely.

"I'm fine now." Leah stepped to the side to walk around him.

Terrell mimicked her movement, "Ah, did you say you're looking for my mother, um, I mean Rosie?" His inquisitive gaze pinned her to where she stood. He clasped his hands in front of him to keep from reaching out to touch her again.

"Ms. Rosie's your mother?" Now she realized why he looked familiar—the graduation photo taped to the mirror of Ms. Rosie's station at the shop. So this was Terrell Pierce, Ms. Rosie's only child, the apple of her eye? She'd heard so much about him and his accomplishments she could probably write his bio. She paused a moment to survey him. Mmm hmmm, he looked every bit the computer geek his mother had described. He was tall—she did like tall men—his light skin clear, darkened only by the thin mustache and goatee he wore. His glasses concealed the true depth of his eyes. Right off the bat she wouldn't call him handsome, that word didn't seem to suit him at all. Yet there was something…

"Yes. I'm Terrell." Unclasping his arms, he extended his hand and waited for her compliance.

Leah moved slowly, calmly taking his hand. For a moment his warm palm gave her a start, but she quickly dismissed it. "I'm Leah Graham. I'm the wedding coordinator." Gripping his hand in a businesslike manner, Leah watched his questioning glare.

"Oh? The wedding…yeah, I guess that's why we're here, right? So weddings need to be coordinated now?" He eyed her suspiciously. Her hands were satiny smooth, and he wondered if all her skin felt the same.

"Some people like their big day planned specifically and want it to go off without a hitch. That's where I come in."

"And they pay you for that?" He sounded incredulous.

"Yes, and they pay me well," she stated boldly. Who the hell was he to question her job? Her credibility?

He made her uncomfortable. She couldn't explain why. Maybe it was the way he seemed to stare right through her. Maybe it was the fact that he continued to block her way. Whichever, she wanted to get away from him as quickly as possible. "Can I have my hand back now?"

Terrell smiled.

Her stomach clenched.

He released her hand. "Sorry about that," he said softly. Staring at her curiously, he noted the quick play of emotions, a sense of loss quickly replaced by rigid politeness. She'd felt it too—that strange tugging between them. "Then by all means you must find your client. My mother went that way." He nodded towards the other side of the room.

Her hand was free yet she still didn't move. His smile had reached those dark brown eyes, warming them until she felt herself being drawn to him. His slow gaze caressed her and she was breathless.

She was a fruitcake for standing there gaping at him that way! For goodness sake, he was only Ms. Rosie's workaholic son, not some gorgeous movie star. "Excuse me," she mumbled and quickly moved away before she could make a further fool of herself.

CHAPTER FOUR

"So what did you have in mind, Ms. Rosie?" Leah asked, sitting at the kitchen table while Rosie refilled the punch bowl.

"Oh I don't know, something small and personal. I want everyone to have a good time, though. But we can talk about this later. Relax, enjoy yourself, baby." Rosie chuckled. Leah was just as serious and career-driven as Terrell.

"I don't think your son's having a good time." Leah thought about the man with the heart-stopping smile and clapped her lips tightly together, hoping she hadn't offended Ms. Rosie.

At Leah's remark Rosie's hand momentarily lost its hold on the punch bowl and red liquid sloshed over its rim. "Oh, lawdy!" she stammered, reaching for the dishrag, her mind instantly registering the connection. She'd just been comparing Leah and Terrell in her mind and here Leah was verbally mentioning him. Wasn't that something?

"I'm sorry." Leah stood, grabbing paper towels from the overhead rack to mop the counter.

"You met Terrell?" Rosie looked at Leah. She'd always been a pretty girl, quiet and very serious. And she never talked about the men in her life as most of her clients did. Rosie often wondered how she could be such good friends with the feisty Nikki.

"Yeah, we sort of bumped into each other a few minutes ago. Maybe he's sad because his girlfriend's not here with him."

"They broke up, but I don't think that's all that's bothering him. My wedding announcement was quite a shock." Rosie finished cleaning the mess. "Sit down, I've got this under control." She motioned to Leah.

"Oh?" Just broke up with his girlfriend? That was interesting. Leah took a seat. "So anyway, about fifty or an even hundred guests, you think?" Her heart skipped several beats at the realization that Terrell was single, and she quickly blamed it on her growing hunger. *Talk about business.* That would keep her mind from wandering into the other room where he was.

"I'd say one twenty-five. That's a safe number. But Donald wants to sit down with us and talk too. Why don't you get your ideas together and we can meet tomorrow to plan things out?" Rosie lifted the heavy punch bowl, preparing to go back into the dining room.

"I have to go to church in the morning, but I guess I could come around about four, if that's okay with you?" *Will Terrell be there?* Thank goodness she caught herself before verbalizing that question. Whether he was there or not didn't concern her.

"That's just fine. Now get out there and get yourself something to eat." Rosie was through the swinging door leading into the dining room before Leah could decline her offer. Besides, the low growl in her stomach agreed with Ms. Rosie.

"I might as well," she muttered to herself, and had just leaned against the door to open it when it suddenly swung open in her direction. Quick reflexes saved her from a broken nose as the person on the other side tried to gain admission.

"What the hell?" Terrell grumbled and leaned against the door again.

Stepping back quickly, Leah caught the swinging door on its next rotation. Holding the door back, she waited for the person on the other side to enter. Hazel eyes clashed with simmering dark brown ones and the air crackled around them.

"Damn, didn't you know…" His words were cut short when he realized who he was about to yell at. "Sorry," he muttered. It seemed he would spend the duration of the night apologizing to this woman.

"Yeah, sorry." Leah rolled her eyes. She was destined to end up embarrassed and lying flat on her back with this guy around. "Are you coming in?" Her gaze fell to his lips and she quickly looked away.

"Yes, I'm coming…in." He was staring at her again. He didn't know why, though. She wasn't beautiful. She wasn't hard to look at , but he wouldn't say she was beautiful. There was something about her—something about her eyes. He couldn't quite place it, and it didn't really matter. He was here to figure out this new situation with his mother, not to fantasize about this woman. Yet he found himself examining her from head to toe again. She was a bit tall for a woman, probably around five-nine or ten. He couldn't tell through the dark pants she wore, but he would bet the entire money clip tucked into his left pocket that she had legs that stretched to forever.

A perky little nose was perfectly centered between high cheekbones, just above thin lips that were now upturned slightly. But it was her eyes that kept him captivated. Her sparkling hazel eyes bored into him with such unbridled intensity that he was speechless for a moment. *Shake it off, man, you just got out of a bad relationship.* "So you're planning my mother's wedding?" he asked, trying to calm the heat heading towards his groin.

Business. She breathed a sigh of relief. Thank goodness he'd brought up business. "Yes, if they like my ideas, I will."

"You've known them for a long time?"

Focusing on his words, and not his understated good looks, she shrugged. "I've known Ms. Rosie for a few years. I met Mr. Donald about a year ago. After he moved back to town."

Her words successfully drew his eyes away from her mouth, about which he was entertaining detailed thoughts. "He's not from Baltimore?"

"I think he is, but after that big investigation he left for a while—waited until things died down, I suppose."

Terrell raised a brow, took a step closer to her. They were standing too far apart, and he didn't like it. "What investigation?"

Leah took a step backwards and bumped into the counter. He was too close. "I don't know the specifics, just tidbits that Nikki told me. But everything's…"

His eyes darkened considerably as he moved even closer to her.

She licked her lips. "Everything's okay now," she whispered.

"Oh really?" he asked, lightly tracing a finger over her chin. This wasn't what he was here for. He wasn't supposed to be feeling the things he was feeling at this very moment. He'd just broken up with Tanya. The plan was to deal with his mother and her fiancé first, then focus on finding himself a wife. Yet he couldn't resist.

Leah shivered at his touch. His toned body was pressed against hers and she could feel the hard contours of a man who worked out a lot. Her fingers itched to touch him. She stared into his face, which was long and angular and had a freshly trimmed goatee. Gold-rimmed glasses sat atop an almost perfect nose and showcased sizzling brown eyes.

She was not doing this. She was not feeling something for this man that she barely knew. He'd insulted her, mocked her job, and now she was standing here letting him touch her, praying he'd kiss her. "I think they make a wonderful couple," she stammered, hoping her words would break this foolish spell. She had a boyfriend, or whatever it was that Leon was to her. And Terrell was not her type. Ms. Rosie said he was quiet, reserved, focused on his job. Well, right now he was quietly driving her mad with his gentle touch and sexy voice.

"That remains to be seen." He'd heard her words, remembered feeling as though he'd seen Donald somewhere before, and vowed to investigate further. But now, right at this very moment, this woman intrigued the hell out of him. What he was feeling, what he was imagining doing to her, was totally new to him and he couldn't seem to stop himself. Yet she purposely held herself away from him while her eyes all but seduced him into kissing her.

"I'm meeting with them again tomorrow to lay the groundwork." She didn't know why she told him that, or why she remained in that kitchen alone with him. Leon was waiting for her. "They're celebrating tonight and don't have time to sit down and go over details the way we need to. So I'm leaving." So she said, but her feet remained planted where they stood. As unwelcome and foreign as she knew it was, she finally put a name to what she was feeling...lust, pure and simple. But she shouldn't have been feeling that with Terrell. Leon was the man in her life.

Terrell's finger found its way up to her lips. He lightly touched them and watched her tremble. Desire soared through his loins so powerfully that he had to take a step back or else he'd have to put her up on his mother's counter and take what he so desperately wanted right now. Folding his long arms across his chest, he continued to watch her. "You don't look like you're leaving."

If it were possible, his already deep voice went deeper, lowering to a husky growl. Her knees wobbled, actually knocked into each other at the exact moment he reached out again and touched her lips one last time. She closed her eyes, shook her head, felt the soft curls against her face. She was not affected by their close proximity, his sizzling gaze or his sexy voice—or at least she told herself she wasn't. Lifting her hand, she brushed his away from her face and looked him squarely in the eyes. "That's because you're again standing in my way."

Her brisk tone snapped him out of his trance. Abruptly, he took another step back and out of her way. She was distracting him. Making him think of something other than Tanya, other than his mother and her impending nuptials. "I'm not in your way now," he quipped.

Just that quickly his rich, sexy tone turned cold and dismissive. That was fine with her.

She was out the door before his decision to keep his hands off her could be tempted again. And it was a good thing, he told himself. He wasn't here for this. He'd just been betrayed by a woman; he needed time to re-evaluate what it was he wanted, just like his mother had said. Ms. Leah Graham, Ms. Wedding Planner, was not a part of that re-evaluation.

It didn't matter that with her casual good looks and cool demeanor she'd managed to stir him more than any other woman he'd ever met. She wasn't on his agenda.

Leah had been up half the night, scribbling notes for her proposal to Ms. Rosie and her fiancé that afternoon. She'd finally decided on two suggestions that she thought would work really well for the couple.

Her first suggestion was an early ceremony to be held at the church around noon. The ceremony would be followed by a luncheon reception scheduled to begin at one-thirty. Depending or whether they wanted her to plan the reception as well, she had come up with a satisfying lunch menu and decorative ideas.

The second option was an afternoon ceremony to be followed by the more traditional dinner reception. For this, the food would be more costly, but should they choose this one, Leah had a menu ready.

Her proposals were neatly typed, complete with pictures and a photo album of past affairs. Sliding all of her materials into her black briefcase, Leah was ready to make her presentation.

Her morning had gotten off to a rocky start when her mother made an appearance at morning worship. Marsha rarely ever came to church, so Leah was both stunned and dismayed. Something must truly be wrong for her mother to turn to God for an answer.

Just as she had assumed, something was truly wrong. Daryl, her mother's husband, had suggested they go to marriage counseling. Marsha was absolutely furious.

"Can you believe him? Like I need counseling. I don't need no counseling. He's the one that's got to go," she screeched during the altar prayer.

"Shhh!" Leah tried to calm her mother down as the woman in front of them turned to stare at the commotion.

"I'm not going to no shrink for them to tell me what I already know. I ain't stayin' married to that man a minute longer," she whispered. Wringing her hands together, Marsha shifted from foot to foot, anxious for the deacon to end the prayer.

"Amen," the congregation murmured and returned to their seats.

"Mama, you have got to calm down. Maybe Daryl has a good idea with the counseling. It might help." Sliding into the pew, Leah waited for what she knew would be Marsha's negative response.

"How is it going to help? He's not going to change," she whined.

"What is it that you want him to change? You never told me what the problem is," Leah whispered, hoping that her mother would follow suit and lower her voice as well. But like a child, Marsha seemed oblivious to her subtlety.

"He is so mean, he wants to put my children out. *My* children, Leah. And you know I don't have no man tellin' me how to raise my children."

Yeah, Leah thought to herself, Marsha didn't like anyone telling her how to raise her children. Sammy and DJ were the youngest, and the only two still at home with her mother. Sammy was twenty-one and DJ was nineteen. Neither one of them worked, neither one of them had graduated from high school, and they both were in and out of trouble so often that Leah had stopped counting the number of times she'd been to the police station with her mother to bail them out.

Leah loved her brothers, but she had to admit her mother had no control over them. They always did exactly what they wanted, when they wanted, and that was usually the wrong thing.

"Mama, it is his house." Trying to placate Marsha, Leah placed her hand on her shoulder.

"I don't give a damn. I cook and clean for that man and I wash all his clothes and I live in that house too. If my children go, I go," Marsha said adamantly.

Oh Lord, Leah thought, and where were they all going to stay? Marsha didn't have anywhere to go and, while Leah would have considered taking her mother in, she was definitely not letting her grown, wayward brothers live with her.

For the remainder of the service Marsha complained and threatened and cried and whined. Leah was so emotionally drained by the time she walked out of the church that she almost went home to crash instead of going to her appointment. Luckily, she had a strong work ethic, and the thought of conversing with normal people was a welcome relief.

Then Leon called, furious with her for brushing him off. This was the first time they'd actually had an argument, the first time he'd raised his voice to her. But she was in no mood to deal with him either.

Having had enough drama for the day, she quickly ended the call and attempted to clear her mind. She had business to take care of— even though that business involved the one thing that scared her most in life, at the same time it provided her only escape.

Terrell had suffered through the night. Not only was his mother enthusiastic about this marriage but her fiancé apparently had a blemished past, one he needed to resolve before this wedding took place.

Still, that hadn't been what had kept him awake. Eyes the shade of perfectly aged rum had haunted him through the night. They seemed embedded onto the backs of his eyelids, so that every time he closed his eyes he saw them. Whether piqued with interest or hot with rage, he was enamored of them. Then cold, manipulative black eyes replaced those intriguing eyes, and his anger flared. Tanya. Thoughts of her shattered the pleasure he'd had thinking of Leah.

He'd awakened in a foul mood that he was unable or unwilling to shake. At breakfast, he was short with his mother and agitated by Donald's presence, although he was careful not to show it.

"Terrell, is something bothering you, son?" Donald asked at the table.

"No. I guess I'm just tired." He wanted to ask Donald about the investigation Leah had mentioned, but didn't want to upset his mother. No, he'd collect his information on Donald, then he'd confront the man. He was certain that something wasn't quite right with Donald Douglas.

"Your mother told me how hard you work. Maybe you need to take a break. There's more to life than making money, you know," Donald said as he sipped his coffee.

Terrell found that hard to believe, coming from a man who drove a luxury car, owned his own business and wore diamonds that could blind you. Leaning back in his chair, he asked nonchalantly, "What else is there?"

Donald chuckled heartily, then reached for Rosie's hand. "There's love. Find yourself a good woman so you can experience it for yourself."

That was exactly what he wanted to do. Instead, Terrell's gaze moved to his mother, witnessed her blush. Then he lifted his own cup. "I haven't had much luck in that department," he said gruffly. To his surprise a tall, leggy vixen stole into his thoughts.

"You haven't found the right one yet, Terrell," Rosie said softly. "But you will, and when you do, nothing else will matter."

Terrell stood, having had enough of the love birds for the time being. "Well, when I find her, I'll certainly let you know."

He emptied his cup and left them alone in the kitchen. He had a phone call to make.

The living room was quieter this afternoon. The couch with its cream and burgundy floral print beckoned Leah to partake of its comfort as she waited for Donald to join her and Rosie. Rosie looked tired, her usually gay features tight and restrained.

"Ms. Rosie, is everything okay?" she asked, fearing that she and Donald had experienced a fight or something. Many couples got so stressed out or so scared about the impending nuptials that they often got into silly arguments as a way of venting.

"I'm fine, Leah, baby. I'm just worried about..." Rosie broke off before telling Leah she was worried about Terrell. That wouldn't be appropriate. "I'm fine, everything is going to be just fine." With a timid smile the older woman looked at the younger one.

"Hello." Donald came into the room, bringing an air of festivity with him. "Ms. Graham, it's nice to see you again." He extended his hand to Leah.

"Hello, Mr. Douglas," Leah replied politely. She remembered seeing Donald Douglas occasionally in and out of the shop, apparently checking on his investment. "You can call me Leah."

"Okay, Leah, you can call me Donald."

"How about Mr. Donald?" Leah suggested jovially. "Are you ready to start planning the big day?" She wasn't sure what had happened earlier that morning with the couple, but part of her job was to constantly remind them of the happy occasion they were embarking on.

"That's fair." Donald ran his hand over his graying hair. "I guess I am old enough to be your daddy." They all laughed. "And I don't know how much planning I'll be doing, but I'm ready to hear what you have to say."

Leah began the presentation, pausing to answer Rosie's questions and carefully explain all the formalities of the contract and payments to Donald.

After two hours of invitations, napkins, favors, colors and other matrimonial chatter, Donald rose to leave the room. "Whatever you ladies agree on is fine with me. Leah, you can just send me the bill. And remember, whatever she wants, spare no expense." He looked at Rosie adoringly before leaning over to kiss her.

Packed and ready to leave, Terrell came down the stairs. Earlier he'd gone to church with his mother, and now he just wanted to get home and do some work. Dressed in jeans and one of his more worn Howard sweatshirts, he made his way into the living room.

His mother sat on the sofa turning the pages of what looked like a large photo album. Next to her, a long-legged woman made comments about the materials found on each page. She hadn't said she was meeting his mother here. He felt that same stirring in his gut he'd felt last night, and tried to figure out why only she made him feel this way.

"This invitation is nice, Ms. Rosie, if you decide to go with the ivory and peach we discussed earlier." Leaning closer over the book, Leah pointed to the page with one long, elegant finger.

"Oooh, I like that one. And the rose on the front will be peach?" Rosie inquired.

"Yes ma'am, the basic invitation will be ivory, the rose on the front will be in peach and when you open it the writing will be in black. You can go to the back of the book to pick out the script that you like. You'll also get R.S.V.P. cards in ivory and peach, which will match the invitation, and gold seals to close the outer envelope." She spoke knowledgeably in a sultry voice.

Transfixed by her every movement, Terrell stood watching her interact with his mother. Stopping frequently, but patiently, she answered Rosie's questions and gave advice. The sound of her voice moved through him as smooth and warm as fine wine.

He took a step toward them, so mesmerized he forgot about the weak floorboard that had gotten him into trouble as a teenager when he used to sneak in the house after curfew. The squeak caught the attention of both ladies, and they raised their heads to spy the culprit.

His gaze met hers and held.

"Hello, Terrell. You remember Leah, don't you?" Rosie spoke first.

"We met last night." Moving slowly, deliberately, he stepped completely into the living room. "Hello, Leah."

"Hi, Terrell," Leah replied cautiously. He looked fresh, showered and casually groomed. She'd tried to convince herself that whatever she'd felt for him last night was a fluke, but that fluttering in her stomach was back. The physical attraction was obvious, yet today, in this quiet room as he watched her with elusive eyes, she felt something else.

"We were just picking out invitations. Would you like to join us?" Rosie was hopeful that her son would want to participate. Not that she needed his input. She could handle the decision by herself. She just wanted him to be a part of her very special day despite his recent letdown in the love department. His shaking head dashed those hopes.

"Nah, I'm about to head home." With learned restraint, he tore his gaze from the younger woman. Again, he felt a pull towards her and tried to ignore it. She was a lovely temptation, though.

"Oh?" Sliding the book from her lap to the coffee table, Rosie stood and walked over to her son. "I was hoping you would at least stay for dinner." Reaching out, she took his hand.

Her voice was familiar, soothing, and he instantly felt guilty. He really didn't have to rush off. He'd already called his friend, left a message vaguely describing what he needed. His cell phone was always available for a return call. He looked down into his mother's warm eyes and expectant face. "I'd love to have dinner with you. How about Ruth's Chris? That's still your favorite, right?"

Rosie beamed. "It sure is."

Terrell had already decided he wouldn't let on to his doubts about Donald, not until he had concrete evidence to make an informed decision. So for right now, he'd simply keep his doubts to himself.

Rosie was still smiling. "I'll go and make the reservation. You sit and keep Leah company until I get back." Turning towards the sofa she told Leah, "Excuse me, baby, I'll just be a minute."

Moved by the obvious affection between mother and son, Leah said, "It's okay. We can go over this stuff tomorrow or you can call my office to make an appointment." She felt that she was intruding on a private moment between mother and son. Her relationship with her own mother was nothing like this.

"Well, okay," Rosie reluctantly agreed. "Terrell, help her with her stuff," she directed before shuffling out of the room.

The last thing Leah wanted was to be alone with him again, yet that was exactly where she found herself. She sensed the moment he closed in on her and tensed. "I can do it myself," she said in a strained voice.

"I'll help you," Terrell offered, despite her resistance.

She tried to move faster, keeping her back to him. "That's okay. I've got it." But her clumsy fingers contradicted her, and she dropped the invitation book. With a sigh of frustration she bent down to pick it up.

Terrell bent down with her and they both grabbed the book. "Why won't you let me help you?"

"Because I don't need your help," she snapped.

He made her antsy. She wasn't sure why and was afraid to take the time to figure it out. All she knew for sure was that she was in a semi-relationship with Leon that she needed to figure out quickly and now this man, who was so unlike what she was normally attracted to, had stormed into her life, giving her butterfingers. She was definitely not used to the loss of control of her own feelings, and didn't like the implications one bit.

Terrell saw her struggle and decided to give her some space. He let go of the book, stood up and backed away, watching as she set the book to the side and pulled together her other items. He could have walked her to the door then, could have bid her a pleasant afternoon and gone on about his business, but that would have been too much like right. Instead, he slipped one hand into his pocket and stared at her. "So how well do you know Donald?"

Leah blinked in confusion, not really sure why he was asking her about Donald. "Not all that well. Why do you ask?" She looked around, making sure she hadn't left anything. The last thing she wanted was to have to come back here. She made a mental note to make all her future appointments with Ms. Rosie at her office.

Terrell shrugged. "I'm just curious. How can you plan a wedding for two people and not know if they should be together or not?"

She heard him talking, was oh so aware that he was still in the room with her, and felt a slight panic that she couldn't find her keys. She quickly spotted them in the side opening of her purse and returned her attention to the last book, attempting again to put it into her bag. He grew quiet, and she knew that he was waiting for an answer. She spared him a glance. "It's not really my job to judge if they should be together or not. I simply give them the wedding that they want." He looked really good in jeans, almost as good as she remembered him looking last night in slacks and a sweater. His angular face was void of any emotion, though, his eyes hooded behind glasses that were slipping down his nose.

"So if they end up divorced within a year it doesn't bother you one way or the other, as long as you get paid?"

His raised brow and barely masked look of distaste bothered her. "My job is to plan weddings, Terrell. That's it. I'm not a matchmaker, nor am I a fortune teller. I cannot predict what will happen after the wedding day and I don't try to."

Her curls were looser today, hanging further down her back than they had last night. She wore a long, straight dress that delectably hugged her curves. He still couldn't see her legs, but her plump breasts and voluptuous backside were enough to get his blood heated. Those bewitching eyes had even darkened a shade as she spoke to him.

"I believe that people should make sure they're well suited for each other before jumping into marriage, don't you?" Was she getting angry? Her chin squared and her fingers tightened on the book in her hand as she struggled with it.

Leah gave an exasperated sigh. That damned book just didn't want to go into the bag. "Look, I don't subscribe to that whole philosophy of 'meant to be' and 'happily ever after', so I really couldn't tell you." She didn't know which was ticking her off more, the book or Terrell.

Terrell saw that she was having a hard time and, despite her previous protests that she didn't need his help, he went to stand beside her, taking a firm hold of the book. "Then why plan weddings if you don't believe in them?"

She tried to pull the book away from him, but he held firm, his eyes holding her with an intense gaze. Feeling childish for participating in this tug of war, she loosened her grip and he nodded slightly before slipping it effortlessly into the bag.

"Thank you," she mumbled.

"You didn't answer my question." He caught her wrist when she would have walked around him toward the door.

"I plan weddings because I love to do it. I love creating a fantasy for people even if I don't believe in the fantasy myself. It's my job, not my life. I keep the two totally separate. Now if you'll excuse me, I have to go."

She smelled good. Nothing overpowering, something soft and quietly sweet, just like her. She pulled her arm from his grasp, but he moved quicker than she did, and now stood in the doorway. He wasn't ready for her to leave yet, wasn't ready for their time together to end. "Have dinner with me." He didn't know why he'd said it, hadn't planned on asking her out, but there it was.

Leah gripped her bag and purse tightly, staring at him in disbelief. "What? Why?" Her mind whirled—this guy switched channels faster than digital television.

Terrell chuckled. "Because I like talking to you."

She pursed her lips, looked at him levelly, finally appreciating her own height. "You like grilling me about a job you don't understand? Or is it that you want to find something wrong with your mother marrying Donald, and I'm your only link?"

She was sharp, he'd give her that, even though those reasons had nothing to do with his wanting her to have dinner with him. "No. Because I like talking to you." His eyes fell to her lips and he wondered how they would taste, imagined they'd be as sweet as she smelled.

Leah looked away. His smile was lethal, she'd learned that last night. "I don't think dinner is a good idea."

"Why?"

She had never been good at lying or beating around the bush so she simply blurted it out. "You're really not my type." And with that she took advantage of the element of surprise, turned and hastily walked out the door.

Terrell stood flabbergasted at her admission. *Not her type.* He smiled to himself.

CHAPTER FIVE

Dinner with his mother went well, but then Terrell had assured himself that it would. He wined and dined his mother, catering to her every need, not because he wanted her to talk to him more about Donald, but because she deserved it.

He didn't even care if they talked about Donald again that night. He was going to find out what he needed to know about his mother's fiancé, but tonight he was simply going to enjoy her company. Afterwards, he dropped Rosie off at her house then headed back to his condo.

On the drive home, he contemplated how Leah Graham, the hazel-eyed temptress, fit into his plan, because try as he might, he couldn't get her out of his mind. When he'd questioned her about her job, those luminescent eyes had turned dark, laced with anger. He'd instantly been turned on by this fiery side of her, and wondered if she transformed like that in the bedroom.

He knew he'd been out of line in pressing her about her job, but hell, he was curious. She made her living from planning weddings, yet she wasn't married and according to their earlier conversation, had no intentions to get married. That was interesting indeed. Leah Graham was a puzzle he wouldn't mind finding all the pieces to.

He was supposed to be concentrating on his mother and the upcoming wedding, the one he'd offered to pay for. When his mother refused the offer, he'd settled for buying her dress. Soon he'd walk her down the aisle, giving her to Donald Douglas. A long time ago he'd realized his father was never coming back; a day ago he'd realized his mother had found someone to replace his father. In the span of two short weeks his life had taken some drastic turns, but none as intriguing as bumping into Leah in his mother's living room, or the coincidence that she was planning his mother's wedding. They were bound to see each other again…for business purposes, that is.

Leah was in her office early Monday morning, somewhat recovered from her tumultuous weekend. Her mother's husband had called her late Sunday night to inform her that, despite Marsha's threats to leave him, he had no intention of letting her go. Which was very admirable of him, Leah thought. Maybe Marsha had finally met her match.

As for her new account, Leah all but cringed at the thought of future run-ins with Rosie's son. He was weird and moody. One minute he was asking her about her job, the next he was interrogating her about Donald and Rosie's relationship. Then he had asked her out to dinner. That had really thrown her. Why on earth would he ask her out? Except for a few really heated looks, he mostly seemed irritated by her.

She couldn't quite figure him out and, frankly, wasn't interested in trying. His type she knew well—highly intellectual and unforgiving of anyone who wasn't just like him. She didn't care for those characteristics in a man. He'd talked about her job as if it were beneath him, a menial wedding planner, coordinating weddings she didn't even believe in.

Well, she did believe in them…for everybody else, that is. Marriage just wasn't her cup of tea. Was that so wrong? Hell no, she was good at her job, and damn proud of it. And if Terrell Pierce had a problem with that, then he could just get a life!

Still, she couldn't dismiss the other side she'd seen of him. The compassionate, caring son who would plainly do anything for his mother. As feelings go, she'd been impressed by that. And his touch, each time he'd laid his hands on her in his mother's kitchen, had been so gentle, as if he were touching something very fragile, something special. She shivered with the memory.

The shrill ringing of the phone quickly snapped her out of her reverie. Snatching up the receiver, she answered, "Good morning, The Perfect Day."

"Good morning. Is this the perfect lady?" Leon's smooth baritone voice echoed over the line.

He didn't sound angry anymore, and she was glad. She definitely didn't feel like arguing with him. "Nope, it's just me." Smiling, she settled back into her chair, thoughts of Terrell all but vanishing from her mind.

"I happen to think 'just me' is perfect. How are you? I missed you this weekend."

"I'm good. Listen. About yesterday…I want to apologize." It was the least she could do for blowing him off. It wasn't that she didn't like Leon, she just wasn't sure she wanted to take things further with him.

"Don't worry about it. There'll be more time for us later. Anyway, I met with the guy from Hecht's this morning and he's going to carry the line in the fall."

"That's great! I'm sure Calvin's pleased."

"Yeah, but you know that means we have to work harder to create better merchandise. Hecht's is already carrying Fubu and RoccaWear, and the younger dudes are really into that." He let out a sigh. "I just hope we can compete."

"Well, your target is the urban professional. Professionals can't wear jeans and flamboyant silk shirts to work, however nice they may look."

"I guess you're right. I mean, don't get me wrong, I have a couple pair of Fubu jeans and I generally like the clothes they're putting out. But until corporate America goes more casual, I guess we're pretty safe."

"I think you'll do fine."

"I'd do much better if I could see you tonight." He really had missed her. In the time that he'd known her he had quickly become attached, thinking that they were the perfect couple, two ambitious, struggling professionals on their way up in the world.

Maybe she should see him, Leah thought. She did need a refresher from the last two days. After a few seconds of debate she replied, "That sounds good. What do you have in mind?"

"Dinner, a movie, a nightcap…" Pausing a moment he added, "…Breakfast."

"Let's just stick with dinner and a movie." Steps three and four loomed over her like a dark cloud. Leah knew Leon was more serious about their relationship than she was. So far he'd accepted her limitations, but she knew that the time for her to make the decision about moving to the next step was growing closer.

"I'll accept that for now," he told her, laughter evident in his deep voice. "I'll pick you up about seven, okay?"

"Seven's fine," she answered quickly, making a mental note to give step three some serious thought in the very near future.

Hanging up the phone, she pictured Leon sitting behind the massive, paper-cluttered desk in his office. He would have on a shirt and tie, probably a white shirt, laundered with heavy starch, and a slick silk tie. An Onyx exclusive suit jacket would be thrown across one of the chairs, and glossy black tie-up Eddie Bauer's would be on his feet. Damn, she was shocked she knew him so well. They'd been dating for about four months now, which computed to be about six times with Leon's traveling schedule. He was fine, successful and crazy about her. That ought to be enough to proceed to step three, but somehow it just didn't seem so. Maybe when she saw him tonight she'd get a feeling for what the next step should be. Or maybe not.

At ten minutes to five, Leah was grabbing her purse and looking around for her keys when the phone rang. Racing across the office to get to it, she snatched the receiver out of its cradle and answered, "The Perfect Day."

"Ms. Graham, please?" a male voice requested.

"This is Ms. Graham." Thinking it was a prospective client she abandoned the search for her keys and snatched up a pen.

"This is Terrell Pierce."

The sound of his name had her dropping her pen.

"What can I do for you, Mr. Pierce?"

"Oh? I'm Mr. Pierce now? Just yesterday I was Terrell," he quipped.

"What can I do for you?" she said, dismissing the pleasantries.

"You turned down my dinner invitation. So how about lunch?"

His voice was enticing, and she pinched herself in an effort to kill the fanciful feelings developing in the pit of her stomach. "That's not possible."

"There's something I need your help with," he said, hoping she'd be curious enough to ask what.

"What could you possibly need my help with?"

He smiled. "I need you to explain why I'm not your type."

"You're kidding, right?"

"No, I'm not. If you're going to tell a man he's not your type, the least you can do is elaborate on what your type is. Come on, you have to eat."

"I bring my lunch."

"Then I'll come to your office and we can share."

"No."

"What if I call tomorrow and ask you to breakfast?"

Leah didn't know if she was impressed or annoyed, but either way it had her stifling a smile. "Not my type means, I don't date men like you. Date means any breakfast, lunch or dinner when you pick me up and pay for it. Is that clear enough?"

She hadn't hung up on him, her tone wasn't angry. He was making progress. "What exactly are men like me? And who said I was paying? I understand you own your own company. You should be able to afford your own meal," he said jokingly.

Leah laughed out loud then. "I can, and that's why I eat alone."

"See, we get along really well. We should see each other again. First impressions aren't always accurate. And we met under stressful circumstances."

Leah was perched on the edge of her desk now, twirling the phone cord around one finger as she talked. "Stressful? I wasn't stressed."

"Well, I was. My mother's wedding announcement hit me kind of hard. And I'm still trying to figure out if her fiancé's on the up and up."

She didn't want to discuss that with him. That was his own personal hang-up, and she didn't need to get involved. "I'm sorry to hear you're taking her happy news badly, but that really doesn't concern me. Now if that's all you want—"

"Are you in a hurry or something? Did I interrupt you?"

"Actually, I'm on my way out. I have a date tonight." She didn't know why the information just slipped out—like he cared anyway whether she had a date or not.

"A date?"

His tone had changed quickly. Gone was the joking, light-hearted exchange they were having, replaced by an incredulous tone. She was instantly insulted. "Yeah, you know what a date is, don't you?"

"Of course I know what a date is." He frowned into the receiver, glad she couldn't see him.

"Oh, so you're surprised that I have a date?"

More like agitated, but he didn't offer that tidbit of information. "Yeah. I mean, no…I mean, I can see why you would have a date, I was just a little thrown at the admission." He took a deep breath. "I suppose this guy is your type," he mumbled.

"It sure doesn't take much to throw you, does it, Terrell?" She didn't wait for his answer. "Anyway, yes, he's my type and yes, I do have a date and I'd like to get going, if you don't mind." Why had she even talked to him for this long? She should have hung up as soon as he identified himself.

He did mind, dammit. Just yesterday he'd asked her out. Then he'd been thinking of her so much today that, against his better judgment, he'd called and asked her out again, only to be reminded that he wasn't her type. Well, what the hell was her type? What did this *date* of hers have that he didn't?

The moment he'd heard her voice, the tension in his shoulders had been released. All the things that had been on his mind today—Tanya, his mother, Donald—all of them had ceased to exist as he totally focused on her. Then she'd announced she was going on a date, and he'd gone totally haywire.

His brow furrowed. He wasn't angry, shouldn't be angry. "Nah, I don't mind. You go on your date. I hope you have a good time." But even as he said the words, he knew he was lying. He was definitely pissed off at the idea of her going out with another man, but for the life of him didn't want to accept the reason why.

That curt and cold voice had returned and she could just imagine his lips setting in that grim, non-compliant way. She rolled her eyes skyward and mentally cursed her own foolishness for bothering with him at all. "Thank you and good bye, Terrell." Without waiting for his response, she hung up.

That man definitely had problems. The nerve of him being surprised that she would have a date. There was nothing wrong with her. He was the uptight one, the moody one. It was no wonder he and his girlfriend had broken up. He'd probably driven her crazy with that split personality of his.

Now that wasn't fair, she scolded herself. She didn't have any idea why he and his girlfriend had broken up. For all she knew, he could have broken up with the girl. She doubted it, but accepted that it could still be true.

She was an attractive woman, she *could* get a date. So what if she didn't want to do anything beyond dating? That was her business. And besides, she'd done just fine up until now. There was no reason to change a system that had worked so well for her for the last couple of years. No reason at all.

Leon was at her door promptly at seven. Dressed in the Fubu jeans he'd mentioned earlier and a navy blue ribbed turtleneck sweater, he looked casual and well kept. His broad shoulders and tight biceps strained beneath the material of the sweater. Timberland boots rounded off the casual ensemble.

"What's this, your tribute to urban attire?" she joked when he walked in.

"I thought I'd give it a try just to see how it felt."

"It looks good on you." Closing the door behind her she surveyed him again. Now here was the type of man who attracted her, the confident, suave, astonishingly good-looking type. This was the man who should be putting those butterflies in her stomach.

"You think so? Better than a business suit or dress slacks and casual polo?" With one hand in his pocket and the other poised beneath his chin, he turned from side to side, striking different poses for her.

Chuckling, she went to the closet for her coat. "I like the slacks and polo better but this is good too. It gives you a definite thug-like flavor." She also had opted for jeans tonight, but unlike his baggy ones, hers fit her long slender legs perfectly. The hunter green shirt she wore was tucked in snugly and stretched tightly over her breasts. Her hair, having long since lost the curls that Ms. Rosie had painstakingly put in last week, was pulled back into a neat ponytail secured with a green scrunchie.

Leon's cologne invaded the air as he stepped behind her to help her with her coat. When his hands came to rest on her shoulders and he turned her to face him, she thought she felt a little stirring in her stomach. Concentrating, she waited to see if it were real. Nope. Nothing.

When he lowered his head, she knew he'd kiss her. She waited for the breathlessness that should occur—the way it had Saturday night in Ms. Rosie's kitchen. She was ready; she closed her eyes, determined to give it her all. Tonight would tell which way their relationship would go from here. If Leon stirred something in her tonight, she'd go all the way. That would prove that not only could she have a date, she could also have a relationship.

The actual thought of a relationship made her queasy, but the mocking tone Terrell had taken with her earlier about having a date at all calmed her nerves, making her all the more determined to prove him wrong.

Leon was the epitome of tall, dark and too damned handsome. Even his bald head was sexy as hell. A neatly trimmed mustache touched her lips with his first tentative efforts. Concentrating again, she lowered her eyes and puckered her lips for the assault.

Leon had kissed her before, and it had been pleasant. Not overly stimulating or knee-knocking satisfying, but it had been good.

Tonight it needed to be better.

His lips were warm against hers when they finally fully connected. A peck. Then a slightly open-mouthed connection. She accepted the silky smoothness of his tongue. Wrapping her arms around his neck, she pulled him closer, concentrating on what she wanted her body to feel.

His arms engulfed her, and she could feel his steely maleness pressing against her stomach. She wondered if that was supposed to be arousing. His hands rubbed her back and slowly inched their way to her bottom, where he squeezed the supple roundness. She knew *that* was supposed to arouse her. Instead, she felt a tad irritated. He had used a little more force than she cared for.

Concentrating still, she moved her head against the rhythm he had created, her tongue abidingly dueling with his. Where was that flutter she'd thought she felt a few minutes ago? His low moan told her that he was definitely feeling this kiss. Her clear mind and wandering thoughts told her she wasn't. Oh, well, the night had just begun. She still had time to warm up to him.

The night progressed with no quivers or romantic stirrings for Leah, even though Leon was giving her his very best efforts. She just didn't feel anything. When they got back to her apartment, Leon sat on the couch waiting for her while she went into the bathroom to examine the situation again.

What exactly were these stirrings she was looking for? Had she ever felt them before? She tried to remember back to her two prior experiences in this department and came up blank. She could barely remember the act itself, let alone the feelings that had preceded it. This was pathetic; here she was, a thirty-year-old woman who had yet to truly experience lovemaking.

Then like a bolt of lightning the word hit her—*love*. Maybe that was the reason she hadn't yet experienced it. She'd never been in love with anyone.

Returning to the couch to sit beside Leon, she wondered if she did love him. She liked him, of that she was positive. But did she love him? Probably not, if she had to ask herself over and over again. Wouldn't you know right off the bat when you loved someone? While up until recently, she'd enjoyed being with Leon, she didn't think about him constantly, didn't dream about him, and her heart didn't flutter every time he was near. Come to think of it, her heart had never fluttered around him. Her heart hadn't fluttered until…the chilling memory of bumping into the slim stranger at Rosie's engagement party burst into her mind.

"Leah?" Leon's voice interrupted her thoughts.

"Huh? Oh, I'm sorry, did you say something?" Her hand on her chest, she tried to hide the hammering that had begun during the memory. Oh God! She didn't need this; she didn't need to be thinking about that annoying man while she was sitting here with Leon.

"I was asking you what's wrong. You look a little distracted." Leon stared at her intently.

"Um, nothing. I mean, I was just thinking about my mother and all the stuff she's going through," she lied. She'd told him about her mother and her seemingly endless problems a few weeks after meeting him, so he was familiar with her situation.

"Is everything okay? Is there something I can do?" Concern evident in his voice, Leon moved closer to her, wrapping his arm around her shoulder.

Leaning in to the offer of comfort, Leah let her head rest on his shoulder. "No, I talked to Darryl last night and he said that he was going to take care of it. I hope she listens to him and tries the counseling." Closing her eyes, she tried to block out the memory of the phone call she'd received just before leaving the office.

"I'm sorry, baby. I wish there was something I could do." Leon's strong hand rubbed up and down her arm, his fingertips lightly brushing her breasts.

She felt something. Concentrating, she zeroed in on the feeling and tried to exploit it. The spot where he had just touched was warm. He moved his hand up and down again—yup, it was warm alright. Maybe it was just going to take a while for things to heat up between them.

"Let's not talk about my mother and her problems right now." Turning her head so that she looked into his face, she searched herself again for some stirrings of emotion.

"Okay, what do you want to talk about?" His voice had lowered considerably, his eyes darkening as he watched her.

She knew what he wanted, read it clearly in his eyes. Her heart quickened a bit. Yes! It's starting, she told herself. Compared to Terrell, Leon was perfect for her. She desperately wanted to prove that point.

"You know, Leah, I've been thinking about us a lot lately." With his free hand he caressed her knee.

She was eager to get the emotional ball rolling. She moved a hand to his shoulder. "You have?"

"I really think we have something special going." He spoke almost in a whisper but she heard him loud and clear. His hands stilled both on her arm and on her knee as he watched her with barely contained desire. His voice was husky, his breathing just a little labored.

Okay, this was were she should be lost in his gaze, anticipating his next move, longing for his touch...as she had the other night in Ms. Rosie's kitchen...in Terrell's arms. His voice had been heavy with desire, deep and arousing. His touch, soft, inviting. Terrell's lips had hovered dangerously close to hers and she thought death would surely be less painful then waiting for him to kiss her.

Terrell. His name was a whisper in her mind and she blinked abruptly, focusing again on Leon.

"I'm beginning to develop some feelings that I think are worth exploring. I think about you constantly. I miss you when I'm away." His hand had left her knee to cup her cheek. "What do you think?"

Good Lord, he didn't want to know what she was thinking, she didn't even want to be thinking it. But there it was. She was sitting on the couch in the arms of this handsome man who obviously adored her, and yet her mind had been on someone else. Someone who annoyed the hell out of her. No, she wasn't feeling Terrell Pierce like that, she was sure of it.

But neither was she feeling Leon and it was time she stopped stalling and accepted that. "Leon, I think we have a really good time together." She hesitated.

"But?" He anticipated her next words and couldn't say that he liked them.

She pulled her hand away, let it rest in her lap. "But that's it. I don't think there's anything else between us." His features stilled, his hands on her going cold. "I mean, I'd like us to remain friends. I just don't see any romantic involvement in our future. I'm sorry if that isn't what you were expecting."

Leon took his time, choosing his words carefully. He took both her hands in his and steadied his breathing. "If you need more time, Leah, I'm willing to wait. I know we would be so good together."

I'm glad you know it, because right now I just don't feel it. "I don't know, Leon. And the last thing I want to do is lead you on. Why don't we take a little break, give each other some space to see if this is really something we want to pursue." She was grasping now, trying to let him down gently. She knew that time was not going to change how she felt about Leon, no matter how much she wanted it to. He just wasn't for her.

"I'm a patient man," he told her, bringing her hand to his lips to kiss her palm. "And I usually get what I want."

Okay, well, whatever. She was getting tired of the men around her not taking no for an answer. He'd spoken slowly, methodically, his jaw clenching with each word, his eyes intent on her. Slightly irritated, she slipped her hands out of his and stood. "I'm kind of tired so—"

Leon stood with her, cupping her face possessively before dropping a soft kiss on her cheek. "My motto is, 'good things come to those who wait.' And Leah, I'm positive you'll be good."

His lips were a whisper from hers. *What the hell, let him give it one more try.* She closed her eyes and leaned in for his kiss. What started out as a sweet gesture quickly changed to a passionate assault by Leon. He pulled her closer, thrusting his tongue into her mouth with a ferocity that she wasn't accustomed to. Leah pulled back instantly, staring at him in surprise. "Good night, Leon."

For a moment he didn't move, and she thought he was going to argue with her, but then he gave her a slow smile and backed away. He walked to the door with her slowly on his heels. Donned in his coat and standing on the other side of the threshold, he turned again to look at her. "I'll be waiting, Leah. I'm not going anywhere."

His words annoyed her, but she managed a small smile anyway. "I'll see you later." But she prayed she wouldn't.

With his nod she closed the door and breathed a sigh of relief.

Terrell lay in bed wondering if she were back from her date yet. Had the guy spent the night or had she sent him home at the door? He imagined what she'd worn, probably a skirt or something classy. The dude had probably taken her to some fancy restaurant trying to wine and dine her so he could get her into bed. A mild fury bubbled around inside of him as he thought of Leah and her date having sex.

This was stupid, he berated himself. He wasn't interested in her. She could do whatever she wanted, it didn't matter to him one way or another. He had more important things to tend to. Rolling over onto his side, he reached for the phone perched on his nightstand. Quickly dialing the numbers he knew so well he waited for an answer.

"Hello?"

"What's up, man? You got some news for me?" Terrell spoke into the receiver.

"I was just going to call you. I checked the bank accounts and he looks pretty stable financially. No wife, two daughters, the shop, everything you told me pretty much checks out."

"Yeah?" Terrell didn't hide his disappointment.

"Except?"

His hopes raised, Terrell sat up in the bed, "Except what?"

"It seems he has a colored past."

"How colored?" Terrell held his breath in anticipation.

"Bloody red." The voice on the phone went on with his report. Terrell listened intently, secure in the fact that he had found information that would blow this whole wedding out of the water.

CHAPTER SIX

A week later Rosie's invitations had been ordered and were sched-uled to be delivered in the next three weeks. Rosie had come into Leah's office the morning after Leah's date with Leon, apologizing for cutting their other meeting short because of her son's dinner invitation. Leah brushed it off, telling Rosie not to worry.

Instead they discussed the menu for the reception, the florists and the photographer. Rosie was excited and Leah was happy for her. She liked Rosie, had secretly harbored thoughts of what her life would have been like had she had a mother like her instead of Marsha. Rosie seemed so full of love, so understanding and accepting of people and their faults. Leah wondered whether, if she'd been Rosie's daughter, she would have the capabilities to love and be loved in return. Maybe then she wouldn't be so afraid of marriage for herself.

As Leah talked to the woman she'd known for so long, she couldn't help noticing the similarities between mother and son. They had the same eyes, except Rosie's were calm and caring all the time, while Terrell's seemed to darken at moments, completely prohibiting anyone from seeing what he was feeling.

Rosie was quick to smile, but Terrell gave his mesmerizing grin infrequently. Not that it lessened the effect any, she remembered with dismay. She'd thought about him often over the last few days. Thought of the way he'd looked at her when he asked her to dinner, the way he'd sounded on the phone when he asked about the type of man she liked. Ultimately, though, her thoughts returned to his seeming surprise that she had a date, and she grew angry.

Returning from a meeting a few days later, Leah found a message from Terrell taped to her computer. What did he want now? They'd said all they needed to say to each other. Crumpling the pink slip of paper, she tossed it in the trashcan and sat down at her desk.

"Why do I get the sneaky suspicion that the message you just threw away was from me?" Terrell leaned against the doorjamb of her office. One finger held his leather coat over his shoulder.

Startled, Leah looked toward the door. It was *him*. "What do you want?" Exasperated, she propped her elbows on her desk and prayed he'd make this quick.

"I wanted to speak with you. Isn't that what the message said?" He took a seat across from her, noticing that he was apparently the last person she wanted to see at this moment. *Patience,* he reminded himself. All good things came in time. He'd practiced that motto during his years of schooling and building his reputation and had been well rewarded. Where Leah Graham was concerned, he hoped for the same outcome.

"Have a seat, why don't you?" she said dryly. "And I don't know what your message said, as you saw for yourself I didn't read it." She was purposely flippant, praying that her body didn't betray her.

He gave a crooked grin. "You read it, you just chose to disregard it." After carefully placing his jacket in the adjacent chair he turned again to look at her. She wore a long blue skirt with a split halfway up her leg. Had she not been so quick to sit down, he could have enjoyed the view a little longer. But the view he had now was pleasing enough. Her suit jacket was open and displayed the white button-down shirt she wore, a silver choker at her neck with a blue stone resting quietly at the hollow of her throat. Thoughts of how sweet that hollow would taste blurred his vision for a moment and he blinked furiously to clear his mind.

His visit here today was two-fold. Yes, he'd thought of her constantly since last seeing her over a week ago, but there was something he needed to talk to her about, to ask her. It was best to get that out of the way first. "Luckily I decided to come and see you in person. I have something to tell you."

"What could you possibly have to tell me?" Wearily, she sat back in her chair, trying to still the erratic beating of her heart. Oh Lord, her heart was thumping hard again. It hadn't been a few moments ago. She was positive her heart had beat at its normal pace for the past several days, but as of about two minutes ago she felt as if she were running a marathon.

He wore dress slacks today, charcoal gray. A dress shirt just a shade lighter than his pants was buttoned neatly and accented with a silver tie splattered with what looked like ebony raindrops. His glasses were, of course, sliding down his nose again and those questioning eyes watched every move she made. She clasped her hands in her lap to keep them still.

"It's about Donald." Pushing his glasses up on his nose he watched her closely.

A little hurt that he wasn't here on a more personal level, she straightened in her chair. "What about Donald?"

"He has some things in his past I think you should know about."

His goatee looked smooth, like the kind that might tickle and arouse her if it brushed over the soft skin of her belly. "First of all, why should I know anything at all about Donald's past? All I need to know is that his check cleared." She shifted uncomfortably.

"So this *is* just about money to you?" Terrell asserted.

"What else would it be about? My job is to plan weddings, that's what I do. Donald hired me to plan your mother's wedding. Are you following me?"

"I'm following you." And he didn't like what she was revealing. "You don't give a damn whether the people whose weddings you plan should be married or not. As long as they pay you, you plan the wedding."

"It's not up to me to judge who's fit to be married. I don't make those calls. If you ask me, everybody in their right mind should stay as far away from wedding bells as they possibly can. They're just going to end up divorced anyway. But if they didn't get married, I'd be out of a job." Rolling her eyes, she unclasped her hands and swiped at a piece of lint on her jacket.

"So I guess you don't plan on ever getting married?" Her statement had roused his growing curiosity where she was concerned.

"As a matter of fact, I don't." Watching him carefully, she waited a second for his response to that admission. He was probably thinking she'd never get an offer of marriage. When he didn't respond she continued, "But my personal preference has nothing to do with my job, as I told you before. Nor does it have anything to do with you. So…"

"Just hear me out." Holding up his hands in mock surrender, Terrell slid to the edge of his seat. "What if your mother were about to make the biggest mistake of her life? What if she were about to marry a man guilty of criminal acts?"

Her mother had made plenty of mistakes in her life and Leah was sure she'd continue to make them until her dying day. "Donald was cleared of all that drug suspicion a while ago. I thought I already told you that."

He lifted a brow. So she had known. "No, you only mentioned an investigation. But this goes beyond the local police surveiling him for suspected drug activity."

Now he had her attention. "How far beyond?"

"His drug activity isn't just local, and his illegal activities have expanded over the years. His business was funded by some less than honest money."

"So what? He's making honest money now," she said.

"Is he?" Terrell let the question hang in the air, watching as her mind began to click.

"What are you saying?"

"I'm saying that even though the local authorities dropped their charges against him, the Feds seem to still be pretty interested in him. I can't help wondering why."

Shaking her head, Leah stood. "I don't care. I don't want to hear anymore. This is none of my business. I'm just the…"

"You're just the wedding planner. I know." Terrell stood, quickly blocking her path to the door. "But I'm her son. And I owe it to her to protect her. If my information is true, my mother could be getting involved in something very dangerous."

"Ms. Rosie knows all about the suspected drug activity. Hell, everybody in the shop knew. But like I said, Mr. Donald was cleared of all that. It's in the past." She took a deep breath. He wasn't smiling, yet the look he gave her made her weak. Raw determination chiseled his features, giving him an air of danger, a hint of the unknown. "It still doesn't have anything to do with me. It's your mother. It's your job to protect her, not mine. Why are you coming to me?" She was standing too close to him. She could smell his cologne, the strong male fragrance serenading her. She tried to back away but his hands grasped her shoulders and held her still.

"Because I don't have anybody else to go to." His admission, he realized, was the truth. "My mother speaks very highly of you. I suspect you two have a special bond, one that goes beyond stylist and client. I thought you'd want to protect her as well." Somebody needed to protect him from the bewitching eyes that searched his face right now. She was trying to figure him out, to understand the man behind the glasses. He knew the look and only hoped that she'd see the right things.

In that moment she felt his strength, his impatience, his concern, and they all beckoned to her. Her first instinct was to calm him down, to assure him that all was well, to comfort him. "I do care about your mother, Terrell, more than you could possibly know. But she loves Donald very much. Maybe you should just leave it alone. Maybe these criminal dealings are in his past," she told him. "And if not, maybe, just maybe…," she continued when he would have interrupted her, "…your mother already knows about it."

He hadn't considered that. Not since the moment he'd heard the disturbing news had it occurred to him that the man could have told all of this to his mother and she had still agreed to marry him. Gut instinct told him that his mother would never marry a man she knew was breaking the law. Which meant she, like Leah, believed that all this was in Donald's past. Terrell turned his back to her and walked across the room.

She felt a pulling in her stomach and couldn't keep her feet from going after him. "I understand that you're worried about her and it's natural for you to want to protect her, but I honestly don't see this as a way to do it. I mean, what are you going to do, waltz over there and say, 'Hey mom, I've investigated your fiancé and he's not what you think he is'? I don't think she'd take that too kindly. And if it's in his past it may not even matter to her now." Folding her arms across her chest, Leah waited for him to turn around. He looked deflated. His shoulders slumped.

He was vulnerable, something she'd never anticipated where he was concerned. She wanted to touch him, to reach out and take him in her arms, to offer him some sort of security, but she didn't know how.

Turning to face her, he stuffed his hands in his pockets. "What if it's not just drug dealing?"

The question hung in the air for a moment. Leah watched him, noting his seriousness, noting his dedication to his mother and more importantly, noting his fear.

"What else is there?" She knew she shouldn't have asked, knew she shouldn't get involved, but he looked so lost and so completely miserable she didn't know what else to do. If he needed someone to talk to, then it wouldn't hurt anything to talk to him, she hoped.

"Murder."

That simple word had her gasping. This was too much; this was beyond what she was prepared to deal with.

"Terrell, I really think this is just…" Shaking her head again, she couldn't even finish her sentence. "I mean, what can you do? How do you even know this?" Her mind was swarming with thoughts and she couldn't get them all out at once.

At that moment, Terrell could swear he'd never seen a woman as attractive as she was. Her hair was straight today, hanging down her back past her shoulders. She was tall and curvy. Even her legs were well shaped; he could see clear up to her thigh through the split in her skirt. Her breasts weren't huge, but full and beckoning to be touched. She was worked up now, he could tell. She was rattling on and on, walking back and forth, her long arms moving dramatically as she talked, her eyes dancing busily. Maybe getting her involved wasn't such a good idea, he thought as he found himself concentrating more and more on her instead of the situation at hand.

"Alright, alright. I'm sorry. Maybe I shouldn't have told you. I didn't mean to upset you."

"Well, dammit, you've upset me now! How am I supposed to work with them knowing that there's something strange going on?" Still pacing, she thought about the meeting she had scheduled with Donald and Rosie in two weeks.

"I'm sorry, just forget everything I said. I mean, I don't have any proof." All he had was the word of a very good private investigator and a written report with leads to check out. In fact, he planned to check those leads out just as soon as he left her.

"No proof," she whispered, stopping suddenly, turning to find herself right smack in his face.

She grabbed his arm to keep from falling backward. He grabbed her by the waist to hold her steady. The contact caused an instant reaction. Speechless, they stood gaping at each other.

He lowered his head. Oh God, he was going to kiss her! Leah panicked. Did she want him to kiss her? Of course she didn't, that was stupid. But why wasn't she moving? Why wasn't she trying to stop him? Why was she standing there waiting, no, anticipating, the touch of his lips on hers?

Her lips looked so soft. He'd just touch them, just this once. It would be quick, nobody would mind. She wanted him to kiss her even though he knew she was seeing someone else. Her body responded to his, her curves molding perfectly to his body and his blood quickened.

His hands at her hips he pulled her closer until her breasts rested enticingly against his chest.

In a moment he'd have his first taste of her. This was the moment he'd dreamed about all week.

Her palms burned at the warmth coming from where she was now splaying them on his chest. *So this is what it's like to* want *to be kissed.* Licking her lips, she readied herself for the experience, thinking she could already hear bells ringing somewhere in the room. They were inches apart. She could feel his breath against her face.

The phone rang and they sprang apart like two guilty teenagers.

"I should get that," Leah said quickly, not sure if she were thankful or irritated.

"No."

The solitary word was spoken so softly and with such finality that had she not been wrapped in his arms she wouldn't have heard it.

He didn't give her a moment to argue before his mouth took control of hers. His tongue slowly traced the outline of her lips, familiarizing itself with the intoxicating feel of her. Leah melted in his arms, angling her head so that their mouths were perfectly connected. Each movement was slow, deliberate, as she opened her mouth to him, invited him inside.

The first stroke was gentle, tentative, the initial meeting. He drew back, tracing the outline of her teeth, accepting her small whimpers of delight.

He was leading the kiss, driving her mad with his slow torture. Her fingers dug into his shoulders and she waited restlessly for the complete assault.

Terrell sensed her urgency and felt raging desire swoop through his loins. His tongue delved inside her mouth again, seeking hers, wanting hers. He stroked her warm moistness, tasting all the sweetness he'd imagined would be there.

Her hands came around his neck, holding the back of his head, angling him to her complete pleasure. He squeezed her waist, let his hands drift downward until they rested on the curve of her butt. His breathing was erratic as their tongues dueled and fought for control. In a minute he was going to tear those clothes off her and prop her up on that desk, legs spread wide and waiting for him. That wouldn't be good. Dammit, she'd distracted him again.

What was she doing? Enjoying the hell out of this kiss, that's what. She would have never believed this type of passion, this raw strength and urgency lived inside this man—the man with the unreadable eyes and ill fitting glasses, the man who'd rather stare at computers than breathe. Yet here she was, standing in the middle of her office being tongued down by what she could only call a master. She'd never, ever, in all her years been kissed like this and for a moment wondered where he'd been all her life.

Then the incessant ringing of the phone on her desk disrupted the moment, and she pulled away.

Questions registered on each of their passion-filled faces as they stared for endless moments.

He spoke first. "I should go."

"Yes, you should."

Terrell grabbed his coat and headed for the door while she made her way to the desk to grab the phone.

At home Leah sat in her bed trying to erase the memory of Terrell holding her close. How could a man who seemed so simple, so predictable, yet so intense put so much fire, so much yearning into a single kiss? Oh, who was she kidding? The only thing simple about Terrell Pierce was that nonchalant look he gave on a regular basis. But beneath that quiet façade lay something totally different, and she'd be lying to herself—badly—if she said she wasn't interested in finding out what that was.

Ever since their first meeting he'd moved her. There was no denying it now, there was something going on between them.

Something that Leah didn't want, mostly because she couldn't understand it. On the one hand she had Leon—well, she really didn't have him anymore since she'd given him his walking papers the other night—then there was Terrell. The contrast was staggering, from the arrogantly drop dead gorgeous man that any woman would kill to have to the more refined, boyishly good looking man that most women probably overlooked.

Terrell had something, some overwhelming quality that was calling to her, beckoning her to let her guard down and receive everything he had to offer. Was it his gentleness? When he'd touched her face and looked at her she'd felt like a delicate flower that he found entrancing. When he'd pulled her close to him, his large hands on her hips, she'd felt like the sexiest woman alive. When he'd kissed her, she'd melted in his arms, ready to give him whatever he wanted that would guarantee the continuance of such delectable torture.

But outside of the havoc he was wreaking on her personally, Terrell had too much going on. If what he was saying about Donald was true, his life was about to spin dangerously out of control. And she didn't need that. Her mother's life was drama enough for her. Still, she wondered how things would eventually turn out for him.

After incessantly changing channels she deduced that there was absolutely nothing on television tonight. Every month she wrote a check for fifty-seven dollars to pay for one hundred and twenty-two cable stations, and about three nights out of the month she actually watched something interesting on one of them. Annoyed, she hit the off button on the remote, tossed it onto her nightstand, and pulled the covers up to her neck, prepared to sleep.

A shrill ring echoed in the quiet room. Groaning, Leah realized that the telephone was quickly becoming her worst enemy, and she cursed Alexander Graham Bell for his damned bright idea. Snatching the phone off its cradle, she put it to her ear. It had better not be her mother.

"Hello," she barked.

"Leah? It's me, Terrell."

Either the background noise or his cheap cell phone muddled his voice. Leah figured it was the latter, but that didn't stop her heart from racing. "Terrell? What do you want? Do you know what time it is? And how did you get my home number?"

"Will you be quiet and listen to me?" he yelled. "I found something down here and I need you to meet me."

"You found what? Where are you?" Sitting up in her bed, Leah glanced at the clock that now read twelve-fifteen.

"Damn, you should have been a detective. You ask a million questions!"

"If you don't start answering some of them I'm going to hang this phone up."

"I'm down at the Inner Harbor. I need you to meet me. I've got something on Donald."

"So why do *I* have to meet you?" Pulling her knees up to her chest, she cradled the phone between her shoulder and her ear and wrapped her arms around her legs.

"Because I'm kind of on a stakeout and my...um, my car broke down."

As intense and serious as his voice sounded, she couldn't help laughing. "Whose car breaks down when they're on a stakeout?"

Somehow he'd known she'd laugh at him, and was thoroughly embarrassed to have to call her. This definitely wasn't winning him any cool points with her. "Just meet me in the parking lot across from The Gallery."

"You're insane." Shaking her head, she contemplated what she should do. Even knowing that the smart thing to do would be to stay out of it, she debated going to help him. If he couldn't even pull off a stakeout without something going wrong, he definitely needed help. But she wasn't any more qualified than he was. Still, it was Terrell, and like it or not, she felt an overwhelming need to be with him—to help, of course. *I mean, really, if a man is willing to go through this much for his mother, if he's this dedicated to her, he's got to be one hell of a man.*

On the other hand, this wasn't any of her concern. Her better judgment warned her to stay out of it, but she was wide-awake now, and there wasn't anything on television.

"Leah? Are you there?"

"Yes, I'm here. Where did you think I went?" Rolling her eyes at the phone, she felt like strangling him.

"You're supposed to be on your way down here."

"Just hang up the damn phone. I'll be there in a few minutes." Hanging up her own phone, she tossed the covers to the side, willing herself not to think about what she was doing for fear she'd change her mind, and went to the closet to grab some jeans.

She should call Nikki, get some advice. No, Nikki had a big mouth. The whole shop would know by noon tomorrow, and then where would she be? Maybe if she could talk some sense into Terrell, get him to drop this whole silly notion of his, then she could get on with her job.

Searching the living room for her keys, she decided that was what she would do. When she reached him, she'd tell him that this was stupid and that he should just approach Donald like a man and ask him about the allegations. Like Donald was going to fess up to being a murderer, she thought cynically, if in fact that's what he was. Terrell didn't have any proof. He'd told her that much earlier. Then why was he on a stakeout? Lord, a stakeout, like he knew what the hell a stakeout was.

Spying her keys on the table by the door, Leah snatched them up, and tucking her jacket under her arm, left her apartment. Her apartment was on St. Paul Street, which was located in downtown Baltimore, about ten minutes from the Inner Harbor. Turning her car onto Pratt Street, she looked for the entrance to the parking lot across the street from The Gallery. The streets were almost empty except for a few people out and about enjoying Baltimore's nightlife. Tall buildings, housing the bulk of the city's prominent businesses, were mostly dark but for the occasional lights employees had left on.

A. C. ARTHUR

She cursed herself as she drove through the streets, looking for the lunatic that she did not want to be attracted to.

The Gallery, a shopping mall connected to both a hotel and a parking lot, was closed at this time of night. Leah wondered if Terrell had meant the parking lot attached to the mall. But he'd said across the street. Downtown was flooded with parking lots, but luckily there was only one on that particular corner.

Turning into the lot, it dawned on her that she didn't have a clue as to what kind of car Terrell drove. He hadn't told her, and she hadn't had the good sense to ask. So she circled the lot looking for a car with a person sitting behind the wheel. When she didn't see one, she cursed herself for being stupid enough to come out in the middle of the night, put her car in reverse and made a U-turn to the parking lot exit. Slamming on her brakes, she just narrowly missed a black SUV speeding past her through the exit.

"Asshole!" Pressing her palm against the horn she cursed the driver. Angry with herself, angry with Terrell, and now pissed at this fool that hadn't had the respect to give her the right-of-way, Leah swore fluently. She was going to go home and get her ass back in bed, and if Terrell called her again she was going to tell him where to go and the quickest route to get there.

The light at the intersection had just turned green so she had to sit at the opening of the parking lot and wait for the few cars to pass. Drumming her fingers against the steering wheel, she thought of all the things she was going to say to Mr. Terrell Pierce the moment she laid eyes on him.

"Getting me out of my bed in the middle of the night," she muttered to herself while she watched the last of the cars go by. Just as the light turned red and she was about to press the gas, somebody banged on the passenger side door. It was Terrell. She hit the unlock button.

Jumping in, he quickly pulled the door closed behind him and yelled, "Drive!"

"What?" Surprised to see him, and still seething with anger, Leah's foot remained rooted on the brake.

"Drive, I said!" Pulling the seatbelt across his body, Terrell clicked the lock into place.

"I'm not going anywhere. Where did you come from anyway? I've been looking all over this stupid lot for you."

"Will you shut up and drive the damned car!" She was sexy as hell, but, damn, there were times when she simply talked too much.

Rolling her eyes at him, Leah did as she was told. Making a right turn onto Gay Street she proceeded to the next intersection. "Okay, Sherlock, where to now?"

Terrell was looking from one direction to the other. "I think we lost them."

"Lost who?"

"Donald! I saw Donald!"

"Where? In the parking lot?"

"Yeah, he got out of his car and walked over to this other dude's truck and they talked for a while. Then he got in the truck with the other dude and they pulled off.

Leah's mind went to the SUV that had sped past her moments before. "Was it a black truck?"

"Yeah, you saw it?"

"It almost smashed right into me." Rolling her eyes, she looked up to see that her light had changed.

"Alright, I heard them say something about a club. Maybe that's where they're headed. The nearest clubs are...what's up Charles Street?" he asked himself. For some reason Leah didn't strike him as a regular club attendee.

"Unless they were talking about the clubs on Baltimore Street?" she added.

"Baltimore Street?" He frowned, looked at her.

She looked back at him and shrugged. "It's possible."

"I guess so." He looked away, because staring at her had him thinking things that had nothing to do with Donald or where that black SUV had gone.

He wondered if the man she was seeing had any hold on her heart—wondered if she kissed him the way she'd kissed Terrell earlier that day—wondered if she were in love with him.

"Terrell!" Leah screeched to a halt at the corner of Gay and Baltimore Streets. The black SUV was parking in front of one of Baltimore's many adult entertainment spots. The corner of Gay and Baltimore Streets marked the end of Baltimore's well-known 'Block' where the premium prostitutes and X-rated shops were housed. For years Leah had wondered how it was that prostitution, which was illegal in Maryland, could be permitted to go on directly across the street from the city's police head-quarters. Wasn't that a contradiction in and of itself?

"Yeah?" Quickly brought back to the matter at hand, he turned to her. Her eyes glittered in the dark interior of the car and he followed her gaze.

"Do you think that's them?" They both starred at the vehicle parked across the street. There were two people in the front seat but darkness and distance prevented them from being easily identified.

"Yeah, it looks like it. Pull over here and turn the engine off," he directed her.

"For what? We're not staying here," Leah protested.

"Come on, Leah, I just want to see where he goes from here and what they do." When she looked like she was about to refuse, Terrell reached for her hand. "We'll just stay for a few minutes, then we can go home. I promise."

It wasn't the puppy dog eyes that stared at her, and it definitely wasn't the warmth spreading throughout her arm. It was the nagging feeling that everything Terrell had told her that afternoon just might be true. There Donald was, parked in a black SUV with another man, doing Lord knows what. The fact that they were in front of the police station had no bearing on the thoughts going through her mind. And when they both got out of the vehicle and headed toward one of the sleazy nude bars on the opposite side of the street, an annoying sense of dread coursed through her.

Pulling the car over, she switched off the ignition and watched the two guys go into the nightclub. Feeling Terrell's eyes on her, she shrugged. "So they want to see some naked women. That doesn't prove anything."

"It sure doesn't," Terrell reluctantly agreed.

Minutes later the two men emerged from the building with two more men following them. The four men talked for a few minutes before Donald reached into his jacket and pulled out a medium-sized package. Thanks to their location and the lights from all those sleazy little sex joints, Leah could clearly see one of the men who had followed Donald out of the club pulling a wad of cash out of his pocket and exchanging it for the package Donald held.

Leah gasped and Terrell swore, "That bastard!"

"Terrell, calm down. We don't know what was in the package," she rationalized.

"It wasn't hair products, I guarantee you that." He all but spat the words at her. "I knew it! I knew it! I knew he wasn't any good!"

The four men continued their conversation before three other men, who came out of nowhere, joined them. Now there were seven men standing in front of the Club Pussycat. One began yelling, and it looked to Leah as if an argument ensued.

"We should leave now," she whispered, never taking her eyes off the men across the street.

"In a minute." His eyes, too, were riveted on the events taking place.

They both gasped when the man who was with Donald pulled out a gun. While his partner motioned for the other men to move into the alley beside the club, Donald looked around to make sure no one had seen them.

Terrell grabbed Leah's arm, pulling her down into the seat. She crouched down without question. "Terrell, I really think we should leave now," she whispered, her heart beating frantically. She couldn't tell if it was because of her close proximity to Terrell or the fear that was quickly consuming her. Ironically, she hoped it was the fear.

"No, I have to see what happens. I have to have proof. Stay here." Before Leah could stop him, Terrell was opening the car door and stepping out onto the sidewalk.

"Stay here?" she murmured. No, she hadn't gotten out of her bed and gone down on 'the Block' in the middle of the night only to be told to stay in the car. He had clearly bumped his head. She climbed out of the car and ran to catch up to him.

She was so busy looking around to make sure no unmentionable characters were near them that she ran right into his back.

"What?" Terrell turned, startled and confused at seeing her. "I told you to stay in the car. You're the driver, remember?"

"Are you crazy? I wasn't staying in that car by myself."

"I told you we were on a stakeout. Every stakeout has a driver," he said as he pulled her across the street, out of oncoming traffic.

Leah rolled her eyes and kept her fingers entwined with his. "Every robbery needs a driver, idiot. Stakeouts usually consist of watching only. You're entering the stupidly spying category now," she said as they came up on the alley Donald and the men had entered.

Overhead, Leah spied the Club Pussycat and groaned. She'd never been this close to this type of bar before. Naked women, and men doing private things to those naked women, were what she supposed happened there. To her it was repulsive and she cringed at the mere sight of it. Terrell was focused on what was going on in the alley. Leaning his back against the wall, he held Leah's hand firmly. "Stay behind me."

Leah looked at him as if he'd spoken a foreign language. "Did you think I was going to bum rush them?"

Terrell frowned. She really did talk too much. "Just stay behind me," he said in an angry whisper.

Against her better judgment, she flattened her back against the wall and stood stiffly next to him, rolling her eyes towards the sky.

Terrell saw that the men were at the other end of the alley, but he couldn't hear what they were saying. He reached for Leah's hand, pulling her quickly behind a dumpster.

"Ew, it stinks back here." Leah pulled her sweatshirt up over her face in an effort to staunch the stench.

"Shhh!" Terrell warned. Peeping around the dumpster, he got a closer view of the scene. Donald's friend still held his gun on them. All five of the other men stood against the wall.

"You can't kill us all," one of the guys that had arrived after the exchange told Donald.

"You think we can't?" Donald's voice seemed louder now. "I told you not to mess with us. I warned you and your crew several times. Now it seems we're gonna have to show you we mean business."

"It don't matter, Ray Ray will find you. It's only a matter of time," the other guy said.

"That's okay, the morgue is gonna find you first," Donald's companion said. Before the man had a chance to utter another word a shot rang out. The man's body slumped to the ground.

"Oh my God! Oh my God! He shot him! He shot him!" Leah was ready to turn and run out of the alley, but Terrell grabbed her around the waist with one long arm and slapped his free hand over her mouth.

"Shhh! If you don't be quiet he's gonna shoot us too," he whispered frantically to her ear, positioning them both low and out of sight behind the dumpster.

Her heart raced and tears threatened to spill from her eyes. What was she doing here, witnessing a murder, when she should have been home in her bed fast asleep? She'd known Terrell would be trouble, and now he'd gotten her involved. Only fear that he might be right about them getting shot kept her from biting his hand and running like hell.

CHAPTER SEVEN

Just as Terrell was about to remove his hand from her mouth they heard another gunshot ring out, then another. They couldn't see what was happening but they jumped at the loud blasts. Leah trembled in his arms. Guilt, and fear that something might happen to her, had him cursing under his breath. He should never have called her, even though the thought of being in an alley witnessing a murder had never crossed his mind. Still, he'd put her in danger, and for that alone he was a bigger jerk than she probably already assumed him to be.

He'd wanted proof that Donald wasn't good enough for his mother. Tonight he had gotten that in spades, but at what price? Leah was shaking, her body almost limp in his arms as they huddled behind the dumpster. He had to get her out of there as quickly, and as unscathed, as possible. Releasing his hold on her mouth, he grabbed her hand, running across the street and pulling her behind him. He prayed no one had seen them.

When they were safely in the car, they both sat in silence for a moment, trying to catch their breath. Terrell thought for sure the next sound they'd hear would be police sirens, considering the close proximity of the police station, but he was wrong.

"I don't believe it, I just don't believe it! And don't you tell me again that you knew it, because I don't give a damn what you knew! If you knew he was involved in murder, then why the hell did you call me? Why did you have to get me involved?" Leah screamed.

She was absolutely right, and he was kicking himself right now for that very stupid mistake. But her frantic yelling wasn't going to help the situation now. They needed to get going. "You can yell at me later, but now I think it's time for us to get the hell out of here."

For once, she completely agreed with him. But where were her keys? Bending over, she slid her hands beneath the seat, clutching at nothing. Oh no, not now, she prayed. Reaching across Terrell's lap she opened the glove compartment and rifled through the things in there. Cursing, she returned her attention to beneath her seat.

"What are you doing?" He'd surmised that she was looking for something, but he hadn't a clue what. "For a person who didn't want to come here in the first place, you sure are taking your time leaving."

She stifled a smart retort. "I can't find my keys."

"What?"

"I can't find my damn keys! I'm not used to chasing around bad guys, you know. I must have dropped my keys when some lunatic left me alone in the car while he went off to save the day."

Her sarcasm wasn't lost on him, but the missing keys took precedence over her anger about their situation.

"Oh please, don't tell me that."

Terrell was searching for the keys when suddenly she yelled, "Sheesh, they're right here." Leah pulled the keys out of her coat pocket and held them up. But before she could start the car, out of the corner of her eye she saw the men emerge from the alley.

"Terrell, look, they're coming out," she whispered, as if they were going to hear her from across the street.

Terrell leaned over to see out the driver's side window. Donald and his partner had come sauntering out of the alley. There was no sign of a gun and no sign of the five men that had gone into the alley with them.

"Where are the others?"

"Do you have to ask?" Terrell replied blandly.

Abruptly, Leah sat back in her seat and stared straight ahead. "Oh God, they're going to walk right past us."

Looking through the window, Terrell confirmed that they were, in fact, heading in their direction. Thinking quickly, he grabbed Leah by her jacket and turned her to face him. "Just follow my lead," he told her before his lips ground roughly into hers.

Blinking in confusion, it took a moment for Leah to realize that Terrell was kissing her. Well, not exactly kissing. His lips were awkwardly pressed against hers, nevertheless causing an amazing bolt of stimulation throughout her body. His eyes were closed and his goatee tickled the sensitive skin around her mouth. His hands were fisted around the lapels of her jacket; still, she felt the smoldering heat of his knuckles as they brushed against her breasts.

Time stood still for all of the three minutes it took as the men passed the car and climbed back into their truck. Terrell heard their retreating footsteps, but was reluctant to break the connection.

Leah, after conceding that this was their only choice, had relaxed into the kiss. His lips still clung to hers and she itched to take the contact further. Her thoughts scattered as she realized this was Terrell—safe, intellectual, quiet Terrell. But it wasn't the quiet, subdued man she'd thought he was. Tonight she'd seen a completely different side of him, a reckless, bold, intoxicatingly sexy side and he was now kissing her senseless. God, if he had nothing else, he had one amazing pair of lips—and he knew how to use them.

Terrell, about to burst with his own needs, seized the opportunity and pushed his tongue into her mouth. Feverently stroking his tongue against the warm contours of hers, he reveled in her response. While she tried to appear reserved and serious, Ms. Leah Graham was one passionate sister. She kissed him as if she was starving for him—he could only wish. Still, her tongue dueled with his until all he wanted to do was tear her clothes off and make wondrous love to her.

But this was neither the time nor the place.

In the back of her mind, she knew they should be leaving. She should be driving like a bat out of hell to get home. Instead, she relaxed, allowing her tongue to be stroked and caressed by his. She didn't see stars, and bells didn't ring, and yet she was engulfed in warmness that caused her whole body to go limp in the seat. Everything else ceased to exist. The car was their private haven, its close confines blanketing them in intimacy. When his hands moved from the lapels of her jacket to lightly cup her breasts, she thought she would scream with pleasure. Spiky tingles soared through her chest, landing in the pit of her stomach where they expanded and shifted to throb between her legs. The whimpering sound she heard, to her surprise, came from her. She wanted him as she'd never wanted another man in her life.

But this was not the time.

Through the thick haze of his own pleasure, he felt her pushing against his chest. She didn't like it; she wanted him to stop. Disappointment at her rejection clutched his heart.

Reluctantly he pulled away and willed himself not to look at her. He didn't want to see the disappointment he was sure would be clear in her eyes. But once the physical connection was broken, her eyes held him captive. He couldn't turn away, not if his life depended on it.

Leah looked at him. She simply stared into the face that was quickly becoming too familiar. The freshly cut and trimmed goatee looked soft in contrast to the prickliness she'd felt against her skin. His nose was straight, free of bumps and curves, hence the reason his glasses always slid down. Unable to resist the urge, she lifted her hand and, with her index finger, pushed the wire rims up to their rightful position.

He blinked in confusion. *Was that pity in her eyes?* He hated that most of all. "Sorry," he grumbled and retreated to the other side of the car. He didn't need her feeling sorry for him, didn't want her pity.

Hell, he didn't know what he wanted from her. She wasn't exactly what he was looking for in a woman. Mentally reverting back to the little list he still carried in his wallet, he thought pretty didn't describe her. No, sitting in the driver's seat after just witnessing a shooting and with her lips swollen from his kiss, she was absolutely beautiful. She was almost as tall as he was, give or take an inch or two. That wouldn't photograph well, he thought sadly. Lastly, from the way she was looking at him now, she could never love him, of that he was sure. Surprisingly, that was the most disappointing thing of all.

He almost laughed at the absurdity of the situation. Here he was in a car, in the middle of the night, comparing a living, breathing woman with the ideal he'd created as a child. Why had he not thought of the list with Tanya? That surely would have saved him a lot of money and heartache.

But Leah didn't seem at all like Tanya. She was honest, for one thing. She didn't mince any words when she was dealing with him. And her loyalty to her job and her clients impressed him. If she were that loyal to strangers, just imagine how loyal she would be to the man lucky enough to claim her heart.

Spurned by his quickness to be away from her, Leah took offense. "Don't let it happen again," she told him before switching the ignition on.

"What am I going to tell my mother?" He'd deal with the confusion of his feelings for Leah later. Tonight he had to think of Rosie.

"I don't know," she said briskly. She was agitated and aroused. His reaction to their second kiss had royally pissed her off. The first time he'd bolted out of her office so quickly she hadn't had a chance to say anything. This time she could say something, but didn't really know what to say. "Look, Terrell, I don't know what you're going to do about your mother and Donald. All I know is that come tomorrow morning, I'm going to have my secretary draft a letter removing myself as her wedding planner. There's no way I can continue with this with so many unanswered questions."

"Unanswered questions, exactly. There's so much we still don't know."

"Are you crazy? Terrell, what we did tonight was dangerous. People have been killed for stuff like this. The men lying in that alley are proof of that! We need to be getting out of this car and going over to the police station. I'm surprised they haven't come out here in droves." She backed up and turned into oncoming traffic.

"I can't let my mother find out that way. I have to be the one to tell her about Donald. But I shouldn't have involved you. I'm sorry."

"You had good intentions, Terrell, but I really think we should go to the police, tell them what we saw." She was so busy arguing with Terrell that she didn't see the truck pull out in front of her. And, for the second time that night, she slammed on her brakes to keep from hitting the black SUV. Donald looked up and saw her. His steely eyes glinted at her through the windshield. And when he saw Terrell in the seat beside her, his scowl darkened.

Terrell swore. "Just act like we've been out on a date," he said as he watched Donald get out of his truck and come around to the passenger side of the car.

Nervously he rolled down the window. "Hey Donald, what's going on, man?" His voice was surprisingly calm, Leah noted.

"Nothing much. What's going on with you?" Leaning over, Donald looked into the car, recognizing her instantly. "What's your name again?" He was talking to Leah.

"Um, I'm Leah. Leah Graham," she told him in a voice that sounded as shaky as she felt.

"Yeah, Leah Graham." Nodding his head to the other guy, Donald reached for the door handle. "Get out of the car, Terrell." The wedding planner and his future son-in-law—what were they doing here?

"Nah, man, we've been hangin' out all night, and both of us have to go to work tomorrow. I think we're gonna just head home." Clutching the door handle, he prayed for her sake that Donald would let them be. The look on Donald's face told him differently.

Leah's door was pulled open. "Don't be shy, little lady, I won't hurt you." The other man was huge, and his thick hand reached in to grab hold of Leah's arm and pull her out onto the street.

"Be careful, Cable, remember that she's female," Donald's irritated voice informed his partner. His grip only intensified when she tried to pull away. Still inside the car, Terrell cursed the drastic change in circumstances and decided he didn't have much of a choice. He slowly climbed out of the car only to meet Donald's massive chest head-on.

"Now, why don't we just go for a little ride?" Taking a step back Donald cleared a path for Terrell to get into the truck.

Terrell hesitated, knowing once they were in the truck they were completely under Donald's control. Replaying the events that had just taken place in the alley, he knew that definitely wasn't where he wanted to be. "Donald, she's tired. Why don't we drop her off? Then you and I can go wherever you want."

"I was under the impression that I had answered all your questions, put a rest to your doubts. I guess I was wrong." Donald shook his head dismally. "Just shut up and get in the truck."

It wasn't so much the tone of Donald's voice as it was the sight of the black gun the other man pulled from his coat that had Terrell finally walking toward the truck.

In the backseat, Terrell reached for Leah's hand and clasped her fingers. She sat back in the seat, wondering where they were going, almost sure they would be killed. She tried to remain calm. Terrell's fingers were long and warm and gave a sense of safety. Even though Terrell wasn't as built as Leon, his long arms sported pretty thick biceps and his chest, as she'd found out this evening, was broad and tight with muscle. Physique aside, she was shocked that his presence alone comforted her, the little that was possible right now.

They drove through the city in a westerly direction. Leah could tell because they weren't far from the hair salon. When they turned onto a dark, winding road, she held her breath in dismay.

In the front of the truck Donald sat silent. Terrell wondered what Donald was thinking. He wondered what he himself had been thinking to get Leah mixed up in any of this. He should have just gone to his mother and let her handle her fiancé and his unsavory dealings herself. Better yet, he should have minded his own business. Shaking his head, he took that back. The whole purpose in his background check on Donald was to keep his mother from making a big mistake, so if nothing else, he was glad he'd found this out before the marriage. But if he were killed tonight, his mother would never know the person Donald really was. The thought of his mother marrying this man and getting mixed up in the drug underworld was too much for him to stand.

Guilt over dragging Leah into this situation weighed heavily on him. If she were hurt because of him, he'd never forgive himself. As the truck turned off the main road onto the dark, winding path, he figured that if they were both killed, then he'd probably just burn in hell. Ironically, that paled in comparison to the regret he felt.

He looked from the side window to the back one in an effort to figure out where they were being taken.

Sensing his puzzlement Leah whispered, "It's Leakin Park."

Terrell turned to her in the darkness of the back seat. They were surrounded on both sides by tall looming trees. The streetlights were mostly out. Scooting over the soft leather of the seat, he paused only when his body was touching hers. Drawing her close to him, he silently vowed to protect her with his own life if need be.

His body was warm against her side. The night had grown chilly, and her thin leather jacket wasn't doing the job. Both the darkness and the realization of where they were being taken made her nervous. Leakin Park was notorious for the number of dead bodies the authorities found there year after year. Struggling not to panic, Leah leaned into the comfort of Terrell's outstretched arm and wondered what would happen next.

When the truck suddenly stopped, both Leah and Terrell held their breath. Eyes on their kidnappers, they waited for whatever was to come next. Sensing their nervousness and experiencing a flurry of emotions himself, Donald stepped out of the truck first, with the driver immediately following him.

Rounding the vehicle, the two men stood near a small opening that led deeper into the park. "What now?" Cable pulled a cigarette out of his back pocket and proceeded to light up.

"We need to do something with them until I can find out what they know." With his hands stuffed in his pockets, Donald stood with his back to the truck.

Blowing smoke into the brisk night air, Cable shook his head in disagreement. "I say we just get rid of them now. It's too risky to take any chances. You heard what Slick said. Ray Ray's gonna be looking for us by the morning. We can't afford any more delays. Rohan won't like that."

"No, I don't want any more bloodshed." Donald looked back at the truck. Terrell. The look of sheer contempt in the young man's eyes when they'd first met had caused him to consider inviting him outside to settle their differences. But something in Terrell's eyes had stopped him. The man was simply protecting his mother. Donald couldn't begrudge that. But now he'd crossed the line. He'd poked his nose into one sticky can of worms and it was Donald's job to handle it.

Rosie had underestimated her son; they both had. Now he had to take care of the situation.

"What do you think they're saying?" Shifting in the backseat, Leah tried to scoot closer to the driver's side window to get a better view of the two men.

"I don't know. They're probably trying to figure out the best way to handle us."

Abruptly sitting back against the seat, she asked, "And that is?"

"I hope it's not what you think it is, but that seems like their MO." Against his side he felt her shiver. Grabbing her hand, he shifted so that he could look into her face. Fear etched her hazel eyes, and her small lips were pressed into a thin line as she tried to think of something other than her possible impending death. Guilt-stricken and remorseful, Terrell spoke from his heart. "I'm sorry, Leah. You were right, I shouldn't have gotten you involved."

"Ms. Rosie's my friend, Terrell. I care a lot about her. I guess, deep down, I wanted to make sure she wasn't making a mistake, either." Terrell's dark eyes were full of regret, and his shoulders sagged with despair. She wished she could make it better for him, but there wasn't much either of them could do at the moment. "Besides, you didn't hold a gun to my head to get me to come downtown," she mumbled as an afterthought.

"Considering our present situation, I don't think that was a good phrase to use." His lips curved into a bleak smile.

"I guess not. Anyway, what I'm trying to say is that I made the decision to come so, in a way, I'm just as responsible as you are."

"But had I listened to you in the beginning, none of this would be happening."

"Yeah, then your mother would be marrying a drug dealer involved in murder. Get real, you did what you thought was right, and now we just have to deal with whatever comes next."

She was so optimistic. Tanya would definitely have been crying, in a state of panic by now. Yet this woman was offering him words of comfort. He was liking her more and more.

"You know Leakin Park is known for the number of dead bodies they find here each year?" That small fact just rolled right off her tongue, giving birth to a fresh wave of fear. They'd been stopped there for about fifteen minutes, and not one car had driven past. Donald and his thug friend could shoot them both right now, roll their bodies down the incline, and go on about their business. There would be no witnesses, and their bodies probably wouldn't be found for at least a week or two. It was rumored that police made regular inspections of the park for just that purpose. Leah hoped it wouldn't take that long. Not that it would matter, because she'd be dead anyway.

Dead, she thought morbidly. Was she ready to die? There was so much she hadn't experienced, so much more she wanted to do. Take her business, for instance. Leah wanted to expand, maybe branch out into a full-scale event planning company. She wanted to buy a house of her own and she wanted to travel, to finally get out of Baltimore. Although she loved the city and would never dream of living some-where else, there were a few places she'd like to visit.

Considering her words about dead bodies, Terrell frowned. "That's good to know," Terrell added in a bland tone, facing his own thoughts of impending death. If this was how he was going to die, then he hadn't lived much of a life. When he was younger he'd thought going to college and maintaining a secure and profitable career was what life was all about. Of course, in those days he'd envisioned a wife to share everything with. But now, at thirty-three, he was facing death. His career had certainly been profitable, even though he hadn't yet reached the level he'd originally aimed for, but he was alone, without a wife or even a girlfriend for that matter. And to top it off, his mother, the one person in this world he loved above all else, would most certainly marry this man who was bad for her. Closing his eyes, he laid his head back on the seat, seeing no possible way out of this situation.

"Terrell?"

Slanting his head in her direction, he opened his eyes slightly, enough to see her worried face. "Yeah?"

"I'm scared." The words almost lodged in her throat as tears began to well in her eyes.

Stunned at her admission, and angered by his own helplessness to make it better, he tightened his grip on her, resting his chin atop her head. "We're going to be okay. I got us into this, and I'll come up with a way to get us out."

"Good morning, baby, I'm surprised to see you here. I thought you'd be getting packed." Greeting Donald at her front door, Rosie paused for a brief second in surprise.

"I'm already packed. I just wanted to see you before I go." Pulling her into his arms he let her soft, cushiony body relax against him.

"Well, I thought you weren't leaving until tonight." Loving the feel of his bristly beard on her skin, Rosie remained engulfed in his arms. He looked a little worried this morning, and she wondered if something was wrong. Donald didn't talk about business with her, so if that was the source of his worries, she wouldn't even bother to ask.

"I have a few things to do before I get going, so I wanted to see you first. Is that alright?" Holding her away from him slightly, he stared into her pretty, cherub-like face.

"Of course that's alright. It's just that you look a little worried. Is everything okay?"

"Yeah, I'm fine. I just want to get this trip over with. As soon as I sign the rest of these papers and this loan goes through, I'll be able to sell the shop and we can get out of here."

"What do you mean, sell the shop?" Rosie was shocked. She had no idea Donald had been thinking of selling the salon, and where did he think they were going?

"I'm tired of it, Rosie. I want something bigger and better for us. I've been talking with some people, and we're working on something big down in Jamaica. If it goes through, I'm gonna sell the shop and we can move down there for good."

"I don't want to move to Jamaica." Moving out of his arms, Rosie went into the living room and sat down. Jamaica was so far away from her family. So far away from Terrell. This hadn't been a part of the original plan. She'd just assumed that they were getting married, and that everything else would remain the same.

Cursing himself for blurting it out like that, Donald followed her into the living room. "Why not?"

"Because my family and friends are here. You never said anything about Jamaica. I mean, I know your daughters live there, but you never said you wanted to live there." Wringing her hands, Rosie sat on the couch trying to still the rapid beating of her heart.

"Have you ever been to Jamaica?" Donald was afraid that not only would she reject the idea of moving to Jamaica, but of marrying him as well. He had meant to ease her into the idea, but time was running out, and he needed to get things rolling. The deal was about to close, the Feds were getting antsy and he needed to make his move.

He'd made the delivery last night, and now he needed to collect his money and be done with it. Rosie, he found, had become a crucial part of his life. He needed her with him. Taking a deep breath, he decided then that drastic measures would have to be taken.

"No, I've never been, but that really doesn't have anything to do with it. I mean, I would be leaving everything I know and love. My job, my family, my son."

At the mention of Terrell, Donald's eyes darkened. He hadn't forgotten that Terrell had followed him around last night like some renegade spy. Nor had he forgotten what he'd done to ensure that he'd be able to collect his money without any interruption.

"I know, baby. Look, why don't you come down with me? See the island for yourself, and then we'll talk about the move some more. I don't want you to feel pressured into this decision. I want us to enjoy our new life together." Sitting beside her, he took her hands in his, kissing her palms gently.

Her smile told him she was weakening. "I don't know," she began.

"Come on, say you'll come with me." Kissing her lips, Donald worked his mouth over hers persuasively.

"Do I have time to pack?" she whispered breathlessly.

"Hurry up, I'll be back in an hour to get you."

Planting one last kiss on her supple lips, Donald stood and went to the door. Before Rosie could change her mind, he was gone.

CHAPTER EIGHT

Leah's head hurt like hell. The simple act of lifting her eyelids was sheer torture. Groaning, she lifted her arm to cover her eyes and prayed the pain would go away. It was at that moment she realized she wasn't in her bed. Snatching her arm down quickly, she braved discomfort and opened her eyes. Her heart beat frantically as she searched the room for some semblance of recognition.

She found none.

Wooden beams hung above her, heavy and forbidding. What looked like old furniture and boxes were stacked in every corner. An old picnic table and chairs sat at the far end of the room, and boxes of old vinyl records blocked her view of the steps. Where the hell was she? And more importantly, how had she gotten there?

A hand on her shoulder panicked her and she screamed loud enough to wake the dead. "It's just me," Terrell whispered in her ear.

When she stared at him with eyes as huge as saucers, he gently stroked her arm until recognition dawned. "It's okay. I'm pretty sure we're alone."

She spoke hesitantly, afraid of what the answer might be. "Where...where are we?"

"I think we're in the basement of somebody's house." Finally sitting up, he turned to help ease her into a sitting position beside him. He had been awake for some time now, coming to with a start at the unfamiliar surroundings, just as she had. He didn't remember how they'd gotten there. His last memory was that of a big burly man telling him to drink a gritty tasting liquid from a paper cup. His mind was blank after that, until awakening this morning on the floor of a dark, cluttered basement.

Only a few moments before Leah awakened he remembered the big burly man was Donald. The man his mother was about to marry.

"How did we get here?" Leah asked as she looked around. It was definitely somebody's basement.

"I think we were drugged." Bringing his fingers to his temples, he began to rub against the nagging pain.

"Drugged? By who? For what?" As she asked, the answers clicked into her brain. She remembered the sleazy strip club and what had happened in the alley beside it. "Donald." She said his name in the faintest of whispers.

"Bingo." Turning to her, Terrell surveyed her appearance. She wore simple jeans and a sweatshirt that should not have turned him on the way it did. Unfortunately, that sexy leather jacket was made more for fashion than for warmth. Her hair was a bit tousled, as if she had been rolling around in bed with a man, with him. The stab of lust that soared from his brain to rest hotly between his legs was staggering and he hurriedly looked away.

"Oh my God! Can we get out?"

He smoothed back wayward strands of her hair. "I was just about to get up and look around. You sit still and let the grogginess pass."

Terrell got to his feet, stood for a second, then followed the stream of light on the floor toward the door.

"Check all the doors. And check the windows." Struggling to get to her feet, Leah felt a wave of nausea hit her and she wobbled into a table, sending an abundance of noisy items to the floor.

Terrell turned around, saw her condition, and hurried to her side, catching her in his arms before she fell. "Not only do you talk a lot, you have a problem following simple directions as well." He looked down at her grimly.

"Oh shut up. And put me down, I can walk." He was holding her in his arms as if she were a thirty-year-old baby. Her head, curse its betrayal, rested against his shoulder.

Terrell grinned to cover the fact that he was worried about her. Apparently she wanted to show no weakness to anyone. "Yup. You just showed me how well you can walk." He liked holding her close, liked the feel of her soft curves in his arms, but knew it was only a matter of time before she really began to protest. Besides, he needed to find a way out. He turned, looking for something he could set her on, and spotted an old lawn chair in the corner.

"I'm serious, Terrell. I don't need you carrying me around." He was walking with her now, his arm beneath her knees, his hand dangerously close to her butt. She squirmed, but he didn't break his stride. *Damn, he's a lot stronger than I thought.* She let her hands splay over his shoulders and back, almost groaning as she felt the flexing of rigid muscles beneath his clothes.

Before she could say another word Terrell stopped and released her legs gently, so that her body slithered down the front of him. Her eyes locked with his, and they both stood perfectly still.

The smoldering heat between them was instantaneous. His hands were trembling. He didn't release her, and she looked up at him with those enticing eyes and licked her lips. Every drop of blood in his body rushed to his midsection and the throbbing began. He saw in her eyes the moment his arousal pressed against her belly. He thought she'd pull away but instead she moved closer.

It was as if Leah were seeing him for the first time. His strong jaw was clenched, his lips drawn tightly together as his eyes smoldered over her. He held her in a tight grip as if afraid to let her go. She didn't want to move, didn't want to disturb the safety she felt there, wrapped up in Terrell. Her nipples tingled as they rubbed against his chest, and lust swirled in the pit of her stomach like a whirlpool, trickling slowly down to rest between her legs. Maybe she needed to re-evaluate what exactly was her type.

Before this moment led to something he wasn't sure she was ready for, he knew he had to end it. Taking a deep breath, he slid his arms from her backside to rest on her hips, as if to steady her. "I'm going to let you go for just a minute while I pull this chair out. Then I want you to sit." He looked at her intently. "Do you understand? Sit. Don't move."

Leah nodded, still tingling from their closeness.

When he had her settled in the chair, he checked the back door. It was locked—one of those old locks that needed a key on both the inside and outside. Gritting his teeth, he moved to the window. It had a latch on it, and was about big enough for a ten-year-old child to slither through. He jiggled the latch from the inside, thinking that maybe he could pry it apart, but then figured it would only bring in the cold air. And if they were going to be stuck here for any length of time, that wouldn't be such a good idea.

Abandoning the window for now, he went to the stairs, taking them two at a time until he reached the door that led into the house. Of course that was locked and as he rammed his shoulder against it, he realized it was also bolted from the other side. He cursed under his breath. The longer they were in this basement, the more likely they were to starve or freeze to death. Maybe that was the plan. Maybe Donald didn't want to personally kill them, but didn't object to them dying a slow and tortuous death. His heart rate accelerated at the thought. Then, as if he weren't already on a roll, the possibility of someone who worked for Donald coming to finish them off arose. He was building himself up to a fine panic when he looked to the corner to check on Leah, surprised that she'd been quiet *and* still for this long.

"What now?" she asked, meeting his defeated gaze.

He took a second to calm himself. The last thing he wanted to do was scare her more. Taking a deep breath, he checked his jacket pockets. "Damn. Where's your cell phone?"

Leah looked hopeful for a moment, then sank back in the chair. "In my purse," she said quietly. "In the car."

"Okay, that's out." Hands on his hips, he looked around the room, in search of what, he didn't quite know. He refused to think of them as being trapped, refused to accept that there was nothing he could do.

Leah watched him from her spot in the chair. Outwardly, he appeared calm and determined, traits she'd already known he had, but hadn't realized were so endearing. Refusing to sit idle any longer, she stood, slowly this time. In his mind, she was sure Terrell was thinking of an escape. She took a couple of steps towards him, then paused and turned to look around for something to break open the window with. They could yell for help she thought.

Terrell, who should have still been thinking of a way to get them out of this mess, watched the sway of her hips as she moved. Her bottom completely and tantalizingly filled out the jeans she wore. Licking his lips, he wondered if the drug Donald had given him was Viagra.

Here he was, trapped in somebody's basement, and all he could think about was sleeping with Leah, who was sending him such mixed signals he had to concentrate with all his might to keep from losing his mind. First she'd kissed him ardently in her office. Then tonight in the car she'd looked at him as if he were one step down from slime after their forced kiss. But just a few minutes ago he could have kissed her, could have peeled away all her clothes and laid her down on this floor. He could have had his way with her, he knew without a doubt, from the way she'd been looking at him.

Being locked in this basement wasn't what worried him most. Being locked in the basement *with* Leah was the challenge.

Just as she spotted a bat, she realized that breaking the windows would make the damp basement chilly and even more uncomfortable. Turning back, she looked at Terrell in question. "So we're stuck?"

With one hand he removed his glasses and with the other massaged his eyes. *Stop looking at her like that. You're never going to get out of here if you don't.* It was a warning he wasn't sure his mind was listening to, or could listen to when he opened his eyes and found Leah standing right in front of him.

"Are you okay? You think you're feeling aftereffects from the drugs?" She lifted a hand to his brow.

He tensed at her touch, grabbed her hand and held it to his cheek. She was so soft, her nearness so comforting. In that moment he pictured himself coming home from a hard day's work, and finding her waiting for him at the door, asking him if he'd had a rough day. The image was so clear, felt so real, he almost moaned in gratitude. "I'm okay. I just need to think of a way out of this."

Leah let him hold her hand, let her fingers be guided over the face she'd become so familiar with, and realized she liked it. "*We'll* think of a way out of this," she vowed.

When she smiled up at him he realized he was in even deeper than he had thought. His attraction to her had quietly grown into something beyond mere attraction. His heart beat rapidly as he tried not to show her too much too soon. He had things to work through, feelings to get in check, and he suspected she did too. Now was definitely not the time to be thinking of entering into a relationship with her—no matter how tempting she was.

"For the moment it looks like we're stuck here. That window seems to be our only option, but I don't know how viable that is. I sure can't fit through it." He released her hand slowly, took a step away from her. They were trapped in a basement together, in a precarious situation, one that could result in a lot of other precarious situations, and he needed to be strong enough to avoid that.

Leah turned so that she now faced the window, her back to him. Something had just happened between them. The moment she'd touched him, the moment he'd looked into her eyes, their relationship had shifted, moved to a position she hadn't anticipated. "I don't think I can fit through it either."

Terrell looked at her butt again and moaned. "No, I don't think you can."

She spun around quickly. "And what's that supposed to mean?"

When Leah glared at him, he held his hands up in mock surrender, grinning all the while. "It just means that you're packaged pretty well, and I'd hate to see that trying to squeeze through that little window."

Her scowl deepened.

"I messed that all up, didn't I?"

Leah couldn't help laughing with him. "You sure did."

Their smooth banter ceased as they again considered their circumstances.

Terrell, wanting nothing more than to get her out of the situation, went up the steps again to try to get the door to budge. "If we could find something heavy we could probably bust the lock on the door; that would at least get us upstairs."

When Leah didn't respond right away, he came back down the steps. He wasn't prepared to see her balled up on the floor, her arms locked around legs drawn up to her chest, and her forehead resting on her knees as if she were a small child.

Ignoring that voice in the back of his head that warned him about moving too fast, he crossed the room to her. When she made no move to acknowledge he was there, he stooped down so that he was eye level with her. Carefully placing his hand on her back, he called her name. When she didn't answer, he moved his hand in circles.

The moment he moved away from her, a fear so strong and so compelling hit her that she had to sit down to absorb it. Not only were they trapped in a basement, possibly left alone to die, but she was feeling things she'd never felt before, things she'd sworn she would never feel and, up until now, hadn't even had to worry about.

For whatever reason, she'd allowed herself to feel emotions for Terrell that she'd never felt for another man. Sure, she'd offered comfort to Leon when he'd had a bad day, but that was usually only a few kind words. With Terrell she'd wanted to make whatever was bothering him better. At first it had seemed like pity, as if she were simply doing what was needed for some poor unfortunate soul. Now she realized she was doing it for another reason entirely. She'd told him he wasn't her type, yet he'd asked her out again. She hadn't been particularly nice to him, yet he'd come to her again for help, had held her in his arms and kissed her as if she were the only woman in the world. When her stubbornness had prevailed, he'd carried her—actually carried her—to safety instead of letting her fall flat on her face.

Sitting on the floor, she felt tears sting the backs of her eyes. They could die in this basement if they didn't figure out a way to escape. She could die without ever knowing what it felt like to love and be loved in return.

Without another word he lifted her to sit in his lap. She seemed to cry a little harder then. With one hand he brushed through her hair while the other stroked her arms. The strong, feisty, argumentative, talkative Leah he'd steadily been falling for had finally showed a weakness, and he was overwhelmed with the need to soothe her. He whispered all sorts of assurances he wasn't positive he could make good on, but all that mattered to him was making her feel better. "I'll keep you safe, Leah. Always. I promise. I won't ever let anything or anyone harm you. Please believe me."

From the depths of his heart he meant every word he said to her, and not just for this situation.

Leah knew he was sincere, knew that if it were the last thing in the world he did, he'd make sure she was safe. She could believe him with her whole heart because that was the type of man he was—loyal and protective to a fault. His protective instincts had carried over to her, and she knew that she could count on him. He'd given her something no other man had ever come close to—a feeling of security. She'd been so busy proving that she was independent she'd never realized she needed it so much. But now, in Terrell's arms, she did.

"Sweetheart," he whispered against her ear.

The endearment warmed her and she moaned her reply, "Mmmm."

"It's going to be okay. I'll get you out of here. And then I'm going to make sure you're never in danger again." He dropped light kisses along her forehead.

Relationships started under high pressure circumstances never worked. Wasn't that what the guy in that movie *Speed* had said? Maybe what they both seemed to be feeling was a result of their nerves being stretched too thin and the fear of dying. She looked into Terrell's eyes and could swear she saw more there than just fear, but she couldn't be sure. And until she was positive of his feelings for her, she wasn't about to go putting hers on a platter for him to feast on. He thought she was upset about their predicament; she'd let him continue to think that. "I'm afraid, Terrell." *Hell, I'm terrified of what you're making me feel.*

"What if they just leave us here to die? Or if they're upstairs and are going to come down and finish the job later?"

He wouldn't admit his own fears right now, because his focus was to make her feel better. She seemed at her best when they were sparring with each other, so that was the route he'd take. "And what if pigs could fly?" His lips curled into a smile while she contemplated her response.

Only Terrell would say something so absolutely ridiculous at a time like this. Twitching to keep from smiling herself, she pushed against him with her body.

"Exactly," he said, his voice growing a little more serious. "Who cares about what if? Now is what matters." Brushing a piece of flyaway hair from her face, he stared at her, longing for another kiss, wondering if she had any idea how much she affected him. "So like I was saying, if we can find something big then we can try to bust the lock on the door. They're probably not up there anyway." He lifted a hand to wipe the tears from her face.

She blinked once at his soft touch, then relaxed, accepting that this was simply how he was. "How do you know?"

"Because I heard them talking about the boat leaving from the Harbor. I assume they meant this afternoon or possibly tonight. Anyway, if we can get upstairs, then we can call the police or we can just walk right out the front door."

"Or we can just walk right into them, and they'll kill us on the spot." Instinctively she countered his plan.

"If they wanted us dead, we wouldn't be having this conversation." He frowned. What had happened to all her optimism? When he'd originally come to her with his suspicions about Donald, she'd countered every shred of evidence he'd presented to her, and now it seemed she was resolved to believe the worst.

Maybe because at this moment it seemed that they were experiencing the worst, he thought cynically. Still, her defeatism worried him.

"I guess you're right." Shrugging her shoulders she added, "Continue."

"Yes ma'am." With a playful salute, he proceeded, pleased that she didn't sound so desolate now. "I heard them saying something about catching a plane just before they opened the door to give us whatever it was they gave us to drink. Something in the liquid must have knocked us out cold, and now they're probably already gone. The fact that they just locked us down here means that they don't really want to kill us."

He sounded confident of his assessment, as if he had all this information on good authority and there was no reason for her to doubt him. And actually, she didn't. "Well, at least Donald doesn't want to kill us," Leah added. "His friend looked like he'd take us out without a second thought."

"You're probably right." Terrell grinned, pinched her pert little nose. "I'm starting to get used to you being right."

Rosie stepped up onto the ramp that had been extended for passengers. Her white tennis shoes were in stark contrast to the red carpet lining the steel plank. Craning her neck, she stared up at the massive ship she and Donald were now boarding. Up until today she hadn't had any idea that cruise ships like this left from Baltimore. Every cruise she'd ever heard about required flying to Florida and boarding there. According to Donald, cruise liners had been coming up the eastern coast for passengers for the last three years.

Entering the Promenade Deck, as the kind gentleman who helped her over the ramp and onto the ship called it, Rosie took in the luxurious surroundings. To her right was a magnificent winding staircase with royal blue carpeted steps. Beyond the customer service desk were signs pointing the way to Nautica Spa, High Rollers Casino, and Destiny Lounge.

Directly ahead of her was the Promenade Balcony, where it seemed all the passengers were momentarily stranded. A crewmember approached them pulling a cart with their luggage securely strapped on, and directed them to follow him. Taking the elevator, they proceeded to their stateroom on the Verandah Deck.

"Are you okay?" Donald asked when they stepped off the elevator and Rosie appeared star-struck again.

"I'm fine. I've just never seen anything like this before." Looking around, she noted that this floor, in bold contrast to the Promenade Deck, had been carpeted in bright canary yellow. The door to each room was painted a shimmering shamrock green, and the hallway glistened pearly white. "It's all so festive," she said.

"It's a fun cruise. This is all I could manage at short notice, but I didn't think it would be too bad." Stopping behind Cliff, the attendant, they waited for him to unlock the door.

Once the door was opened, Rosie stepped in first. The room was decorated in more subtle tones—beige, rose and turquoise. Immediately to her right was the bathroom, which boasted a large tub and shower, a spacious sink and dressing table. Taking a few steps forward, she saw an oval-shaped bar with a twenty-seven inch television hanging above it.

"We show first-run films in each room. There's a guide over there on the table that will help you with programming," Cliff informed them.

Continuing her survey of the room, Rosie moved to the foot of a king-sized bed with a mirrored headboard that took up one wall. Opposite was a sliding glass door opening onto a balcony as long as the room.

"So what do you think?" Donald asked when the attendant left. He took off his leather jacket and tossed it across the couch.

"It's a little overwhelming, maybe because it's my first cruise." Wringing her hands, she watched as Donald removed his tie and unbuttoned the top buttons on his shirt.

"It'll all sink in once we get moving." Crossing the room to stand in front of her, he placed his large hands on her plump shoulders.

"Please don't say 'sink.' " She rolled her eyes and rested her head against his chest. When she felt the rumbling of his laughter against her face, she had to chuckle herself.

"Come on, let's get unpacked. Then we can take the grand tour."

"Maybe we can just stay in our room," Rosie suggested, her voice sultry. "It would be a shame to put such a big bed to waste." Her arms encircled his waist to pull him closer.

"I guess you have a good point there." Moving his hands from her shoulders, he caressed her back, then slid his hands further down to grip her voluptuous bottom. "A very good point."

Perched on the steps, Leah ripped the tape from a box marked photos. Lifting the cardboard flaps, she explored the contents. "I think we can safely assume we're in Donald's basement." Her voice was bland as she flipped through the photographs.

"Let me see." Terrell abandoned the box he'd been going through to join her on the steps. He'd been looking for a crowbar, or something to wrench the door open, but so far all he'd found were pictures and real estate documents.

Without so much as a glance in his direction she handed him a handful of pictures she'd already viewed. Donald was in almost every one. She didn't recognize anyone else in the pictures. Some showed him with two younger women whose faces she'd seen repeatedly in the photos. She figured they might be the daughters that Nikki had told her about.

Dropping the pictures she still held in her hand back into the box, she sat straight up and stretched. She arched back and lifted her arms above her head. "This is tiring."

Out of the corner of his eye Terrell watched the rise and fall of her breasts. His mouth went dry at the sight of the heavy mounds molding themselves against the cotton of her shirt. Continuing to flip through the pictures, he tried to concentrate on the people in them, or the people that weren't in them, anything but the fact that with Leah he was trapped in this basement, which seemed to be getting smaller and smaller by the moment.

"You didn't find any tools over there, huh?" Unaware of the effect she was having on her fellow captive, Leah spoke calmly as she looked around the room to the pile of boxes Terrell had already gone through.

"Nah, I didn't see anything." Terrell cleared his throat. "I did find some papers that I think might shed some light on the type of person we're dealing with, though." Dropping the pictures into the box, he crossed over to where he'd set a pile of papers he'd pulled from a file cabinet and came back to sit beside Leah. "It looks like Donald owns some property." Tension crackled between them as they touched. Terrell focused on the papers and tried to ignore it.

Leah closed her eyes and tried to ignore it.

"Have you ever heard of Negril?"

"Yeah. It's in Jamaica and it's becoming a pretty hot vacation spot. A lot of my clients go there on their honeymoon." Opening her eyes, she looked down at the papers he held. "What are those? Deeds?"

"Yeah, it looks like it. I guess he owns land in Negril."

"They're dated within the last two years. Why would he buy property in Jamaica?"

"Maybe he's planning to relocate," Terrell mentioned quietly.

"Yeah, maybe." Leah shrugged. Then his silence caught her attention and, taking a chance, she looked at him. He was no longer looking at the papers but was staring straight ahead, a blank expression on his face. No, not blank, she thought, sad.

"What's the matter?" *Besides the obvious*, she thought to herself.

"I was just thinking that he's probably planning to take my mother to Jamaica with him."

"And that would bother you?"

"Of course it would bother me!" he yelled. "What kind of question is that? Would you want your mother living an ocean away from you?"

"Actually—" She thought of Marsha and all her problems.

"Never mind, you wouldn't understand." Gathering the papers into a neat stack, Terrell started to get up from the steps.

"You're right." With her hand on his arm she stopped him. "Why don't you explain it to me? I know that you love your mother. When I see you with her I know there's nothing in this world you wouldn't do to make her happy. What I don't understand is why—before you found out all this about Mr. Donald—why you didn't want her to get married."

She wouldn't understand, he thought. He barely understood it himself. Still, he found himself preparing to tell her. He looked into her hazel eyes. "You really want to know?"

"Yeah, I really want to know." Placing her hand on his knee in what she meant as a purely innocent gesture to reassure him, she continued, "It might help you to talk it out with someone and, as it stands, I don't have anywhere to be just now, so I'm all ears."

Her lips curved in a smile that both melted his heart and threatened to destroy him. "My father died when I was ten years old. He was killed in a car accident."

"I'm sorry," she whispered and took his hand in hers.

"So it's been just me and Mama all these years. She was always telling me how she wanted me to make something of my life, to be successful...to be happy. So I went to college and I studied hard. I found my niche in computers and was offered a six-figure salary in my senior year. I figured this was the life meant for me—so I set out to live it." The only thing missing was the family he'd wanted so desperately, but he wasn't about to divulge that information.

"Ms. Rosie's really proud of what you've accomplished."

"I know. But she always cautioned me not to get too caught up in the success. I just wanted to make things better for her, to repay her for all that she'd done for me. I wanted to take care of her the way she took care of me."

Because she was curious, because her house had always been a revolving door for father figures, she asked, "Was it bad growing up?"

He sensed the part of her question she'd omitted. "Without a father, you mean? Yeah, it was bad. We always seemed to have what we needed, but Mama worked and worked. I just knew that if Daddy had lived, things would have been much different. Mama and I are very close. We both shared the same tremendous loss the day my father died. I wanted to be the one to fix that for her."

"You can give her all the material things in the world, Terrell, but it won't fill the gap that losing your father left. That's not for you to fill."

Terrell frowned. Her words were true, but they made him seem like some perverted freak. "I never thought I could fill her husband's shoes. I just wanted to make her comfortable so it wouldn't hurt as much anymore."

Leah saw an opening to lighten the moment. "Oh, okay. For a minute there I thought…"

He looked at her. "You did not."

Leah's smile spread. "Of course I didn't. I'm not stupid, I knew what you meant. But still, you can do only so much. And Mr. Donald seemed to give her what she needed at the moment. Were you really going to begrudge her that?"

He shook his head adamantly. "No. I wasn't. After I spent the weekend with them, saw how happy he made her, I really wanted it to happen—for her sake. Something just kept bothering me about him. I remembered his name from somewhere. Now I realize it was the papers. I found a huge stack of old clippings at the library that outlined the investigation into him and his business dealings a while back. I understand that she loves him and that even after I tell her this she probably still will, but I won't let him hurt her. I won't let him involve her in his illegal activities."

"For the record, this time and probably this time only," she grinned as he looked at her with raised brows, "I think you're right."

Their close proximity was quickly changing the moment to something more sensual and she was instantly uncomfortable. *Not under these circumstances*, she reminded herself. She'd thought that talking to him about his past would alleviate some of the sexual tension. Instead, it had brought her closer to the realization that he was one hell of a man. Everything he'd worked for, everything he wanted in life, took a second seat to protecting his mother.

In a sense they were two of a kind. He was just as determined to protect his mother as she was to not repeat her mother's mistakes.

Because she felt she was reading way too much into their connection, she gently removed her hand from his knee and reached behind her head to free her hair from its ponytail.

Leaning back, he rested his elbows on the step above and stared at the ceiling. He'd told her something he'd never uttered to another living soul, and it had been so easy. Keenly aware that she was sitting very close to him, he dared not look at her. The way he was feeling right now he just might start blubbering about his feelings for her.

"It's getting dark outside." Looking down at his watch, he confirmed that it was evening. "Six o'clock. We've been down here probably about twelve hours now."

"I'm hungry." *Maybe that's the true cause of the fluttering in my stomach.*

"There's a deep freezer way back in the corner." Rising from the steps, Terrell walked across the room. "And, I thought I saw..." His voice trailed off while Leah stood and stretched again.

"You thought you saw what?" Hands on her hips, she watched him going from one corner to the next.

"I thought I saw...yup, I did. Here it is." Stooping down, he moved a box from atop a white surface. "A mini refrigerator," he announced as he pulled open the door.

"Who puts a mini refrigerator in their basement?" Leah asked as she joined him in his perusal of the refrigerator's contents.

"Maybe he worked down here late at night and got the urge for a snack. I don't know, but there's some bottled water, a carton of milk..." Putting the carton to his nose, he sniffed. Frowning copiously, he sat the carton to the side. "...That's no good at all, but here's an unopened pack of bologna and some Kraft singles."

With his bounty in hand he turned to Leah. "My dear, we have a feast."

"Yeah, a feast." She tried to muster up her excitement. "I'm not a big bologna fan." Opening the bottle of water, he handed it to her and she took a few big gulps.

"Me either, but I'll make the sacrifice." Passing her the meat and cheese, Terrell grabbed some blankets that they'd thrown beside the boxes in their earlier search and began to spread them out on the floor. After putting three blankets on top of each other, he took a fourth one and rolled it into one long pillow. Then the last two he set to the side saying, "We'll have to use these to cover us."

Leah watched him in silence. The makeshift bed was anything but encouraging, but she couldn't help thinking of lying on it with Terrell.

"Leah?" Terrell called her name again.

"Hmmm?" she answered, her eyes never leaving the blankets on the floor.

"Are you alright?" She looked funny, he thought, as if she were dreading something. Dreading sleeping next to him, he figured. The thought made him angry. He knew he was no Denzel Washington but damn, he wasn't ugly and disgusting either. She was acting as if she expected him to rape her or something.

He thought of taking half the blankets and moving to the other end of the room but the floor was cement—cold cement. Should he continue to be unsuccessful in finding a way out of here, they were going to need the cushioning, as well as the warmth, the trio of blankets layered on the floor would provide. So he quickly dismissed the idea of splitting the blankets just so she wouldn't have to suffer lying next to him. She'd simply have to deal with it.

"No. I'm fine." Dropping to her knees, she began to pry the plastic wrapping from the bologna.

Taking a seat across from her, he opened his bottled water, took a refreshing sip. "There's a bathroom beneath the steps."

"Really? A bathroom?" She couldn't imagine a bathroom being in such a limited space.

"It's just a toilet, but since we found the water, I'm sure it'll come in handy." His lips melted into a smile. Once he assured himself that she was comfortable he'd resume his search for an escape.

"I'm sure it will." When she removed the wrapping from the container she peeled off a slice of meat and held it out to him.

Terrell, in turn, removed the wrapping from the cheese and held a slice out to her. The exchange was a sort of truce, both of them quietly accepting their circumstances and mutually agreeing to deal with them the best way they knew how.

CHAPTER NINE

Leah rolled her bologna and cheese into a log before taking a bite. In no way did it compare to a real meal, but it would have to suffice. At least she wouldn't starve, she thought to herself.

"Why did you roll it like that? Does it make it taste any better?"

"Not really, but when I was a little girl my mother bought only bologna, I guess because it was cheaper than other lunch meats, and she had so many of us to feed." She didn't know why she'd added that last statement, but shrugged, since it was already said. There was nothing she could do about it now. "Anyway, I didn't like the taste of it, but if I didn't eat what she prepared, then I didn't eat. So I would roll it with the cheese, which was always sliced thicker than the bologna because we used to get the government allotment. That way, I'd taste more cheese than I did bologna. I'd fill my stomach and not get yelled at."

"Oh, I see." He didn't really. Since he didn't have any siblings, food had never been rationed in his house. There had been times when it wasn't his mother's pay week and they'd had to eat leftovers two nights in a row, but Rosie always cooked more than enough for the two of them.

"How many sisters and brothers do you have?" Mimicking her movements, he rolled his meat with his cheese and took a test bite.

"I have four brothers, all of them younger. Two are still at home."

"That's why you're so bossy." Terrell decided that the bologna was much easier to stomach when accompanied by the cheese, and took another bite. She was right again.

"I'm not bossy," she pouted. "I just know what I want."

"And what is it that you want, Miss Wedding Planner?" The last was said in a prissy, girlish voice that made her giggle.

"I want my business to be successful." Unaware that she was still smiling at him, she stretched out on the blanket on her stomach.

"That's all you want?" The bologna and cheese almost got stuck in his throat and he coughed. Did she have any idea how seductive she looked right at that moment? Her long legs, extending from a magnificently round bottom, stretched across the blanket. Her elbows were propped and supported the weight of her upper body. Her breasts hung low, brushing the blanket.

"Yeah, for right now anyway. Why? What do you want?" She popped the last of her bologna concoction into her mouth and chewed.

"We're not talking about me." At least not anymore. He'd told her enough already. "You don't want to get married or have a family?" Finishing his bologna roll, he took another drink of water.

Adamantly, she shook her head in the negative. "No. Definitely not." Even as she answered she wondered how truthful she was being.

Taken aback by her response, he stifled the disappointment coursing through him. "Why not?"

"Marriages don't last," she said simply.

"Some do," he countered.

Her eyes remained steady on his. "Mine wouldn't."

"Why not?"

"Because," she answered, hoping that would be enough.

"Because what?"

She should have known he'd be persistent—payback for her inquiry into his personal life. Figuring it didn't matter one way or the other, she answered, "Because my mother can't seem to stay married, so why would I be any different?"

"That's stupid." Pushing his glasses up on his nose, he frowned at her.

Offended, she tried to remain calm. "Why is it stupid?"

"Because you and your mother are two different people, and maybe your mother just hasn't found Mr. Right yet."

"There's no such thing as Mr. Right. You date people, you sleep with people, and you marry people. Then you argue, you fight and you get divorced. That's the way the world turns."

"That's the way your world turns. If my dad were still alive, I'll bet he and my mother would still be married."

"Then they would have been the exception to the rule."

"What makes you so sure you won't be the exception to the rule?"

She wasn't so sure, not anymore. "Because I don't intend to play the game," she quipped.

"Chicken."

She frowned. "I am not a chicken."

"Then what do you call it? You're afraid that if you commit to marriage it'll one day end in divorce. So what? Then you pick up and start all over again, because evidently you picked the wrong person."

The wrong person—that was an understatement. A few weeks ago she'd thought the wrong person was the one sitting across from her giving unsolicited advice. "Well, you asked me what I wanted and I told you. It's not open for discussion." She fidgeted, because she now saw the foolishness of her own thoughts, but she wasn't about to admit that to him—not yet anyway.

He sensed her mood shifting and wasn't quite ready for her to shut down completely, so he changed his line of questioning. "So what about that dude you went on a date with the other week? Does he know you don't want to get married?" This was very important to him. How serious was her relationship with this guy? Maybe it was nothing at all. Maybe it was just like she'd said: You date, you have sex, then you get married. Maybe she was just omitting the marriage part. He doubted that. Leah wasn't the type to take anything lightly—least of all sex. So was she just dating for the hell of it? That didn't make too much sense to him, considering his dating scheme had a purpose.

"Who? Leon?" Rolling onto her back, she stared at the beamed ceiling. "Leon and I have been seeing each other for a couple of months now. He's cool." She wondered why it had been so easy for her to categorize Leon as just 'cool' when off the top of her head she could come up with at least ten adjectives to describe Terrell.

"Oh, he's *cool*, huh? Cool enough to sleep with?" The words were out of his mouth before he could stop them. Then he realized he hadn't wanted to stop them. He wanted to know if she planned on sleeping with Leon. He needed to know about his competition.

She'd rolled onto her back, and he'd watched her breasts spill across her chest. Visions of stripping those clothes from her, glimpsing her complete nakedness, teased and tantalized his senses. At the same time, alarm about whether or not she was already sleeping with someone spoiled his fantasy. When her head snapped in his direction, he stared at her intently, clearly expecting an answer to his question.

"Not that it's any of your business, but no, I haven't slept with him." Bringing her arms up to cradle her head, she went back to staring at the ceiling.

"Why not?" He prayed his sigh of relief hadn't been audible and figured as long as she was answering questions, he might as well get them all in.

How much of the truth should she tell him? "Because I wasn't ready." Which was really weird because she'd known Leon for months, whereas she'd known Terrell for only a few weeks, and if he touched her right now she'd be putty in his hands.

It wasn't any of his business, still she felt the need to expound on her simple statement. "See, I have this system."

"A system?" He thought of the piece of paper in his back pocket with his criteria for a wife. She couldn't possibly have something as ludicrous as that in her pocket, too. As tight as those jeans were, it didn't appear anything could fit in her pocket.

"Yeah, a system. Relationships have steps, just like I said before." She used her fingers to count them off. "Step one is the second date. Step two, the second through fifth dates, which mean you really like this person. Step three is sex and step four is marriage. I try to stay on the first step as long as humanly possible."

"And where's the logic behind that?"

"No logic, just my system. I wasn't ready for step three with him, so I…I ended it."

"You what?" Terrell almost choked on his water.

"I explained that I just didn't see any romantic involvement between us and he said something about waiting, taking things a little more slowly."

Waiting wasn't going to do him any good. Now that she'd admitted she had no romantic interest in Leon, it was on. He'd have Leah Graham for his own, it was just a matter of time. *Sorry, Leon, you snooze, you lose.*

"Yeah, I think he's a good guy." *He's just not for me.*

Chancing another glance at her chest moving rhythmically with each breath she took, he shook his head. *But not nearly good enough.*

Rosie sat in the Blue Wave Restaurant, waiting patiently for her date. Donald had left the cabin two hours earlier, telling her to meet him here at six. It was now six-fifteen and she was seated at the table he'd reserved for them, but he was nowhere to be found.

Finally she admitted to herself what she'd been denying since yesterday morning when Donald had walked into her living room and told her of his plans to move to Jamaica: Something strange was going on with Donald. He'd been distracted from the moment they boarded the ship. Last night, he'd suggested that they stay in the cabin, continuing to enjoy the amenities offered, but he'd spent most of his time closed up in the bathroom with his cell phone. When he'd finally come to bed, she'd been restless, wondering what was going on. She'd broached the subject, only to have him brush her off. Before she could bring it up again, he was kissing her. And then the kissing led to other things, which ultimately took her mind off the way he was acting. Which, she thought now, was probably his plan.

This morning she'd awakened to a wonderful breakfast on the balcony. They ate in silence as the waves slapped against the side of the ship. The sky was a pale blue backdrop with a few puffy white clouds. Rosie enjoyed the scene and pretended there was nothing wrong with the picture she was a part of.

After staying in their cabin the better part of the day, Donald decided he wanted to hit the casino for a while. Knowing that Rosie detested gambling, he opted to go alone and meet her later. Rosie wondered if that hadn't been his plan all along, to get out of the cabin without her. But why?

A little voice in the back of her head had been yelling warnings from the moment Donald had waltzed into her house talking of Jamaica. She'd known when she met him how he'd started his business, how he'd once been a big time drug dealer. He'd sworn to her that that part of his life was over. And when the police had investigated him, she'd watched him leave town and come back a totally different man. When they first started dating, he'd told her his past was behind him. She'd believed he was on the up and up.

Then the strange cars started appearing in the shop's lot. Donald began getting a lot of calls on his cell phone and their time together had become less frequent. The marriage proposal had come as a shock to her, especially since she hadn't seen him at all that entire week—he'd been away visiting relatives. Relatives she now doubted existed.

Okay, it was now six-thirty and still no Donald. He was testing her patience and that was something she would not tolerate. Oh yeah, it was definitely time to find out what the hell was going on. She wasn't about to marry a man who was so obviously hiding something from her. Pushing her chair back, she stood to look around the elegant room one more time. No Donald. Snatching up her purse, she walked out the door.

She didn't have a clue where she was going. All she knew was Donald was somewhere on this boat. Somewhere, she thought, with a small fist of hurt clutching her heart, doing Lord only knew what. She opted to go left, the direction of the casino. Maybe he was on a roll and had lost track of time. For that, she'd only torture him slowly.

There seemed to be an awful lot of people in a hurry to get to the casino, Rosie noted. "Idiots," she said to herself. Like they hadn't spent enough money on the cruise itself. Now they were eagerly giving it right back.

Slot machines whirled and chimed with winners, dice rolled across the green felt-covered tables, and a money wheel clicked incessantly before stopping at a number. Scantily-dressed women moved from one end of the room to the other, carefully balancing trays full of drinks, and stopping occasionally to pass one to a thirsty gambler. People were everywhere, and it made her hunt for Donald difficult. Still, she searched each row of slot machines and each aisle of gaming tables.

Half an hour later, she was back at the entrance and still alone. She hadn't seen Donald anywhere amongst the crowd of people eagerly giving away their money. Glad to get out of that negative surrounding, she began her search in the opposite direction.

An hour later Rosie was both exhausted and thoroughly pissed off. She'd searched everywhere she could think of and hadn't seen Donald. She'd even gone back to the restaurant to ask if he'd shown up, which he hadn't. Fuming now, she began to make her way back to their room. If he was there, she vowed to forego the slow torture she'd thought of earlier. Now she was ready to kill. She didn't know what was going on but she was going to put a stop to it—tonight!

Since she was closer to the stairway than the elevator, and they were only on the floor directly below the restaurant, she decided to take the stairs. After the first few steps, she stopped a moment to rest. That was when she heard Donald's voice.

Plain as day she could hear him talking. He was saying something about meeting the man in Negril. What man? And why was Donald planning to meet him? He was supposed to be wrapping up a business deal and then showing her around the island. Leaning over the railing carefully, she could see two men standing on the landing beneath her. One was Donald and the other she had never seen before.

"Was the money in the account?" the other man was asking.

"I haven't been able to get through to the bank yet. I tried all last night. I'm not getting a real good connection on this damned boat," Donald told him.

"Well, as soon as we hit land, you check it out, and then we go see Rohan. If my money ain't there, I'm killin' that bastard."

"Just chill, Cable. It'll be there and then this will all be behind us."

She should leave. She should go back to the room and wait for him. To hell with that! She was going to get her answers, and she was going to get them right now! Anger and fear of what this situation really meant stirred inside her and she started down again. When she reached the next level, two pairs of shocked dark eyes focused on her enraged features.

"I know you better have a damned good reason for standing me up to talk to some man on the stairway." Hands on her hips, her big chest heaving more from anger than exertion, Rosie glared at Donald and waited for his reply.

Still shocked to see her there, Donald couldn't find any words. Cable spoke up instead.

"Hello, ma'am. My name's Cable McDaniel." The man extended his hand and quickly snatched it back as Rosie ignored it. "Um, I just met Mr. Donald, and we were talking about some business ideas we both had, and were thinking about getting together once we're back on land. I understand this is your first trip to the islands."

She didn't believe this shady character for one minute, not any more than she was believing her fiancé, who still hadn't said a word. "Donald, tell your friend I'm not interested in words from him. All the answers and explanations I want need to come from you."

Dragging his hand over his mouth, Donald cleared his throat and prepared to speak. Something in her eyes stopped him. He knew that whatever he said had to be good. Rosie wasn't going to believe just anything and, not that he hadn't tried, but Cable's little recitation had only angered her more. So, instead of explaining right there on the staircase, he decided it would be best to get her alone. That way if she hauled off and hit him, which was exactly what she looked like she was ready to do, he wouldn't be embarrassed in front of his friend.

"Rosie, come on, let's go back to our room. I'll explain everything there." Keeping his back to Cable, Donald gently placed his hand on Rosie's elbow.

"Oh, now you want to go back to our room?"

From behind him Donald heard Cable say, "Yeah, that's a good idea, Donald. I'll catch up with you later. It was nice meeting you, ma'am." The last was muttered as he quickly made his way through the door.

Folding her big arms across her chest, Rosie stood perfectly still. If he thought he was going to shuffle her off to their room and talk his way out of this, he had another thought coming.

She could no longer ignore the fact that something was definitely wrong. She was looking at the man she loved, the six foot, three inches, two hundred and eighty-five pound man she'd fallen madly in love with, the man she was about to marry. The gray slacks and gray button-down shirt looked the same as they had when he'd left her in the room earlier this afternoon. His hair, thin graying beard and mustache looked the same. Dark eyes she'd spent long nights staring into were still there, only hooded by something she couldn't quite fathom. He was the same, yet he was different.

"Innovations." Loosening his tie, Marty Blum stared at the elegant script on the window of the beauty salon. "That's a fitting name, don't you think?"

Jeffrey Tobias slowly sipped hot coffee from a Styrofoam cup. "How so?"

"They've certainly come up with new and innovative ways to smuggle drugs into the U.S." Marty chuckled at his own wit.

Rolling his eyes, Jeffrey turned his attention from his goofy partner to the building they were staking out. "We haven't seen or heard from Douglas in a few days now. I think something's going down." Watching as two young women unlocked the door and walked into the building, Jeffrey flipped through a manilla folder.

"That's Nicole Ayers and Keesha Jones. They normally work from eleven in the morning to around ten at night. They have a steady clientele. Nicole lives in Woodlawn, Heraldry Square Apartments, alone. Keesha lives in Randallstown, Liberty Apartments, with her cousin Jasmine Johnson. They're both single and pretty hot, if you ask me," Marty rattled off between bites of a Boston cream donut, courtesy of the Dunkin' Donuts across the street.

Confirming Marty's recitation with the information in the file, Jeffrey continued to flip through his papers. "Been doing your homework, I see."

"That's my job." Marty smiled. "Rosetta Pierce, hasn't been in for a few days. When was the last time we heard from Douglas?"

"We talked to him on Sunday night. He said the drop was scheduled for Tuesday and things were expected to go smoothly." Rubbing the stubble of beard that had begun to grow at his chin, Jeffrey sat back against the seat, thinking intently. "That was the last time we heard from him. I knew we should have put a tail on him."

He'd been heading up this investigation for the Bureau for the last four years; it was time to bring it to an end. The pyramid of players was complete, pinned up on the wall in his office in D.C. They knew every one of them from the kingpin to the delivery guys. All they needed now was the big bust and he'd be on his way to Special Investigator.

But Douglas was becoming a glitch in the plan. A couple of months ago Jeffrey had begun to notice something different about the man. His comings and goings remained the same but his actions had changed.

"You think she's with him?" Marty pulled another donut from the bag.

"I don't know." Staring into the window of the building, he conceded that he'd been thinking the same thing himself, but he didn't dare verbally agree with Marty. His younger partner was cocky enough as it was. He wasn't about to add to his already-inflated ego. "Let's go talk to them."

"You sure? It might tip them off."

"Something's going on, I can feel it. Douglas is gone. His senior stylist is gone. A million dollar deal was supposed to go down three days ago, but we haven't heard a word. Yeah, something's going on." Stuffing the file between the seats, Jeffrey checked the weapon holstered just beneath his left shoulder blade and, with a glance, advised Marty to do the same.

Cramming the uneaten portion of his donut back into the bag, Marty quickly wiped his hands on a nearby napkin and checked his own weapon. Getting out of the car, they both pulled their jackets closer around them and crossed the street.

The door swung open, setting off a jangling melody. Glancing above, Jeffrey spotted a wind chime made of miniature blow dryers and other hair salon equipment. Frowning slightly, he made a quick scan of the room. The waiting area was currently empty, the radio blared Baltimore's most popular R&B station, and the two women sat at their stations chatting about this and that. The other four stations were empty.

"Good morning, ladies." Marty's voice cracked just a bit at the sight of the women up close.

Keesha was up and out of her chair first, walking with her confident stride, sashaying hips that a skinny woman prayed for, thumbs hooked between the belt loops of tight hip-hugger jeans that showed the rim of a sexy black thong. She'd gotten her hair done yesterday, so long black and burgundy braids hung seductively down her back except for one lengthy, wayward plait that dangled between the two lush mounds of her breast.

Jeffrey thought Marty's tongue would fall out of his mouth as the young woman approached. *Young boys*, he thought cynically.

"Good morning, ma'am. My name is Jeffrey Tobias. I'm with the Federal Bureau of Investigation. I was wondering if I could ask you a few questions." Removing his badge from his back pocket, he flipped it for the woman who stood staring at him with huge brown eyes.

"Well, well, well. What have we done to be honored with the presence of two such gorgeous men?" Sparing a cursory glance for the badge the taller guy flashed, Keesha was more intent on choosing which one she preferred. The one with the badge was tall, dark-skinned and fairly handsome, while the one with the cute smile had a creamy coffee complexion, curly hair, dancing brown eyes and a killer dimple in his left cheek. She wanted that one. Nikki could have the tough cop, she'd take the cute one.

"Did you say you're with the FBI?" Nikki approached the group, eyeing each man suspiciously.

"Yes, ma'am. We'd like to ask you a few questions." Jeffrey looked at the woman now standing in front of him. She was a lot prettier close up than in her pictures. Her face had been carefully made-up, with peach toned lips, and she directed a frown at him. Her skin was a shiny bronze accented by glittering gold eyes. She was a very attractive female.

Shaking his head, Jeffrey cleared that thought from his mind. He was here on business. "You're Nicole Ayers, am I right?" The quiet shock in her eyes told him she now believed he was with the FBI.

"Yes. Is that what you wanted to ask me?" Nikki's cool stare and poised stance gave the impression that she wasn't the least bit bothered by being questioned by the FBI. But in truth her stomach was clenched, and, at any moment, she feared she'd relieve herself of her breakfast, right on this agent's feet.

"No, ma'am. I have a few more questions." Jeffrey cracked a small grin at her brashness. This wasn't going to be as easy as he'd initially thought. She wasn't as silly as her profile made her out to be. If she knew anything, she would be very careful about what she told him. A part of him prayed she didn't know anything.

"I want to ask you about the owner of the shop, Donald Douglas." Recognition flickered in her eyes.

"What about Mr. Donald? Is he in trouble?" Keesha's loud voice shattered the private conversation between Nikki and Jeffrey, bringing Jeffrey quickly back to the matter at hand.

"I don't know. We were just trying to get in touch with him. Do you know where he can be reached?" Marty asked.

"We have his home number." Keesha smiled into Marty's excited eyes.

"If you're the FBI, you have his home number too, don't you?" Nikki asked Jeffrey. She ignored the other guy, who was clearly lost in the cleavage Keesha so bodaciously displayed.

Jeffrey was beginning to like her sassy nature. He stared into those mystical eyes and answered, "We have his address and his phone number, but we haven't been able to reach him. I was wondering if maybe you knew where he was. Did he say anything about a business trip, a vacation or something?"

"No, he doesn't discuss his personal life with his staff." Her answer was cold and brittle. But beyond that, Jeffrey thought, it was probably true. The odds of Donald Douglas discussing his personal affairs in the beauty shop were slim to none. The man wasn't that stupid.

"Okay, what about Rosetta Pierce? Has she been around lately?" A small flicker of something Jeffrey couldn't quite put his finger on flashed in her eyes for a brief second.

"No, I haven't seen or heard from Ms. Rosie," Nikki responded quickly.

She would protect the woman, Jeffrey noted. But did she really know where the woman was? Probably not, he figured. "Is Mrs. Pierce involved with Mr. Douglas?" This question had been on his mind for the past few weeks, so he was eager to finally have an answer.

Marty stood beside his partner, a little taken aback, because this wasn't in the file. They hadn't even discussed this as a possibility. He'd have to pay attention to the conversation and not the hot little number in front of him so he wouldn't miss anything important.

"Oh yeah, they're engaged. They're getting married in May," Keesha chimed in.

Nikki's angry glare toward the other girl confirmed to Jeffrey that she had been prepared to deny any knowledge of that fact.

"Really? Well, that's…interesting," Jeffrey managed. This changed things drastically.

"Is that all, officers?" Nikki folded her arms over her chest, her eyes glued on Jeffrey.

"Ah, yeah, I think that'll be all, for now." Jeffrey turned to leave.

Something in the way he'd said those last words had Nikki shivering. She wanted these men out of the shop. She didn't know what was going on, but she didn't like it. Ms. Rosie had called the other day saying that she and Donald were going on a cruise. Nikki had been taken aback because Ms. Rosie hadn't mentioned a cruise before, and something like that she definitely would have told them about ahead of time. But Nikki figured it was what engaged people did. Now all sorts of thoughts were going through her mind. She was going to call Leah as soon as these men left. Maybe she would know what was going on with Ms. Rosie and Donald, since she'd been working so closely with them on planning the wedding.

"Ah, we'll be in touch, ladies," Marty said as he turned to follow Jeffrey out of the shop.

"You know where to find us." Keesha hurried to Marty's side and walked him to the door.

"We sure do." Jeffrey turned before opening the door, his gaze locking once again with Nikki's. "We know exactly where to find you."

The words seemed to be spoken to her alone, scaring her, so that Nikki rolled her eyes and turned to walk toward her station. For a moment—a brief moment that seemed to last an eternity—Jeffrey watched the gentle movement of her bottom and the tenseness of her shoulders. Swallowing quickly, he turned and left the shop.

"Dammit! Where is she?" Nikki muttered for the millionth time today. She'd been calling Leah ever since those FBI men had left the shop. Melinda had wondered why Leah hadn't come into the office, and told Nikki she'd been calling both Leah's house and cell phone all morning as well. A call to Marsha didn't help matters, since she hadn't talked to her daughter in a couple of days.

It wasn't like Leah to just go off and not tell somebody where she was.

As soon as she was finished with her last client, Nikki was going over to Leah's apartment to see what was going on. She wished she had the phone number of Ms. Rosie's son. Maybe he knew what was going on. If he didn't, he probably should know that the FBI was asking questions about his mother.

"It's gonna take a few hours to get a search warrant for the house. But getting in there is the best chance we have of finding some clue as to where he went. Until then, we're gonna sit right here and wait." Jeffrey and Marty were parked in front of Donald's house. They'd gone there right after leaving the shop.

"So what do you think about this engagement thing?" Marty asked.

"I don't know, Marty. I just don't know." Shaking his head, Jeffrey tried to think of something besides Nicole Ayers. "I told you something was going on."

"Yeah, something's definitely going on," Marty agreed as he opened a pack of peanut M&M's.

CHAPTER TEN

"Tell me about your girlfriend," Leah said suddenly. They had been lying on the blankets trying not to think of the situation at hand. The quiet was driving her crazy. How could they not think about what was going on? They were trapped in a basement, for goodness sakes.

After their meager dinner, they'd talked about her relationship with Leon, causing her to rethink that whole situation. Why was her four-step method so baffling to him? Did he really think that dating was all about marriage? Of course he did, he'd said as much. But who cared what Terrell Pierce thought?

Reluctantly, she forced herself to admit that she did.

"I don't have a girlfriend." Quietly, he said the words that remained a sore spot in his mind.

She'd known that already, but didn't want him to know that she knew. Instead, she hoped he would confide in her the way he had about his mother. And she wanted to see if he still had feelings for the woman. "Why not?" she persisted. "I mean, you *are* looking for a wife, aren't you? According to your little theory you won't ever find that wife if you don't date and pursue a meaningful relationship."

She lay on her back with her hands tucked behind her head and with the soles of her feet planted solidly on the pad of the blankets, which elevated her knees. She'd taken off her boots earlier because they'd been wreaking havoc on her tired feet. Terrell hadn't seemed to mind; in fact, just a few minutes ago, he'd discarded his own shoes as well. They both seemed to accept the fact that they were stuck here, at least for the night.

Terrell hadn't talked about what happened between him and Tanya since telling his mother, and even then he hadn't gone into great detail. He and Leah seemed to be getting closer and he didn't want to alienate her now—not when he was feverishly thinking of a way to make her want him as much as he wanted her.

And oh, how he wanted her. The thing was, at first it had seemed to be only sexual. She'd told him he wasn't her type, and he'd been bound and determined to find out why so he could change her mind. Now, after spending time with her, after talking to her, she seemed to be everything he wanted in a woman, despite the contrasts to his little criteria list. Leah was definitely beautiful; there was no question she'd passed the cute stage in his book. And she was successful. He'd done his homework. In the four years she'd been in business she'd seen major profits and had a good reputation. She was outgoing and courageous, compared to his more introverted personality, which made them an obvious mismatch. Yet there was a connection, he could feel it.

"I had a girlfriend. Her name was Tanya," he began. After the first few words, he found it was surprisingly easy to finally get it all out. Leah listened patiently, just like his mother had when he was younger and he'd gone to her with a problem. Another plus in Leah's corner— she reminded him of Rosie.

"So she was a 'ho'?" Leah surmised after Terrell's recitation of how his relationship had gone bad.

"I wouldn't say that." He chuckled at her tone. "Well, okay, I would. But I played a significant part in the relationship's end too. I know that now, even though I couldn't see it at first."

"Okay, admit your faults so I can tell you how they don't compare to her being a 'ho'."

He wanted to laugh, but thought it wise not to; Leah wasn't smiling. In fact, she looked more than a little irritated. "I didn't pay a lot of attention to Tanya's needs. I was so focused on working and making sure she had everything she wanted I guess I never thought she might only want me."

Leah chewed on his words for a moment. "And sleeping with another man in your house, in your bed, made up for your neglect? Hmmm. I don't think so. She could have handled that differently."

Curious now, he propped himself up on an elbow and looked down at her. "Really? How would you have handled it?"

Leah mimicked his movements and they were face to face, on their sides. "I love my job and I tend to work really weird hours as well, so I probably wouldn't have much more time than you did. But when I did have time I would expect to spend it with you. Keeping in mind that you're a workaholic as well, I would make allowances for that, occasionally. But as you said earlier, I'm kind of bossy, so that means I'm used to getting my way."

Terrell smiled. "You would have demanded I spend time with you?" He could almost picture her doing just that.

"Not demanded. I would have persuasively suggested that you spend time with me. Then I would have tortured you until you did."

He raised a brow. "Tortured? In what way?"

Leah's grin was slow, seductive. "A woman's most lethal weapon."

Terrell groaned and fell back on the blankets. "Ahhhggg. I would have given you whatever you wanted."

His words left a hush in the air as Leah looked down at him. His glasses were crooked again and she lifted her hand to straighten them.

Terrell took her hand before she could finish the task, turned her palm and planted a soft kiss in the center.

She sucked in a ragged breath as his lips moved to her wrist. He pushed up her shirt sleeve and proceeded up her arm until the shirt would reveal no more skin. She was hovering over him now and, with his free hand, he removed his glasses and set them gently to the side before pulling her down.

"Terrell," she whispered just as his lips brushed across hers.

Greedily he took her mouth, pouring all the pent up desire he felt for her into that one kiss. She matched his fervor and he moaned. *My God, Leah, where have you been all my life?* Leah shifted so that she was completely straddling him now. She'd think about what she was doing later. Right now, right at this very moment, she was taking everything Terrell Pierce offered her. His hands moved to her butt, pulling her against his now rigid erection. She sucked his tongue and undulated to match his rhythm.

Having her on top of him, moving over his arousal so sinuously he could scream, just wasn't enough. Terrell's hands moved swiftly beneath the ribbing of her sweatshirt, tracing a heated path up her bare stomach until he found her heaving breasts. He cupped them both in each of his hands and she nipped his bottom lip before moaning.

"I want to see you. Now!" he growled.

Leah dragged her lips away from his long enough for him to pull her sweatshirt over her head and unclasp her bra. Her breasts tumbled free, falling heavily into his hands. Moving to a sitting position, keeping her comfortably on his lap, Terrell looked from her face down to her bare breasts. "You are a beautiful woman, Leah."

Leah's heart beat frantically as she tried to digest what he'd just said. "Nobody's ever called me beautiful before."

Cupping her face, he dropped feather light kisses on her nose, her cheeks, and her lips again. "Then I'll have to make up for all the stupid people who've obviously overlooked you."

His kisses trailed down her neck and Leah arched her back to accommodate him. When he closed his mouth over one puckered nipple, she almost screamed. Nothing, absolutely nothing, had ever felt as good as his mouth on her. Kneading one breast in his hand, Terrell sucked the other one until Leah's legs began to shake with intensity.

Stopping suddenly, Terrell lifted her off him. "Not yet, baby. I don't want to bring you to release just yet."

Leah was too dazed to ask any questions. All she knew was that she felt awfully incomplete and, if Terrell didn't do something about that soon, she might have to resort to drastic measures. "Terrell," she said in a ragged voice.

"Shhhh, sweetie. Trust me." He unbuckled her jeans, slid them down the length of those legs he'd known would be long and enticing, and over her feet. From her ankle to her inner thigh, he placed hot, titillating kisses.

"Mmmmm, Terrell. I never knew," she moaned, her head thrashing from side to side.

The mere sound of her voice pushed him on, and he hooked his fingers into the rim of her panties, pulling them down and off as well. When she lay splendidly naked, waiting for him, he thought about what he was about to do and what it would mean to their future. He wanted this. He wanted this woman more than anything he'd ever set his sights on in his life. And at this moment she wanted him too. But he needed more than that. He needed her to trust him, to feel completely safe with him. And he knew just how to achieve that goal.

"Are you ready, baby?" he asked as his hands moved to her knees, lifting her legs into the air.

"Terrell, hurry," Leah panted.

With her consent he lowered his head, stroked his tongue from the tip of her honey glazed core to the center and back again.

Leah sucked in a breath, filled with intense pleasure.

Gently he slid his tongue over her puckered nub, back and forth, up and down, repeatedly, until her hips were lifting from the floor. He inserted two fingers into her center and had to use his other hand to hold her still. "It's alright, baby." He spoke softly as his fingers loved her earnestly. "You can let go. Trust me, I'll take good care of you."

She looked at him for one dazed moment. Then her eyes closed as his mouth returned to stroke her so efficiently. Between his fingers and his tongue Leah wasn't sure where the most pleasure began. And didn't really care. All she knew was that her previous sexual encounters had never reached this point, had never made her reach this point. That scared her momentarily. Then he was stroking her slowly, talking her into release. She cleared her mind, let his words and his ministrations guide her, strengthen her as she felt herself rising, floating, soaring into oblivion. "Terrell." His name was a jagged cry from her lips before the final descent into ecstasy.

Terrell lay beside her, cradling her in his arms. "But I didn't give you anything," she murmured.

"Sweetie, you gave me more than you know," he told her before pulling the blankets up and settling them in for the night.

Though Leah fell asleep quickly, Terrell lay wide awake, thinking. There was no turning back now. What they'd just done sealed it for him. Leah was the woman he wanted, the woman he was determined to have. But when she awoke, when a new day dawned, how would she feel about him? He didn't know, and tried not to think about it.

Easing away so that she wouldn't wake, he moved around the basement, resuming his search for an escape. She was important to him, her life was important to him, now more than ever. He had to make sure she was safe. He'd deal with his mother and he'd deal with Donald Douglas, but for now, the first thing on his mind was getting Leah out of here.

He returned to corners they'd searched previously, moving things lightly and with the least amount of noise as possible. Both repetition and frustration threatened to overtake him but persistence eventually prevailed. There was a box of tools behind the bathroom door, a place he was sure he hadn't personally searched earlier. And in that box was a crowbar.

With quick steps he took the stairs two at a time. He positioned the crowbar near the door latch and began working it loose, all the while being as quiet as he could. He didn't want to wake Leah until they were home free.

Terrell gave an audible sigh at the sound of cracking wood and with a deft shove watched as the basement door opened before him. Dropping the crowbar, he ran down the steps to wake Leah. She was still asleep, cuddled into a ball. Her arms cradled her peaceful looking face.

He stopped, bent down and ran his fingers lightly over her cheek. He'd told her she was beautiful, yet that one word didn't seem enough to describe her. She stirred. "Baby?" he whispered.

Shaking her shoulders gently, he dropped kisses along the line of her jaw until she moaned.

"Terrell?" she asked groggily.

"I'd better be the only one kissing you awake," he replied lightly.

Leah opened both eyes, focused on the man who had brought her such pleasure. "Hi." She smiled up at him.

"Hi, yourself. Come on, get up and get dressed." He pulled the blankets down, purposely averting his eyes. They didn't have time for another round, no matter how much he wanted her. He'd vowed last night that the next time he lay with her naked would be in a bed, with enough protection to keep them there for a good long while.

"Where are we going?" They were still in that damned basement and, as far as she knew, they didn't have a way out, but she was rapidly pulling on her clothes.

"We're going home. " Grabbing her boots, he slipped them on her feet.

"But how?" She stood still, staring at him in obvious disbelief.

He swelled with pride as she looked to him for the answers. He wanted to kiss her pouty lips, but knew that would only delay their departure. "I got the door open." He tweaked her nose instead.

A broad smile spread across her lips, and those sexy eyes lit up with pleasure. "You did? When?"

He almost ran to the steps but stopped short at the sight of two men, guns in hand, coming down the stairs. Leah bumped into his back and gasped when she saw them.

"It's okay, baby. Just stay behind me," Terrell instructed her.

"Hold it! FBI!" the first man to stop at the bottom of the stairs yelled.

"FBI!" the man immediately behind him echoed.

Terrell stood perfectly still, not sure if these guys really were FBI or some of Donald's men.

"Who the hell are you?" Jeffery roared at the man standing across the room. "How did you get in here?"

"I…I'm Terrell Pierce and this is Leah Graham." He kept Leah shielded by his own body, but knew they had seen her because he'd felt her head peeping around him. "We were abducted and locked down here yesterday."

"Abducted?" Marty moved closer to Terrell. "Put your hands up, both of you," he ordered.

Terrell and Leah put their hands up in the air.

"I'm going to ask you again, how did you get here?" Jeffery still had his gun aimed directly at them. The name Pierce hadn't been lost on him, and he wondered about the man's true involvement in this case.

Leah rolled her eyes and Terrell spoke.

"Just like I said before, we were abducted by Donald Douglas and his big goon friend. They drugged us and left us here early yesterday morning."

"Why would they do that?" Jeffery eyed them suspiciously. Gaining access to Donald's house had led him to the two people who'd most likely been the last to see him. There was definitely something above and beyond their operation going on here, and these two were going to help him figure out what.

CHAPTER ELEVEN

"So let me get this straight." Jeffery sat on the edge of the couch in Donald's living room. "You and Ms. Graham, who's the wedding planner for Donald Douglas and Rosetta Pierce's wedding, were tailing Donald. You saw him and another man go into a strip club, then come out and go into an alley with five other men. You followed them into the alley, where you heard several gunshots before running back to your car.

"When you got back to your car and would have pulled off to return home, Donald and his friend almost crashed into your vehicle, at which time he spotted you and pulled you and Ms. Graham out of the car. Then they took you both to Leakin Park, where they drugged you and brought you here to lock you in his basement."

Terrell nodded. "That's correct." The detective's recitation of the events sounded so unreal he wouldn't have believed it had it not happened to him.

"So why didn't they kill you too?" Marty asked.

"I suspect because Donald's about to marry my mother." Terrell glared at the shorter detective, the obviously less experienced one, he surmised. "That would put a major glitch in the wedding plans, don't you think? 'Ah, I'm sorry, honey, but I had to kill your son.'"

Holding up his hand, Jeffery stifled Marty's next comment. He was in no mood to watch two grown men bicker. "Mr. Pierce, please, we're trying to conduct an investigation here. Okay, so you woke up here. Do you know where Donald is now?"

"I heard them say something about a boat leaving from the Inner Harbor," Terrell said. Leah sat on the chair beside him, her hand firmly held in his. She hadn't spoken much since they'd been rescued from the basement. He planned to talk to her as soon as they were alone. Things had changed between them, and he wanted to make sure they both had a good understanding of just how much.

Leah listened to the men talking around her. She'd heard enough to know that the FBI was looking for Donald and had obtained a search warrant to get into his house. That wasn't good. She wondered how she had gotten involved in this whole mess. How could planning a wedding lead to witnessing a murder and being abducted?

Still, none of that rivaled the embarrassment she now harbored. Memories of what she'd allowed Terrell to do to her last night were still vividly fresh in her mind. So much so that she was having a hard time focusing on the two agents who were talking to them. Terrell held her hand firmly in his, a gesture of comfort, no doubt. But what must he think of her now? *How could I have let him go that far?* She took a deep breath. *Oh, please, like I really could have stopped him once he got started.*

Terrell probably thought that the FBI and the millions of questions made her nervous, which in a way they did. She'd never had any run-ins with the authorities. That was totally her brothers' territory. So sitting here—in Donald Douglas' living room of all places—being interrogated, was a bit disconcerting. Terrell was his usual calm self, answering their questions and even giving one of the agents attitude. She wasn't sure what that was about, but at this point didn't really care. What she wanted more than anything else at this moment was to be allowed to go home, take a long bath, climb into bed, pull the covers over her head and hide for a while. That's what one did when they'd thoroughly embarrassed themselves in front of a man.

"Okay, we're going to take you two home to get some rest. But I'll have to advise you not to leave town or anything like that. I want to meet with you again tomorrow to go over some of your story one more time." Jeffery stood, tucking his notepad into his jacket pocket.

"That's fine. Whatever you need, I'll be glad to help," Terrell was saying. "I'll be staying with my mother." He had to talk to Rosie, so he planned to make her house his first stop once he made sure Leah was settled into her place. "If you're investigating Donald, that means he's dangerous and I don't want her left alone until he's caught."

Terrell stood to shake Jeffery's outstretched hand. Leah seized the opportunity to move away from him. Distance was better, she told herself.

"Your mother is Rosetta Pierce, right?" Marty asked Terrell.

"Yeah, I told you that already." Terrell really didn't like Marty. He wasn't sure why—hell, he was sure. The guy had been looking at Leah like she was a five star dessert since the moment he'd entered the basement, and he didn't like it one bit.

"Your mother hasn't been seen at the shop, so she may be with Mr. Douglas." Marty seemed to take pleasure in giving Terrell that bit of information.

"What?" Terrell began to pace the floor, cursing fluently.

At Marty's words, Leah immediately returned to Terrell's side, grabbing his arm to still him. She turned to the agent. "Are you saying that Donald has taken Ms. Rosie with him?" she asked.

"We can't really say she was taken. We don't have any proof of that. And if they're engaged, it's safe to assume she consented to the trip."

Terrell pushed his glasses up further on his nose. "My mother would have told me if she was going away. She wouldn't leave without telling someone," he said more to Leah than to the agents.

Leah rubbed a hand up and down his arm. "It might have been a last minute thing. Don't think the worst. If Donald didn't hurt us, he won't hurt Ms. Rosie." She kept her eyes on his, wanting so badly to take away the pain she clearly saw etched in them.

When he didn't respond, she extended her arms, waited for him to react and when he did, she simply held him. A moment ago she'd concluded that distance was best for the moment, until she'd had time to figure out last night. But in an instant none of that seemed to matter. All that mattered now was the man in her arms. His mother was in danger, of that they were certain. He needed someone to help him get through this.

He needed her.

"He loves her, Terrell. No matter his other faults, I'm sure of that. He won't hurt her. Trust me," she whispered as her hands rubbed his back. Leah was startled to find that she believed her own words. She'd seen Donald and Rosie together. He clearly adored the woman. No, she didn't think Ms. Rosie was in any danger.

Terrell couldn't speak. He'd needed somebody, he'd needed her, and she was right there. Last night he'd asked her to trust him and she had. Now she was asking him to do the same thing. He didn't like the idea that his mother was possibly with Donald, but he'd put enough drama into Leah's life and he wouldn't add anymore. "You're probably right," he whispered, then pulled slightly back from her. "Again." He gave her a wry grin.

Inside, he knew he had to find them. He had to make sure for himself his mother was safe, and then he had to warn her about Donald.

Donald's excuses about what had happened to him last night on the cruise were insufficient, but after two hours of arguing, Rosie decided to give it up. He wasn't going to tell her anything more than he already had, so she'd have to keep her suspicions to herself. If something wrong were really going on, she'd find out soon enough. Besides, what else could she do? She was in a foreign place with no one to turn to but Donald. No, she'd keep her mouth shut for the time being—and her eyes open.

Her decision, however, was short-lived. As soon as they docked, the man Donald had been with on the stairwell appeared. Cable was his name, she remembered. He was tall and broad and dark. He looked damn near evil, she thought. He and Donald conversed in private for a few moments before Donald came back to inform her that Cable would be traveling with them because his parents had a house in Negril. Rosie could care less where the man was going, or where his parents had a home, but she bit her tongue and rode in silence to the airport.

Once there, Donald discovered that there was no small plane available to charter and announced he'd now have to rent a car. Rosie was furious at the thought of now sharing a two hour drive with the strange man.

"If you wanted a threesome, you should have found yourself another woman," she told Donald before Cable got in the car.

"We're just giving the man a ride, Rosie. That's all, calm down." He spoke to her in that slow, placating voice he'd used last night, and Rosie suppressed the urge to scream.

Negril was beautiful. Its white sand and sapphire blue water beckoned to her, and her heart leapt with joy as childhood memories burst into her mind. When she was young, her grandfather had taken her to the beach a couple of times, and she'd loved it. Now she lived in the city, so it was public pools for her each and every summer. She wondered absently what it would be like to live on a beach, on this beach, with her husband.

The sky was filled with big, puffy white clouds streaked with golden rays from the sun. There was a light breeze moving throughout the palm trees, rippling the water. Inhaling deeply, she sucked in the tropical air, letting it course through her very soul.

"Do you like it?"

"It's pretty," she said simply, but couldn't keep from staring.

Donald chuckled at her attempt at boredom. He knew she liked it, he could see the lights dancing in her eyes. She was excited. This was good. Maybe she'd be excited enough to want to stay here forever.

Using his key, Terrell let himself into Rosie's house. As he stepped into the foyer he inhaled the undeniable smell of Rosie, of home, of stability. Closing the door behind him, he fought the urge to plow his fist into a wall. Was she safe? Had Donald taken her against her will? These questions had plagued him from the moment Agent Blum told him his mother was most likely with Donald.

Leah had said that Donald wouldn't hurt her, and Agent Tobias was pretty sure of that fact as well. At this moment Terrell didn't care what either one of them said. He wanted his mother home, safe and sound, with him. And as far away from Donald Douglas as he could get her.

He'd already called Seth, his investigator friend, and had him researching the ships leaving the Inner Harbor in the last two days. Seth could get a complete guest list and let Terrell know exactly where Donald had taken his mother.

Taking the stairs two at a time, Terrell headed first to the shower. After all that had transpired in the last two days, he needed to shower, needed to refresh his mind so he'd think clearly enough to save his mother. But once he stepped under the spray of hot water his entire body came alive with thoughts of Leah and the previous night.

Her body was as gorgeous as he'd pictured it to be. Even in the dim light of that basement he'd seen her clearly. And she'd given herself to him willingly—she'd trusted him just as he'd asked her to. Closing his eyes, he dipped his head under the nozzle and let the water pour over him. He could still smell her intoxicating scent, could taste the sweet nectar that he'd feasted on. He hardened painfully. Last night he hadn't been prepared to properly love her, but that would come in time. He had big plans for Ms. Graham, plans that they were both going to enjoy.

Grabbing the soap, he quickly scrubbed his body. After getting out of the shower, he brushed his teeth, almost choking on that awful toothpaste. After all these years he was shocked to learn that Rosie still used Aqua Fresh. He grimaced at the memory it brought back of medicine mixed with mint taste.

Grabbing his duffle bag, which he'd retrieved on his way to Rosie's, he pulled out his laptop and plugged it into the wall. While it booted up, he slipped into clean boxers and donned jeans and a clean t-shirt. Moving over to his mother's dresser, he searched for some lotion that wasn't too girly. Just like the toothpaste, Rosie hadn't changed her brand. Terrell poured the creamy lotion into the palm of his hand and began smoothing it up and down his arms and over his face, the smell of cocoa butter wafting through the room.

His laptop beeped, signaling that it was ready for his password. Punching the keys quickly, he waited for the appropriate program to boot up. He had limited information but was sure this database would come up with something. He keyed Leah's name, the city and the state and waited for a response. In seconds an address appeared on the screen.

Finding a pen on his mother's bedside stand, he jotted the information down and stuffed it into his pocket, determined to let Leah Graham know exactly how he felt about her.

Leah walked into her apartment, thoroughly relieved to be back in her own familiar place and out of danger. She switched the lights on and threw her coat on the sofa. As she turned to go into her bedroom she was startled to see an African fertility statue sitting on top of her television. Tilting her head to the side she wondered why it was in that particular place. Because it was tall and a bit bulky, she distinctly remembered putting it on the bookshelf.

Shaking her head, she lifted the heavy piece from the television and put it back on the bookshelf. *Maybe I moved it, who knows?* All she could think about right now was a nice hot bath. Then she'd be ready to deal with the world and all the things that had changed in it.

She passed the answering machine on her way to the back room of her apartment and decided to at least listen to the messages, even though she wasn't planning on returning any calls until after her bath. Most were from Nikki, a few from Melinda, some from her mother, who was clearly agitated that she hadn't been there when she needed her, and two from Leon.

Definitely deciding she'd deal with the messages later, she went to the bathroom, turned on the water and poured in her favorite vanilla-scented bubble bath until the bottle was empty. Closing her eyes, she let the soothing aroma tickle her senses as she tried to relax while the tub filled.

So much had happened in the last forty-eight hours her mind didn't even know where to begin. The best starting point was probably that first kiss, the day Terrell had come into her office looking serious yet debonair. He'd thrown his jacket on the chair as if it belonged there while he'd watched her with those smoldering eyes of his. Even shielded by glasses she'd still felt their intensity as they followed her around the room. Before meeting him, she'd taken one look at the picture at Ms. Rosie's station and assumed he was your classic nerd. Then she'd met him at the party and realized that nerds were coming in better looking packages these days. His quiet strength had called to her, pulling her closer and closer...

A ringing phone interrupted her thoughts. Taking a deep breath she tried to push thoughts of Terrell out of her mind as she moved to the other room to answer the phone. "Hello?"

"It's about damn time! Where have you been? I've been looking all over the city for you! Girl, I got some news for you. You are not going to believe what's going on!" Nikki's voice rattled on the other end.

"Let me guess, the FBI's looking for Donald, who is off somewhere on a cruise with Ms. Rosie. Two agents came to the shop yesterday morning and questioned you and Keesha, and you're calling me to find out what I know." Rolling her eyes toward the ceiling, Leah listened to her friend's silence. "Is that about right?"

"How did you know? What's going on, Leah? You're not telling me something."

"I know, there's a lot I'm not telling you, but right now I desperately need a bath. Can I call you back later?"

"Hell no! Not after I've been searching high and low for you. Uh-un, I'm comin' over right now. You go on and get in the tub but leave the door unlocked so I can get in. I want to hear everything, and I want to hear it now."

Before Leah could respond Nikki disconnected. Slamming the phone down, Leah walked over to the door and disengaged the lock, then hesitated for a moment. Was it wise to leave her door unlocked with all the mess that had gone on around her in the past two days? But this time of morning traffic wouldn't be too bad on the highway, and Nikki would be here in a few minutes. Besides, if Donald was on a cruise somewhere he couldn't hurt her. Shrugging, she went into the bathroom and began to undress.

Five minutes later she was in a tub full of hot water with steam rising to cloud the bathroom mirror. Lying with her back against the porcelain, Leah closed her eyes and tried to block out the events of the past two days.

Terrell knocked several times without getting an answer. He was sure this was the right apartment because he'd read her name on the mailbox. Fear simmered below the surface as he thought of some of Donald's henchmen finding her. Desperately, he tried the doorknob. It was unlocked, further panicking him. Stepping into the apartment, he glanced around the room quickly. It was empty.

Walking into the kitchen, he surmised that she wasn't in there either. Without hesitation he started in the opposite direction. The bathroom door was ajar but he didn't hear anything. When he cautiously poked his head in the doorway, his heart stopped, his tongue swelled in his mouth and his manhood throbbed painfully as he watched Leah pick up her loofa sponge, fill it with water, hold it aloft and dribble water over her breasts. Repeating the motion, she drenched her back and neck. Eyes closed in apparent deep relaxation, she reached along the wall until her hand found the soap and lathered the sponge. In long, languid movements she washed her arms, lifting them above her head, one at a time.

Terrell swallowed as her breasts rose and fell with each movement.

Dragging the sponge over her neck, she applied a soapy film to her skin. As she lifted one breast at a time, the sponge left a bubbly trail around and between the twin mounds.

Terrell licked his lips.

Lifting one long leg she covered it with soap. Then she lathered between her thighs.

Terrell's heart stopped as the ache in his groin grew too much for him to bear. He had been holding his keys and his fingers—curse their clumsiness—chose that precise moment to drop them.

The crowded key ring fell to the floor with a loud clinking.

Leah's eyes shot open.

Terrell's closed with embarrassment.

In the bathroom, alone, Leah rinsed the soap off her body. As the water rolled in heavy rivulets over her smooth skin she tingled all over at the memory of Terrell standing in the doorway. His desire had been undeniable, giving her ego an overwhelming boost.

She knew she should be upset, outraged at the nerve of him walking into her house and watching her while she bathed. But all she felt now was desire that was stuck in her throat like an unmovable lump. Quickly she finished in the tub and got out, pulled the heavy terrycloth robe over her shoulders, and knotted the belt around her waist.

When she entered the room, Terrell braced himself for the attack he undeniably deserved. He couldn't believe what had just happened. He'd only been concerned for her safety. He hadn't meant to spy on her. But when he'd seen her in that tub, gloriously naked, only an act of God could have taken his eyes off her. His feet had been glued to that spot as he watched her lather her gorgeous body.

"Well, hello." Standing behind the sofa, she looked at him calmly.

"Hello. Ah…Leah, I'm sorry. I didn't mean to—" Stuffing his hands in his pockets, he stammered over the words.

"What? You didn't mean to be a Peeping Tom?" She chuckled to cover the anxious feelings bubbling inside her, threatening to come rushing to the surface.

"Yeah, I guess that's what I was doing. But really, I didn't mean to. I knocked and knocked and didn't get an answer. Then I found the door was unlocked and I got worried."

He was worried about her. It was a good thing she had already decided she wasn't angry with him, because the look he was giving her now, combined with his admission of concern, would have diffused any anger.

"So what are you doing here? I thought you would be heading back to Agent Tobias' office." Moving quickly before her knees gave out, she sat on the far end of the couch and motioned for him to take a seat.

"Thanks," he muttered before sitting at the opposite end. "I am going to see him, but I needed to see you first."

"See me? What for?" He'd showered and shaved. She could smell the soap still fresh on his skin. She knew it wasn't her because it was a fresh deodorant smell and she used a beauty bar that smelled more feminine. He wore jeans and a neatly tucked-in button down plaid shirt. The rim of his crisp white t-shirt showed at the base of his neck, where he'd left the first few buttons of the plaid shirt undone. Briefly she let herself imagine what he hid under all those clothes. His goatee had been trimmed, and the stubble that she'd felt against her face a few hours before was long gone.

He was nervous and his clouded eyes danced as he watched her. But that was the only giveaway.

"I know where my mother and Donald went," he began.

"Really? Where?" A bolt of disappointment moved through her—he wasn't here to talk about them at all. It was about his unwavering concern for his mother's safety.

"I know a PI who owes me a lot of favors." He took a deep breath. "They boarded one of those fancy cruise ships heading for Montego Bay, Jamaica, on Wednesday afternoon. I've booked a flight out tonight." His legs were spread slightly, his elbows resting casually on his knees. He folded his hands beneath his chin and looked at her.

LOVE ME CAREFULLY

"Oh." He was going to Jamaica to get his mother and confront Donald, no doubt. A feeling she'd gotten too used to surfaced, and she struggled to keep it at bay.

"I wanted to see you before I left." He looked at her seriously. "There's something I need to say before I go."

"Terrell," she began. She stopped because she wasn't sure what to say. She was certain he was going to say something about what had happened between them. An hour ago she'd known exactly how she was going to deal with this moment. But right now, sitting mere inches away from him, she wasn't sure.

His two fingers to her lips silenced her. "I heard everything you said about your relationships, and while I don't understand your reasoning, I can clearly see what prompted you to think the way you do. But you're wrong, Leah. Relationships can work, marriages can last. I believe that, and I want to prove it to you."

She started to speak, raised a brow at him, then moved his fingers from her lips, giving him a leery gaze while she did.

Terrell shrugged, gave her a crooked grin.

"I've been thinking over my little four-step method and realize that it may have been a little rigid."

"A little?" Terrell sighed. "Falling in love is as natural as breathing, Leah." He turned to her, his hand cupping her cheek. "And ever since that night I bumped into you I've been having problems taking a deep breath whenever you're not around. You are like air to me, sweetie. Do you understand?"

His brown eyes were intense as they bore into her. She understood alright—she understood that she was about to suffer a breathing deficiency of her own. He was so close, his words so surreal, she wondered if she could possibly be dreaming. All her life she'd secretly wondered what it would feel like to be loved—and even though he hadn't said the words, the look on his face, the gentleness of his touch, gave her hope. She tried furiously to blink away the tears forming in her eyes. "I understand that, since meeting you, something in my life has changed. You've changed me, and I'd be lying if I said that didn't scare the hell out of me." She chuckled even as one fat tear rolled down her face.

Terrell's heart swelled with emotion as he watched her struggle with new feelings. It couldn't be easy for her after believing for so long that she'd never be in a meaningful relationship. But that was where he came in. He'd show her what it felt like to be loved, to be cherished. He'd put all her doubts to rest, that was a promise. "It's okay to be afraid, baby. But I'm right here to chase all those fears away. I'll take care of you." He pulled her close enough so his lips could lightly brush hers.

Leah allowed the contact, reveled in the sensations swirling through her and sighed. "If we do this, it's all or nothing, Terrell."

He pulled back slightly, his fingers moving to massage her scalp, the nape of her neck. "I'm willing to give you everything I have, Leah. That's how serious I am about us."

Leah shook her head. "I don't want all your material possessions, I have my own," she said, thinking of the end of his previous relationship. "I want you, all of you."

Terrell heard her words, knew exactly what she was saying. Now he was the one overwhelmed with emotion. "Tanya was a stepping stone in my plan for my life, Leah. I know now that was all she ever was. But you, you *are* my life. I don't want a future if it's not with you."

With an unsteady finger she pushed his glasses up on his nose and smiled. "I'm going to hold you to that, Mr. Pierce."

He smiled. That smile effectively melted every bone in her body, and she knew that she was doing the right thing. No four-steps could have ever led her to this moment. She hadn't dated Terrell, not one time, not six or seven times. He'd simply waltzed into her life and shaken her to the core, reducing that plan of hers to gibberish.

"I just want to hold you, Ms. Graham." And with that he pulled her into his arms, placing light kisses on her neck as she embraced him.

She was locked in his arms when the sudden potential for danger hit her and she felt panic creep slowly up her spine. "You're going to Jamaica to confront Donald, aren't you?"

Terrell heard the panic in her voice. "I have to make sure my mother is safe."

"But Donald is involved in things that are way over your head, Terrell. You can't save her all by yourself. You have to think logically for a minute." He had to think of how she'd feel if something happened to him. "Your mother would much rather you be safe and cautious than for you to do something irrational. It would kill her if something happened to you. Why don't you just let the FBI handle it?"

"I can't." Pain and turmoil were clear in his voice. "I owe her everything. Don't you understand?" His eyes softened as fear and concern for one woman mixed with desire and longing for another.

His words gripped her heart, squeezing desperately. He would go to Jamaica, she knew it positively, regardless of what she said or did. He had to save his mother. She'd think less of him as a man if he didn't at least try. She realized then that he was so much more than just a good man—he was *her* man.

"I do understand, baby. I do." She caressed his freshly shaven jaw, biting her lip to keep from crying and begging him to stay.

"When I get back—" he began.

This time it was her lone finger on his lips asking for silence. "When you get back I'm going to make you never want to leave again," she whispered.

Oh God, I don't want to leave you now. He kissed her finger, then the next one, until he'd loved each one and moved to her lips.

Opening his mouth, he deepened the kiss, drowning in her sweetness. On a soft moan Leah granted him access. Tongues dancing, mating, joining them in a way words could not. They clung to one another with hopeless longing.

Nikki walked in to find her best friend in a heavy lip lock with Ms. Rosie's son, of all people. Yeah, Nikki thought, Leah had a lot of explaining to do.

Clearing her throat loudly she said, "Hello?"

Cold water could not have been more effective than the shocked sound of Nikki's voice. Leah backed away from Terrell who, for a brief second, stared irritably at the woman who'd entered the room.

"Hey Nik." Leah pulled her robe closer and faced her friend. "Um, you know Ms. Rosie's son, Terrell," Leah said, chancing a quick look at him.

Terrell pushed his glasses up on his nose and closed the space between him and Nikki. With an outstretched hand he spoke. "Hi, Nikki. Nice to see you again." He remembered her from the times he'd gone to pick his mother up at the shop.

Nikki shook his hand with a barely suppressed smile. They both looked like two teenagers that had been caught necking by their parents. "Even though I've never seen you like this, I suppose it's nice to see you again, Terrell."

"Ah, look, I have to go." He turned then to Leah. "I'm gonna go and see Agent Tobias, and then I need to go back to my apartment to pack some things. I'll call you when I get back."

"Terrell." Her voice cracked. She was moving toward him now, wanting to hold him one more time.

He held his hands up to stop her progress. If she touched him again he'd never make it out that door. Nikki's interruption was a good thing, because he'd been headed straight to the bedroom with that kiss. Once he secured his mother's safety, he and Leah would have the rest of their lives together. Of course he planned to start in the bedroom, but they'd have sufficient time after that. "When I get back, Leah. I'll talk to you soon." He turned and left the room before she could say another word.

The clicking of the door closing was like a knife through Leah's heart, and she plopped down onto the couch, her arms folded, her lips pouting like a child's.

"Well, well, well, we certainly have a lot to talk about." Nikki dropped down beside her. "Shall I order lunch?"

CHAPTER TWELVE

"I know we've already talked to the authorities in Kingston. This guy here," Agent Tobias pointed to a picture on the bulletin board in his office, "he's the head man, Rohan Bernal. He's been controlling the shipment and sale of massive amounts of marijuana between the U.S. and Jamaica for about ten years now."

"You've known this for ten years and you haven't caught him yet?" Terrell asked incredulously. He stood in front of the bulletin board and looked at the pyramid of pictures the FBI had assembled. He didn't see Donald's picture anywhere.

"It's taken ten years to build up enough information to finally arrest him, Mr. Pierce," Agent Tobias said with a grim look.

"You can call me Terrell, since we'll be working together." Terrell turned to face the agent and waited for his argument. He'd been in his office for about an hour now, going back and forth about the pros and cons of him going to Jamaica to get his mother.

"Terrell, you have to understand that this is a very delicate situation. I can't just let a civilian walk into a carefully planned operation and start shaking things up." Moving to his desk, Agent Tobias sat down. More importantly, he didn't want this civilian messing up the case he'd spent years building.

"My mother is also a civilian. I just want her safe. I won't bother Donald or whatever investigation you have going on. I just want to bring my mother home."

"I understand," Agent Tobias began. And he did, even though he doubted Terrell would agree. For a brief second he entertained the thought of telling Terrell everything. Maybe then the man would relax and let him do his job. But he couldn't risk it. He couldn't risk anything more going wrong at this point. It was bad enough Donald had disappeared on him.

Any more shake-ups and his case would quickly go down the tubes. That he couldn't have.

"Do you? Do you really understand?" Slamming his fist down onto the agent's desk, Terrell leaned over so he was closer to Tobias' face. "This is my mother we're talking about here! What would you do if it were your mother, or your wife, or someone you loved? Would you sit on your hands and hope that everything turned out right or would you go and make things right yourself?"

Agent Tobias stared at the man for a moment. His eyes were wild, and the veins in his hands pumped with the anger and outrage soaring through his body. He knew the feeling, knew it all too well. Just as he knew that he couldn't stop Terrell Pierce. Unless he handcuffed him to a chair and locked him in a closet, Terrell would be on the next thing smoking to Jamaica. The only thing he could do was stall him.

"Alright, look, if you're gonna go down there we need to put some sort of game plan in place. You can't just go waltzing around on foreign soil playing rent-a-cop. The native criminals will sense you without a doubt. I'm coming with you. And we'll go by boat."

"But flying's faster. I don't want my mother alone with him any longer than need be," Terrell argued.

"As I explained to you before, Mr. Pierce, I really don't think she's under any duress. Despite what you think you know, we don't have any evidence that Donald Douglas is a violent man."

"But the people he has dealings with, can you say the same about them?"

Jeffrey shook his head, truthfully. "No, I can't."

"Exactly," Terrell said grimly.

"That's why we're going to follow their same route to Jamaica. We'll take the same cruise, and investigate each stop that boat makes. For all we know, they could have gotten off at one of the other ports and not be in the Montego Bay area at all." Despite his words, Agent Tobias had already checked this out and now knew Donald's precise location. A few of his top men were already on their way there. He'd originally planned to stay put a day or two longer, but, staring at Terrell now, he figured things were likely to get worse if he waited.

Terrell looked at the man, who appeared to be his age or maybe a few years older. His jaw was strong, his eyes determined. "Thank you, Agent Tobias." Terrell held out his hand in gratitude.

"Don't thank me yet. Things could get pretty hairy once we get down there. And call me Jeff. We'll be spending a lot of time together in the next week or so." Gripping the man's outstretched hand, Jeffrey Tobias prayed he wouldn't regret this decision.

"Girl you've gotten yourself in the middle of one crazy love triangle." Nikki sat on the couch rolling her eyes after hearing all about Leah's night in the basement with Terrell.

"Tell me about it." Leah folded her legs beneath her at the other end of the couch.

"So where does Leon fit in all this?"

Dropping her head on the back of the sofa, Leah sighed, letting out a whoosh of breath. "He doesn't. I tried to tell him that the last time I saw him. I don't know why he's calling me now."

"You said he told you he'd wait. And you didn't exactly tell him not to."

"Nik, you're not helping," Leah whined.

"Sure I am. An hour ago you were about to carry little Terrell right off into your bedroom and I stopped you." Nikki sat up on the sofa, pushing the half-eaten carton of pizza out of her way. "Wait a minute. You're not stressing over Leon at all. You're sitting here all uptight because of what happened between you and Terrell."

Leah groaned. "I just told you something happened—actually I told you exactly what happened. Weren't you listening?"

"Oh, I was listening, all right. You got your thing off in the basement of Donald's house. So what? Only it's not 'so what' to you, is it? That wasn't a 'farewell, it's been nice, catch you later' kiss I walked in on, was it?"

"I've always been afraid of the unexpected, Nik. I like things planned and organized, you know that. But Terrell is…I mean, he was…totally unexpected. I wasn't looking for these feelings and I damn sure wasn't looking in his direction for them. Yet somehow he found me." She could still feel his hands on her, could still see his face as he promised her everything. And she'd let him walk right out that door, not knowing if she'd ever see him again.

"Oh my God. I never would have guessed. None of us ever would have guessed that the person so against marriage and relationships would be swept away. But it seems Ms. Rosie's son has done just that." Nikki shook her head. "So what are you going to do now?"

Leah smoothed her hair back, squelched any lingering doubts, and looked Nikki right in the eye. "I'm going with him."

"Going with who? Terrell? To Jamaica?" Nikki gave Leah a frazzled look. Her girlfriend had completely fallen off her rocker.

"That's right." Leah's voice was soft. "I won't let him do this alone."

"You can't be serious!" Nikki yelled. "What about work? You're right around the corner from the wedding season!"

"I know, I know. But my next one isn't for another three weeks. I'll call Melinda and go over the checklist with her. She's competent; she can handle things until I get back. I don't see that we'll be gone for long." Sighing, she grabbed one of the pillows from the sofa, crumpling it beneath her arms. " 'I have to do this.' That's what he said to me. You don't know him, Nik. He's hell-bent on saving his mother. He might do something irrational, something dangerous, something…" She couldn't bring herself to say it.

Nikki covered Leah's hand. "Alright, I get the picture. Calm down. I'll help you. Call your office. I'll use my cell to book you a flight."

Leah sighed, giving her friend a hug. "Thanks, Nikki."

"If you really want to thank me, give me Leon's phone number."

Leah frowned. "Uh-uh, don't even go there."

Laughter erupted between them.

Rosie was amazed by the view from the balcony of their suite at the Samsara Resort. The Caribbean Sea spread out around them like a giant blue carpet, its rock formations a drastic but stunning contrast to the soothing backdrop.

A light breeze moved through the tropical trees, gently lifting Rosie's hair from her neck. Leaning over the balcony, she took in the beauty of her surroundings and wondered again what it would be like to wake up to this each and every morning. Her heart fluttered momentarily, the thought so exciting she almost screamed with joy.

Then, like a weight on her heart, Terrell's face crossed her mind. How could she leave her boy, her only child, the one steady person in her life for the last thirty years? She'd be so far away if he ever needed her—which he hadn't, since he left for college.

Terrell had his own life, his own goals; he was a grown man and he could certainly make it on his own. Still, she struggled with the sense of abandoning him as he'd felt his father had done.

"Hey, beautiful." Donald came up behind her, wrapping his arms around her waist.

"Good morning," she said, allowing herself to lean back into his steady hold. She felt comforted, loved, emotions she hadn't felt in a long time. Was she ready to give that up? No, she didn't want to give that up. But she didn't want to live her life wondering either.

"What are you thinking so hard about?" He'd seen her out here and wondered what was going through her mind. In their short time on the island he'd felt something different from her. She'd questioned him that night on the boat and he'd lied to her, one of the hardest things he'd ever had to do in his life.

He loved Rosie with all his being. Everything he'd done for the past few months was because of her—for her. He thought then of Terrell. He'd never had a son of his own, but figured if he had he would have wanted him to be as strong and persistent as Rosie's son, the son he'd left locked in the basement back in Baltimore.

By now the young man and his wedding planner friend would be free. He was sure Terrell's persistence would have seen to that.

"Just that it's beautiful here." She looked down toward the pool. "Let's go for a swim." There seemed to be a wall between them now, a wall she had no idea how to approach.

"I'd love to, but I've got to take care of something this morning. How about as soon as I get back we grab some lunch, then camp out at the pool for the rest of the afternoon?" He hoped she wouldn't ask too many questions about what he needed to take care of, but could almost see them reeling through her mind.

"Is it something about the house you're looking into?"

"Ah, yeah, it is. I need to meet with the realtor and give him a picture of what I'm looking for." He was glad for the excuse she'd given him.

"Okay, well, I should go with you. I mean, if I'm going to consider living here I should see some of the homes they have to offer."

Damn, he swore in his mind. She had a good point there. "This is just a preliminary visit. We'll just be talking price ranges and stuff like that. I don't want to take you away from enjoying the scenery. I can handle that alone. You stay here and get some rest. We've been traveling for a few days now and you're probably tired." His fingers caressed her jaw and tucked strands of hair blown out of place by the breeze behind her ear.

"No, I'm not tired, and if we're about to be married I should be as aware of our finances as our living quarters, don't you think?" He was trying to brush her off. She could tell, and she didn't like it.

"Well, call me old-fashioned, but I'd like to take care of the financial stuff like a man should. I'll be back before twelve, and we can go out then." Before she could come up with another retort, he kissed her quickly and walked back into the room.

Oh, no you won't, Rosie thought. You will not leave me in the dark. She stalked through the balcony door a few steps behind, only to stop short when the front door slammed, with him on the other side.

"Dammit!" Rosie cursed and sat abruptly on the bed. She was getting damn tired of Donald and his secrets.

Terrell boarded the ship and followed the directions of the staff. He'd never been on a cruise before, so he tried to take in some sights as he followed behind the other passengers trying to find their cabins. The atmosphere was festive, the staff gay and friendly. He wished this voyage could be focused on pleasure, but he had a mission that he was bound and determined to carry out.

Agent Tobias and the rest of his men had probably already boarded. They'd secured special privileges to board the boat early so that the other passengers wouldn't see them. As they'd be operating undercover once they reached the island, they didn't want to chance that someone might notice them and blow their cover at an inopportune time.

After a few minutes of walking up the yellow painted hallway and back, Terrell finally found his cabin and, with the key card, let himself in. The room was spacious and boasted a view of the water, which now was simply Baltimore's Inner Harbor, a sight he'd seen a lot during his childhood years.

Throwing his bag on the bed, he began to unpack, slipping things into the small drawers of the dresser on the opposite side of the room. When the bag was empty, he tossed it to the floor and collapsed on the king-sized bed, closing his eyes and trying to relax. He needed to focus; that was what Agent Tobias had told him to do. This way he wouldn't endanger himself or the other men working with them.

His heart pounded at the thought of his mother being held captive or worse, not even knowing what she had gotten herself into. That made Terrell all the more anxious to put an end to it.

Out of the blue he wondered about Leah. Thoughts of their last moments together brought on a new kind of excitement as familiar stirrings in his groin had him adjusting himself. If the circumstances had been different, he would have asked her to join him on this trip. But things in Jamaica were sure to be uncertain. He'd risked her life once, he wouldn't do so again.

Strange as it might seem, he felt somehow stronger when she was with him, as if he could do anything, be anything. Her confidence and no-nonsense attitude brought out the best in him. That made him all the more certain they were meant to be together. Earlier this morning he'd thrown away his criteria list, sure he'd found the woman he was looking for.

Once he had things with his mother situated, he'd have all the time in the world for Leah. Working didn't seem so important anymore. Although he'd checked in on the SISCO project, he didn't feel compelled to rush back to D.C. to resume the reins. Leah was the only project he was interested in completing right now.

Her four-step plan had been carefully laid out and catered to the needs she thought she had. But he saw something different. A person so dead set against marriage couldn't possibly build a business around the blissful event. Her mother's failures had blurred her mind, convincing her that she would never be good in a marriage. The best marriages took loyalty, honesty, trust and love. So far, she'd proven three out of the four requirements to him. She was definitely loyal to her clients, her honesty could at times be brutal and he trusted her with his life. Now if he could only make her love him as much as he knew he already loved her.

It was just her luck that all the flights out were booked. But determination and Nikki's quick thinking had her resorting to a ship. She'd be there after Terrell arrived but she'd get there nonetheless and the ship was leaving tonight. With Nikki's help Leah managed to secure passage on the ship, pack her bags, fax Melinda the checklist for the Ortega wedding, get her hair braided and call her mother, all in the space of five hours. Now she crossed the walkway with the last of the straggling guests boarding the Carnival cruise ship.

Terrell was probably in Jamaica by now. He hadn't called her before he left, but he'd said he'd call when he returned. For a moment she wondered how he'd feel when she showed up there. Would he be angry or happy to see her?

Whatever his feelings, she'd be there, and they'd handle this business with Donald together.

She found her room without problem, let herself in and dropped her stuff to the floor. After a quick stop in the bathroom and a cursory check of her makeup, she was in the hallway again. A cruise hadn't been on her list of things to do, but since she was here she might as well enjoy the ride. She walked the deck until her legs screamed and her stomach growled. She hadn't eaten since that pizza shared with Nikki earlier.

Too tired to even think about going back in the direction of the restaurant, she headed for her room instead.

Terrell had been in Jeff's room going over pictures and possible scenarios. His feelings about Donald Douglas had become contradictory.

On the one hand he'd read all the history and obtained a copy of his criminal record. On the other hand he'd sat across the table from the man and shared a meal, all the while watching the way the man pacified and coddled his mother.

The elaborate FBI investigation seemed unreal to Terrell. He was a simple guy with a life embedded in computer codes. Now, with the announcement of a wedding, he found himself traveling to a foreign land to help save his mother. He walked along the deck leading to his room, his mind full of scenarios, gunfights, drugs and tropical islands.

He was more than a little preoccupied, so concentrated on his thoughts that he never saw her. Never looked up before crashing into the tall, soft form.

Leah had picked up a room service menu from the customer service desk and was busily making her dinner selection as she walked when something hard and unforgiving bumped right into her. Strong arms came around her waist as she looked up to see who or what had rammed into her.

The scent of vanilla caused Terrell's heart to thump. He knew that smell, remembered the bathroom full of the aroma, the thick foaming bubbles, the luscious nude body…

"Terrell?" she gasped.

"Leah? What are you doing on this boat?"

Leah bent down, retrieved her menu from the floor. "I could ask you the same question," she said, rising. "You said you were booked on a plane."

"My plans changed." In a moment he took in the peach-colored sundress that barely skimmed her knees, the skinny braids cascading down her back and the abundance of bare skin she displayed, courtesy of two barely-there straps holding her dress up.

His jaw clenched with a combination of arousal and anger.

Fortunately they were only a few steps from his room. He grabbed her by the arm and pulled her the rest of the way. "Come on," he grumbled.

"Wait a minute," she argued futilely. "Terrell?"

Closing the door soundly behind them, he released her arm and took a deep breath. "Why are you here?"

Okay, so she could rule out jumping for joy as his reaction to her surprise appearance but this manhandling was a bit much. "This is still a free country. And I wasn't left under lock and key." She found the closest chair and dropped down into it, slipping her strappy sandals off to rub her tired feet. "Now, I've answered you. You can tell me why you're traveling by sea at any time."

In a minute he was going to kick himself for being so harsh with her, but her presence here was insane. He took a seat in the chair across from her.

"Jeff—Agent Tobias—thought it would be best to take the same route Donald did to the island. And you didn't answer my question."

Leah sat back, let her feet fall to the floor. "I decided you need me."

That was an understatement, he thought. "You decided?"

"Mmm-hmm. Since you tricked me into that stakeout, I figure we're a team now. So I'm here to help you save your mother."

He couldn't be angry with her, even though he wanted to. However, this was a dangerous situation. He didn't want to have to worry about her and his mother at the same time. He'd been comfortable with the fact that she was safe in Baltimore. "This isn't a game, Leah." His voice was a tad louder than he'd intended.

"Good, because if it was, I'd have to say it sucks."

"You could get hurt," he roared.

Leah was quickly growing tired of his attitude. Here she had put her life on hold to help him and he was acting like a gigantic ass. "Look, Terrell, you're the one who coerced me into that stakeout." She sat up in the chair. "And you're the one who had me standing in an alley witnessing a murder."

Terrell shook his head. "I told you to stay in the car. You never listen."

"And if you'd agreed to go to the police that night I wouldn't have been drugged and locked in a basement."

"You're right," he said quietly.

But Leah didn't hear him. She stood, hands on her hips, in front of him. "I tried to tell you to let the police handle it, but oh, no, you wouldn't listen. You've got to go off playing Shaft all by yourself. But I won't let you, Terrell." She was yelling now, her head rocking from side to side. "Not when I've changed my whole course of thinking because of you."

Her hands shook, a slight movement he noticed only because she was standing over him. Her voice caught on those last words. He mentally added another kick to himself for upsetting her like this.

Terrell stood, caught her trembling hands in his.

"I mean it, Terrell—"

"Shhh."

"—you are not a cop. You don't know the first thing about...tracking...criminals."

"Shhh. Leah, baby, listen to me."

"And if you think I'm just going to sit back—"

To shut her up and because he couldn't resist any longer, he kissed her, trapping her lips beneath his until she relaxed and opened her mouth. He wanted to wrap all his emotions around her so tightly and so securely he wouldn't have to wonder about her safety.

Breaking for air, he rested his forehead on hers. "I just don't want you hurt, baby."

Leah sighed. "I don't want you hurt either, you big idiot. That's why I'm here." She hiccupped.

He was an idiot. He should have realized how upset she was, should have anticipated she'd worry about him, the same way he was worried about her. "I know, sweetie. I'm sorry. Sit down."

He eased her back onto the small couch, sat beside her, lifted her feet into his lap and began to rub them. "You're here now. I can't very well throw you overboard, now can I?"

She rolled her eyes at him. "Not if you want to live yourself."

He grinned. "So what now?"

Leah's stomach growled. "Dinner."

"Well, Starsky had a partner, and so did Clyde. I guess if they made it, we can make it too," Terrell said after they'd finished their hamburgers.

Leah let loose with wild laughter. "Starsky and Hutch and Bonnie and Clyde. Are they the best you could come up with?"

He liked the sound of her laugh, so much so he joined her. "I was going to say Lois and Superman but thought you might take offense. Lois didn't do much besides get herself into trouble."

She nodded. "I'm more of a Wonder Woman type of gal."

"Yeah, you're a wonder, alright." He gave a teasing grin.

There was that boyish smile, that look that made her want to fight all his battles, then make mad passionate love to him through the night. "Besides, you can't go to some tropical island looking for my client without me there to help. Donald's still under contract, and he owes me his next installment."

"Yeah? Well, you let me handle Donald. I don't want you near him. Understand?"

Leah frowned. "Wonder Woman never took orders."

"Leah," Terrell said in a dangerously calm tone.

"Alright. Alright. Whatever you say, Shaft."

"Shaft and Wonder Woman. What a pair we make." He looked at her. Her long braids rested on one shoulder, the curly tips just barely brushing her left breast.

Leah watched as his eyes darkened. She was thinking the same thing. Now that one hunger was filled, she was ready to tackle the other. She rose and stood in front of him. "Funny, I've been thinking we'd make a pretty good pair." She traced a finger along his jawline.

Terrell sucked in a breath. The look in her eyes said they were no longer talking about superheroes.

"Oh really? What else have you been thinking?" Spreading his legs, Terrell grabbed her hips and guided her between them. Her dress was paper thin, the tropical-colored material falling gracefully over her curves. He licked his lips as his eyes roved over her hungrily.

Her hands went to the first button on his shirt, released it, then proceeded to the next. "I've been thinking that it was awfully unfair what you did to me in that basement." She pushed the shirt open and marveled at his bare chest. She'd known he'd been hiding his goodies under all those shirts he liked to wear. Pectoral muscles bulged, nipples puckered as she pinched them. His honey-tone skin appeared glazed in the dimly lit room. Slowly, torturously, she let her fingers travel further, splaying over his tight abs.

Terrell sucked in a breath. "I got the distinct impression you were enjoying it." He dragged his hands up and down her sides, his thumbs brushing past her breasts.

She gave him a sly smile, then let her hands fall to his belt buckle. "Oh, don't get me wrong, I'm not complaining." She undid the belt, unclasped the button on his pants and slid his zipper down. "I was just thinking that I hadn't held up my end of the bargain."

The moment she touched his zipper, his vision blurred. He swallowed, hard, even as his grip around her waist tightened. When she reached inside and claimed him, he almost lost all train of thought. "Leah." Her name came out as a ragged moan.

She smiled even as she stroked his ever growing length. "Yes, baby?"

"Ahhh, you are not going to believe this," he started but quickly stopped when her thumb grazed his tip. "I'm…ah…I wasn't expecting…ahhhh. Leah, I'm not prepared for this," he finally managed to say.

Leah paused for the briefest second before leaning closer. She stroked her tongue over his partially open lips. "Don't worry, baby. I've got this," she whispered.

When he would have spoken, her tongue entered his mouth in one swift intoxicating swoop before leaving him again. Her light eyes had darkened, and her slender hands still worked their magic between his legs. "Well, then." He grinned and sat back.

"That's right, just let me do all the work."

She didn't release him even as she lowered herself to her knees. Terrell fingered her braids, twirling a few between his fingers, as he marveled at the turn of events. Thoughts of throwing her overboard or even sending her back to the States were the farthest thing from his mind at this moment. He was thinking more of…

"Mmmmm," he moaned as her warm lips kissed the head of his penis. Then her tongue did some sort of swirly motion and he gave up all conscious thought.

Leah took her time, taking him in slowly, inch by glorious inch. She gave herself completely to the task at hand, soliciting soft moans and ragged growls from Terrell as she mastered him. But it was when she took his entire length, sucking and twirling her tongue around his member until she felt her own moistness seeping between her legs that she received the reaction she wanted.

"Ahhh, baby. Please, baby. I can't take this, it's too much." Even though he said it, he still grabbed the back of her head, guiding her down again.

A smile covered her face as she tasted him again and again until his control slipped and he gave her what she sought.

Hours later after they'd talked and enjoyed each other some more, Terrell escorted Leah to her room. There was no way he could sleep with her and not have her completely.

They walked down the corridor hand in hand until they stopped in front of her door. He pressed her back against the door and covered her lips again, squeezing her breasts as his tongue plunged deeper and deeper into her mouth.

"Mmmm," Leah moaned as she held his butt in a death grip. "I'm so enjoying this cruise."

"Yeah?" Terrell fingered her nipples.

She moaned. "That's wonderful."

He agreed and reluctantly pulled away from her. "But now we have to get some rest." She'd already given him her key card, so he swiped it and opened the door for her. "Goodnight, my love."

She ran her finger along his jaw one last time and winked at him. "Goodnight, baby."

The moment the door clicked shut, Terrell groaned, took a deep breath and then returned to his own room.

He walked down the quiet corridor and was just about to turn the corner when he saw a flash of something out the corner of his eyes. He turned back but there was nothing there. Maybe somebody else was making a booty call.

CHAPTER THIRTEEN

As the ship docked, Terrell stood at the railing, marveling at the clear blue waters and brilliant sunlight and thinking about all the time he and Leah had spent getting to know each other. At this point he felt as if they'd always been together. But the real purpose of this trip had never been far from his mind.

Somewhere on this island was his mother with a man she considered her fiancé, but Terrell considered him—at this point he didn't know what he considered Donald. Was he really dangerous? If so, why hadn't he killed him and Leah when he'd had the chance? Even if he was simply a drug dealer, he had to get his mother away from him. That was the bottom line. Fear and distress sat on his shoulders like dead weights. He prayed for the strength to do what had to be done.

"Hey, you okay?" Leah came up behind him quietly. His long, lean legs were clad in khaki shorts and he wore leather sandals. A black shirt hung loosely over his muscled shoulders, exposing the light skin of his arms. From his posture she could almost tell what he was thinking, as she'd spent some time harboring those same thoughts herself.

While the last couple of hours had passed almost blissfully, danger beckoned to them the moment they set foot on the island.

"Yeah, I'm cool. Just thinking about how things are going to turn out." He didn't turn toward her, not yet ready for her to see him this vulnerable.

She'd placed her hand lightly on his back when she spoke to him, and now he relished her touch. She was there, quietly offering her support. Wasn't that what a wife did? She'd made herself at home in his heart, and the thought of her not being there permanently was too painful to conceive.

"It's beautiful, isn't it?" A light breeze ruffled her shirt as she inhaled the fresh tropical air. When she caught the scent of his cologne, she resisted the urge to nuzzle closer.

"It is. I was wondering." He let his voice trail off, wondering if now was a good time. "You were wondering what?"

He took a deep breath. "If when this mess is all behind us we could come back. I mean, would you like to come back here with me?" He turned toward her then, his eyes searching her face earnestly.

She looked into his warm, sensitive eyes and smiled.

"I think that would be really nice," she answered.

He smiled, happy with her response. Circling her waist, he pulled her closer, loving the feel of her soft curves against him, remembering the things they'd done to each other the night before. "I'm really happy you changed your mind."

"So am I." He was going to kiss her, she knew it the way she knew her name. And she wanted it, needed it, needed it like a desert needed water. So instead of waiting for him, she brought her arms up behind his head and pulled his lips down on hers.

The contact was soft and enticingly sweet at first. Then urgent need struggled to break free. Their tongues delved and clashed, stroked and massaged until moans of pure pleasure echoed in the air surrounding them.

"Alright, can you two try to remember you're here on official business and this kind of stuff can get you both killed?" Tobias approached, annoyance clear in his voice.

"Yes, sir." Leah smiled when she finally tore herself away from Terrell. Tobias wore dark glasses and a baseball cap, she suspected in an effort to appear inconspicuous. In his hand was a travel guide.

Terrell was too pleased with Leah's response to give the arrival of the FBI agent much attention. But as he looked beyond the boat, caught a glimpse of the tropical island, he remembered what his true mission was. "Where to now?" he asked Agent Tobias as the ramp was being assembled for persons to leave the ship.

"My man said they rented a car and drove to Negril. They're staying in a hotel down there, so we'll charter a plane and go down. I've booked you two at a hotel a few miles from the one your mother is staying in, and I want you to stay out of sight tonight. I'll meet with you first thing in the morning to go over what our first step is going to be."

"That sounds like a plan. Where will you be staying?" Leah asked.

"Some of us are going to stay in the same hotel with your mother, and the others are going to spread out across the island, try to get a feel for what's going on down here before we set up the operation." He turned to walk toward the ramp. "Wait a few minutes after I get off, then meet me at the location on this paper and we'll fly down."

"Aye aye, captain!" Leah made a mock salute and Tobias frowned before smiling. "You two are really something else." He shook his head and walked away.

The Rockhouse Hotel stretched across the cliffs of what the natives called Pristine Cove in Negril. It was a sturdy three-story structure nestled amongst lush trees and bordered by white sand beach and blue water.

Tobias had booked them connecting rooms. "Good 'ol Tobias." Terrell smiled when the room clerk gave them their keys.

Both rooms had a private sun deck, four-poster queen-sized bed, mini bar and a door connecting that she chose to unlock.

Leah put her bags down and walked out onto the sun deck. The sun was setting over the beautiful island of Negril—brilliant hues of purple, orange and gold streaked the sky above the turquoise water. Finding a wicker chair on the deck, she sat down, relaxing, and inhaled the tropical scent. A sound at the door jolted her, and her eyes flew to the spot where Terrell stood on her deck.

He watched her, silently wondering if and when he'd finally have her. She looked at peace, as if she hadn't had a care in the world. With his hands stuffed in his pockets, he walked over to the railing of the deck. The water smelled fresh and beckoned to him. The hidden cove the hotel was situated in gave a secluded feeling, a romantic atmosphere no doubt a hit with tourists.

But they weren't here for romance.

He reminded himself of that fact and let his mind drift back to their main purpose. "You should really keep that door locked. You never know who might walk in." He turned to look at her with a grin.

"Yeah, like you," she retorted lightly. She'd seen his pensive gaze, noticed the slump in his shoulders as he'd walked across the deck. He was worried, and he had every right to be. "Yeah, like me."

He stared at her then, his lopsided grin sending shivers throughout her body. "Terrell?"

"Mmmmm."

He never took his eyes off her, which made the question she was about to ask all the more disconcerting. There were things she wanted to know, things she needed to know.

"Did you love her?" she blurted out. "Tanya, I mean. Did you love her?" she explained when he only blinked in response.

"No, I didn't. Like I told you before, she fit this image that I had for a wife. I met her, we clicked and it just seemed like the right thing to be with her."

"Oh." Leah nodded her head as if she understood.

"I don't think I've ever loved anyone." Taking his hands out of his pockets, he braced them on the railing and leaned back. "Until now."

Her head shot up and she stared at him blankly, wondering if she could really trust that he meant it. But this was Terrell. If nothing else, he was honest and loyal. She knew that if he was saying he loved her, he damn sure meant it. "And now?"

They both remained quiet while water rippled and splashed against the shore beneath the deck. The sun completed its descent, taking with it the wonderfully color-streaked sky.

He moved to sit on the lounge chair beside her, took her hand in his. "Now I'm so completely in love with you I can't tell where I end and you begin."

Could a body physically melt? Could her heart beat only to the rhythm of this man's words? Leah could only answer yes to them both. "I never thought I'd be in love. Never thought I'd find someone I trusted with my heart."

"You can trust me with your life, Leah. I would never do anything to hurt you." He lifted her hand to his lips for a brief kiss.

With her free hand she rubbed the back of his head. "I do trust you, Terrell. I trust that you will be everything you say you are."

She hadn't said she loved him back, but that would come in time, he knew. Right now she needed assurance that he was sincere. She said she trusted him but he still felt compelled to show her that she could. "Let's get some dinner. You haven't eaten in a couple of hours so I know your stomach will be protesting soon." Standing, Terrell pulled her up with him.

"Are you saying I'm greedy?"

Terrell tweaked her nose. "No, of course not. You have a healthy appetite and I enjoy watching you cater to it. Now let's go before the rumbling starts."

After a playful punch to his arm, Leah reached up and fixed his glasses.

"I must have walked around for the last thirty years with my glasses lopsided on my face," he laughed.

"Why do you say that?"

" 'Cause nobody's ever fixed them as much as you do." His voice lost its laughter as he stared into her eyes, one of his hands still holding hers while the other snaked around her waist.

"Maybe nobody ever noticed you the way I do," she said, snuggling closer to him.

"Then I'm flattered," he whispered before his lips sought hers.

"So am I," she breathed as her eyes fluttered shut and her mouth opened to greet his. It was the sweetest kiss, slow and satisfying, his tongue sliding over hers in sinuous movements that made her wish they were closer to the bed.

His hand fanned out over her bottom, pulling her closer as her fingers clenched at his shoulders urging him to deepen the kiss. His mouth opened wider as if to swallow her. She responded hungrily, wrapping both arms around his neck and pulling him closer to the brink.

"So sweet," he moaned into her mouth before lightly nipping at her bottom lip.

"How much longer?" she asked, breathless from the assault and shaky from overwhelming desire.

"How much longer for what?" He was kissing her chin, her jaw, her neck and moving towards her ear.

She was melting in his arms, praying she wouldn't fall onto the floor. Each time his lips grazed her skin, her knees weakened more. "How much longer before you go back to your room and grab those condoms?"

His tongue dipped in and out of her ear while his hands groped and kneaded her bottom.

His heart beat erratically and hers was thumping wildly in her chest. "Five seconds tops," he said, then darted through the connecting door.

When he returned she was standing beside the bed. "I think you broke your own record," she grinned.

Terrell didn't say a word, simply tossed the box on the nightstand and walked to her. Planting both hands firmly beneath her bottom he lifted. She obediently clasped her legs tightly around his waist and they fell, more like collapsed, onto the waiting mattress, both laughing and kissing.

Pulling himself up to rest on his elbow he looked down into her eyes, rubbing his thumb over her swollen lips. "We are going to be so good together."

He definitely didn't have to tell her what she already knew. So without further preamble she removed his glasses. Stretching her arms to reach the nightstand, she set them down. "We're going to be great together." She smiled as her eyes returned to his.

His heart skipped a beat. In her own subtle way, she'd told him what he so desperately needed to hear—she loved him. Dropping his head, he took her lips again briefly, teasingly, before unbuttoning her shirt.

She was still as a stone as he undid the buttons one by one. Then his long fingers splayed across the span of her stomach, their warmth easing her nervousness. When his hand moved to cup one swollen breast, she held her breath. Then he leaned closer, suckling through the material of her bra one hardened nipple. She moaned into the quiet of the room.

With one hand still attending the breasts he'd dreamed about so frequently, his other hand reached between her back and the mattress to unsnap her bra. Then he removed both the shirt and the bra.

A few braids had fallen forward with her movements and now hung between and around her breasts. One by one he moved them around her shoulders to lie against the mattress and brushed the back of his hands against the creamy brown swells. Because he couldn't resist, because the mere sight of darker brown nipples, puckered and hard from his lips, called to him, he cupped each breast hungrily, kneading the mounds through his fingers. Again, he lavished them with his tongue, pushing them both closer together, attempting to suckle each nipple at once, then blowing on them in brief succession.

Leah clenched at the sheets as her head bobbed from side to side. She'd never felt this before, *never*. From her neck down she was on fire, her body heating like hot lava waiting for the ultimate eruption.

With trembling hands he finished undressing her. Finally, blessedly, she was gloriously naked, lying on the bed, her braids haloing around her head. "You are so beautiful." He looked down at her with clear admiration in his eyes.

Leah almost sang with joy. Nobody had ever looked at her like that, never said anything like that to her and it surprised her how much she'd needed it to hear it, how much she'd actually longed for someone to want her that way. Holding her arms out, she reached for him.

Falling into her arms was the easiest thing Terrell had ever done. He felt so comfortable there, so right to be in her arms. The tighter she clung to him, the more positive he was that she was the woman for him.

When his lips grazed the sensitive skin beneath her ear, she purred with pleasure, arching up off the bed. Her legs wrapped around his as she felt the burning length of his desire covered still by his shorts rubbing roughly against her center.

Slipping her hands between them she eased her hand down his belly, grasping his arousal. He jerked. Heady with her newfound power she quickly undid the buckle of his belt and unfastened his shorts. With both hands grazing the hardened contours of his bottom, she slid his shorts and boxers beneath his waist. Not wanting to wait another minute to feel him skin against skin, she grabbed the full length of him, stroking him slowly at first, then picking up the pace.

Struggling for each breath, Terrell closed his eyes in ecstasy and buried his face further into the crook of her neck as her hands glided back and forth, pulling from him those premature drops of completion.

"I want you," she whispered.

With those words, stars burst beneath his lids, his heartbeat accelerated and his mouth went dry. He wouldn't make her beg, wouldn't keep her waiting, would no longer deny himself. Reluctantly pulling away from her, he stood and quickly pulled his shirt over his head and let his shorts and underwear fall to the floor.

"Open for me," he murmured spreading her thighs further apart. She lay naked beneath him, her secret place unfolding, the musky scent of her arousal sifting up through his nostrils, intoxicating him, enveloping him. He rubbed one finger down her center, watching the rise and fall of her breasts, the sudden intake of her breath. With soft rhythmic motions his finger circled around the stiff bead at her center.

Leah sucked in a tremendous amount of air and released it moments later on a long, exaggerated sigh. Her hands grasped the sheets as her legs began to tremble beneath his stimulating ministrations. When his fingers slid slowly, deeply inside her, a sound echoed throughout the room. Later she would realize that the sound had come from her. Her catlike moans escalated as her hips met the rhythm of his two fingers planted securely inside her. With his free hand Terrell deftly massaged her right breast, rolling the pebbled nipple between his fingers.

"Terrell." His name was torn from her throat.

"You are so wet, so damned wet," he whispered as his fingers slid deeper into her moist center.

Lifting her right hand, she placed it atop his over her breast, guiding him to grip the softened mound harder as she climbed higher, to where she had no idea. Something was going on inside her, something was building and building, something so intense she was almost afraid of what would happen when it finally reached its peak. These were new sensations for her and she couldn't quite get a handle on what to do or say. Going on instinct, she murmured, "I want to touch you."

Removing his hand from her breast, he guided her hand to his swollen sex. She quickly lifted her other hand, slipping both hands around him, admiring him with her touch.

A low growl rumbled in his chest as he pulled his fingers from inside her and grabbed both breasts in his hands. She continued with quick up-and-down strokes, and he pumped against the continuous movement.

When his arms grew weak with the steady rising of arousal he bent over her, first kissing her neck, then her ear, then her cheek. Quickly turning her head, she opened her mouth to his, inviting him to take all she had.

"Oh my God," he gasped just before her tongue delved back into his mouth.

Each moment, each second, each touch of his hand pulled her closer to the brink where anticipation bloomed and waited to burst free.

"Terrell." Taking a breath, she tried to verbalize the feelings inside her.

Words were not needed for he had been holding on to his own desire for far too long. He heard the desperation in her voice, felt it in the frantic ministrations of her hands, and thought he'd lose himself right there at that moment.

But he'd told her he would make it good. He wanted to make it good for her. He wanted to make her love him the way he so desperately loved her. So losing himself now in the palm of her hand would be the act of a horny boy, not of a man soliciting a woman's heart. With iron will he pulled out of her reach to lie on the bed beside her. His hands were quick as they spanned her waist, pulling her so they both lay on their sides entwined by legs and arms.

"Leah, I've wanted you for so long," he told her, his fingers twining through her heavy braids.

"I never thought I could want like this," she sighed into his mouth, denial of her feelings towards him a distant memory.

For endless moments they kissed, their tongues sealing the bond between them. Leah thought she'd explode when he finally pulled his mouth away from hers. Blinking, she stared into his eyes. They simmered with passion, glistened with pleasure. There was so much she wanted to say, so much she wanted him to know, but the words didn't come.

As if he knew exactly what was going through her mind, the backs of his fingers glided slowly over her cheek, his chest heaving beside hers. "There's no turning back, Leah." His voice cracked both with desire and fear. "I need you to know that I want all or nothing."

"I know that," she told him. And she was prepared to give it, she wanted to give it.

"You have to want that, too." His voice was stronger now as his erection jutted and poked against her stomach. When she didn't answer, his fear grew while his eyes questioned her again.

"I don't know what to say, Terrell. I just know that I want to be with you, now. Is that enough?" She sure as hell hoped it was.

"As long as you know where I stand." It wasn't enough. He had wanted her to tell him that she wanted the same things he did, that she'd give him those things willingly, but she hadn't and a small part of him said he should walk away—the bigger part elected to stay.

From the nightstand he grabbed the box, tore it open and returned to her with a small packet in hand. "You want to do the honors?" he asked.

Leah quickly shook her head. She'd been bold enough when they'd been caught up in the passion, but now that they'd had a moment to regain their senses she was feeling a tad shy.

Terrell smiled, ripped the wrapping off and covered himself. Pushing her onto the mattress, he covered her, bringing his lips down to take her mouth in a kiss designed to muddle her mind, to make her forget there was anyone else in the world except the person kissing her.

To Leah, the kiss did all those things and then some. Her arms twined around his neck. The beauty of Negril paled in comparison to this man who was preparing to love her.

He entered her slowly, painfully slowly, and her heart ached with the connection. He inserted himself deeper and deeper until she could feel his testicles against the swollen lips of her vagina. He stayed there for endless moments deep inside her, surrounded and engulfed by her.

Terrell held his breath and only the thought of dying on top of her had him expelling it in one great whoosh. After all these weeks he couldn't believe he was finally here. He was finally inside her and it was beyond anything he'd ever imagined. Her muscles clamped around him, taking him deeper still. When he finally possessed enough energy he pulled out of her gently, raising up on his elbows so he could look into her face.

Her eyes were closed as if she were regaining herself as well. Brushing light kisses along her cheeks he murmured her name with each long, sensuous stroke he made.

Leah moaned, her hands gripping his shoulders, her hips matching his rhythm, her mind soaring into the clouds, as the sensations of his manhood moved through the depths of her, inciting new sensations throughout her body.

"Oh, Terrell," she murmured into his neck, nipping lightly at his skin.

Terrell moaned with absolute satisfaction, "Leah."

As they moved together to the melody known only to lovers, his soul shook with the intensity of the feelings. He loved her beyond words and wondered if he told her what her reaction would be. Her bucking and twisting beneath him tore his mind from those thoughts. He hardened to an almost painful point and stroked longer, harder, slamming into her with uninhibited ardor. Her legs clenched around him tighter, her bottom lifting off the bed as the convulsions began to overtake her.

She'd reached it, she realized. She'd reached the top of that mountain and, with Terrell's persistent but pleasing thrusts, she'd fallen right over and now floated somewhere between heaven and earth. A ragged cry, a gasp of pure pleasure bounced off the walls and filled her ears. She'd screamed, she'd actually screamed. For years, she'd laughed at Nikki when she'd described a man making her climb the walls and yell with pleasure, and now she was sure she'd just done the same thing.

He'd pleased her, he could tell by the sound of her voice, the strength in her legs still wrapped tightly around him and the tightening convulsions of her walls around his penis. He was elated with the thought that he'd kept his word. A small part of him wondered if she'd faked it, thoughts of Tanya coming to mind. Then as quickly as that glimmer of doubt appeared it was replaced by the sound of her voice.

"I've never been *there* before," she whispered against his ear, taking the soft lobe into her mouth, suckling.

Nothing could ever surpass this feeling he'd just evoked. She seemed so content, so blissfully sated he ached to join her. Lifting above her, he untwined her legs from his waist and placed an ankle on each of his shoulders, plunging deeper inside her. "How about I meet you there?" A passion-filled grin spread across his face as he pumped into her fiercely.

Though Leah thought it would take hours to recover from her latest ride, Terrell's demanding strokes started the climb all over again.

His hands gripped her ankles as he balanced himself on his knees, lifting her up to meet every thrust. "Leah!" Her name was torn from his very soul as her muscles pulled at him, twisting his insides and making him quake.

"Oh God, Leah!" His thrusts quickened, the friction of his hardness against her silken walls coaxing him, guiding him to oblivion. "Damn. Damn, this is so good." His lips contorted, his face twisted.

"Terrell." She was breathless. This couldn't be possible, she couldn't be taking the same trip again—so soon. Her heart raced, her hands clenched at the sheets as she opened her eyes to see him.

He was on his knees above her, holding her legs tightly at his neck while he plunged into her mercilessly. In that instant he looked strong, confident and definitely male. Her heart ached with a feeling she knew had to be love. For all that he'd seemed to be when she first saw him—nerdy, geeky, nervous and confused—now he controlled her. He owned her and he worked her until she thought she'd crumble into a million pieces.

"Oh baby, it's…" The words seemed stuck in his throat. "Leah, baby." His movements stiffened and he came with what almost seemed like pain. "Oh, oh…Leah." The muscles in his arms bulged as his hands gripped her ankles and he froze over her.

Leah felt a dizzying sense of spiraling in the air. Her vagina throbbed and pulsated as her release oozed out slow and hot.

Terrell collapsed on top of her, afraid that he'd die right there, but knowing that if that were the case, he'd die one happy man!

CHAPTER FOURTEEN

"Straight to step three," Leah mumbled, the side of her face cushioned by Terrell's chest.

"Hmmm?" His eyes didn't open, and his hands didn't move from where they rested on her back.

She sighed contentedly. "Nothing, I was just thinking aloud." She snuggled closer.

But Terrell remembered her silly notion of relationships and the four-step method. "So I guess we're moving backward, huh?"

Her head lifted slightly and he knew she was staring at him. He cracked his eyes to see her shocked expression. "I remember your four-step method. I guess we're moving backwards. Now we'll start dating." His tone was casual but his heartbeat accelerated.

"Since we've clearly gone off course I'm not sure where we go next," she told him honestly.

"We could start a new method," he told her in a cheerful voice. "First step—admitting the attraction and acting on it, what we've been doing the last couple of days." His arms extended to make a sweeping motion toward their naked bodies. "Second step—admit we're madly in love." He waited a beat for her denial. "Third step—marriage and family. Bam! Happily ever after!" He smiled down at her when she made no effort to stop or correct him.

After a moment of regarding the small cleft in his chin she hadn't noticed until now since his goatee practically concealed it, Leah wondered at his logic. "That sounds as foolish as the plan I'd come up with."

"Maybe," he shrugged. "But a man can dream."

"Yeah, I guess you can." Lowering her eyes, she thought about his dream and how much she wanted it to be her own.

One arm slid from her back and his finger slightly lifted her chin. "It doesn't have to be a bad thing, Leah." He looked into eyes teetering between her deepest desire and the mistakes of the past.

"When my father left I thought it was the end of the world. My family was destroyed. And I wanted so much to hate him for leaving, but I knew that if he'd stayed they would have continued to argue. They would have continued to hate each other and, as much as I wanted my family, I wanted the fighting to stop more."

Terrell absently lifted a braid and twined it around his finger as she continued.

"Then when my mother said she was getting married again, I thought I'd been given another chance. And then she had a baby and I was so excited. Not only did I have a mother and a father, now I had a little brother. Then that was over too. By her third marriage I stopped hoping that I'd ever have a real family. Mama just kept getting married and having babies and getting divorced. And I kept getting older, swearing I'd never go through that kind of heartache or disappointment."

"So your four steps were designed to shield you from a broken heart?" He'd already figured that out, but thought it would be good if she admitted it.

"That and the realization that I was no better than she was when it came to commitments."

"But that's not true. You've committed to your business and from what I can tell you're doing a great job."

"That's a different kind of commitment," she reasoned. Laying her head back on his chest, she let the rhythm of his steady breathing soothe her. He was listening to her, hearing thoughts she'd never before voiced, seeing a part of her even Nikki had yet to see.

"It's still a commitment, and it took a lot of guts. You didn't fail when you opened the shop, so why are you so convinced you'll fail when you enter a relationship?"

"I thought that's how things worked. I guess I never really took the time to see if I'd be good at a relationship or not." In the last few days she'd come to realize that she wasn't her mother and in so many ways she'd already proved that. Instead of using her mother's mistakes as a crutch all these years she should have used them for strength.

As enlightening as her thoughts toward relationships were, they paled in comparison to the fact that she'd never before thought of entering a serious relationship, until Terrell. She'd never before allowed herself to truly examine what she wanted and how she could get it, until Terrell.

"You'll be good at whatever you put your mind to." Terrell stared down at her. He wasn't going to hold back anymore. He wanted so desperately to take his time with her, to get her used to the idea of him loving her, but he now realized that Leah liked to see the whole picture at one time. She needed to see exactly how good they were together on a regular basis before she'd be totally convinced. He had a plan of just how to make that happen.

His hand slid up and down her back, each stroke adding to the flicker of desire growing inside him. He craved her like no addiction ever before. She had filled him completely and the thought of her backing away, refusing to give herself to him, was heart wrenching—something he knew he couldn't bear.

"I'm afraid," she whispered against the taut muscles of his chest as the last of her resolve began to crumble.

"I won't hurt you, Leah. You have to believe that I would never hurt you."

She believed him, which only added to her despair. "I know."

Shifting so that he was now on top of her, he looked into her face, his free hand cupping her chin while his other hand remained wrapped around her. "Let me love you, Leah. Let me show you how good we can be together." His eyes pleaded, his voice begged, his lips, when they touched hers, persuaded.

It was morning when Leah began to stir. The sweet tropical breeze floating through the room added to her already sated mood. She stretched like a cat, yawning in a release of energy. Her outstretched arms came down, startling her when they landed against something solid.

Her head jerked, and she saw Terrell lying next to her. Memories of the previous night came flooding back, and Leah trembled with embarrassment. She'd never spent the entire night with a man. After a moment's hesitation, she snuggled closer to him and realized she liked it.

Terrell turned to face her as if it were the most natural thing in the world. "Mornin', beautiful," he said sleepily, his eyes remaining closed.

"Good morning," she mumbled and pulled the covers up closer.

When his arms extended beneath the covers, grasping her at the waist and pulling her toward him, she hissed in surprise. "Come on now, we are not going to act shy after what we did last night." He opened one eye to peek at her.

Her cheeks flushed as she remembered all the things she and Terrell had done. Not just last night but the night before that on the ship. She'd done things she never imagined herself doing. But she'd done them because she felt so safe with him. Still, this morning things were totally different—they'd gone all the way this time. "Don't do that," she protested.

"Don't do what?" he said when she was cuddled with her backside against his front. "Don't make you remember how uninhibited you were last night, or don't make you remember how good it was?"

Despite herself she smiled at both. "Either."

"Get used to it. I like you uninhibited." Pushing wayward braids out of his way with his chin he nuzzled her neck.

"I'll just bet you do." Admitting she loved being held by him, she allowed herself a few more minutes of bliss.

This could be real, she thought. She could really be with him this way all the time. All she had to do was allow it to be.

"You're too quiet. What are you thinking?" he asked, his hand finding her breasts.

"Mmmmm, just that we have quite a day ahead of us." Through the mist of their glorious lovemaking the reason for being here on this island at this very moment was never far from Leah's thoughts. And she knew it haunted Terrell as well.

He let out a whoosh of breath. "I know. I've been wondering how everything will play out myself."

"I still don't think Donald wants to hurt her," she added.

"It doesn't matter to me what his initial intentions were. Now that we know just how serious this whole situation is, any involvement on her part is too much." He hugged her tighter. "I just want her away from him."

"I know." She did understand his need to protect his mother. Still, she couldn't shake the feeling that things weren't exactly what they seemed where Donald was concerned. She'd seen him with Ms. Rosie, seen the obvious love shared between them, so she was reluctant to believe that Donald had used her as a part of his cover. And even though she couldn't intelligently deny that Donald was into something pretty dangerous, she was sure it had nothing to do with his feelings for Ms. Rosie.

But she wouldn't dare say this to Terrell. Because as much as he talked about love and relationships, he seemed to be blind to the feelings his mother and Donald shared. Leah knew it was because he was reluctant to accept his mother marrying another man. She remembered him saying he felt that she was leaving him, and a part of her longed to tell him that she'd be there for him after his mother married, so he wouldn't be alone, but she held that back as well.

The phone on the nightstand rang, shaking both of them free of their thoughts. Terrell loosened his grip on her, but didn't let go completely, while she rolled closer to the edge of the bed, stretching her arm until her fingers curled around the receiver. "Hello?" she answered.

"Yes, Tobias… Yes, he's here… In an hour? That's fine… We'll meet you in your room… Very funny." She smiled wryly before replacing the phone in its cradle.

"Tobias?" Terrell asked.

"Yup, he wants us to meet him in his room in an hour." Their intimate solitude had been interrupted by apprehension and anxiety. Terrell rolled onto his back and pulled her closer, so that she lay halfway across his body. They stayed that way in silence for a few more moments.

Then Leah sat up and threw her legs over the side of the bed, taking the sheets with her. "He advised that we not try to squeeze in another quickie because things were hot last night and he wants to move in as soon as possible." She turned just in time to catch Terrell's broad grin.

"How'd he know what I was thinking?" He reached for her but grabbed a handful of the sheet instead. When he pulled on it unexpectedly, it slipped out of her hand and revealed one plump breast.

Terrell's eyes immediately fell to the exposed skin and his mouth went dry. Leah stared at him, watching as desire crept into the smooth features of his face. Elation filled her. He still wanted her. After all they'd done last night, he still wanted her. She smiled at the thought, pulled the sheet back around her body and stood. "No quickies," she reminded him.

"I didn't say it was gonna be quick." Feeling empowered by her obvious arousal Terrell lay back against the pillows, his arms cradled behind his head. He was gloriously naked and Leah's eyes took in every inch of him.

She saw him in a whole different light now that he was unclothed. He didn't look so skinny anymore. *Can you say buff to the third power?* Just below his navel a line of dark hair led the way to that part of him that had given her so much pleasure just hours before.

Her heart thudded in her chest as desire simmered low in her stomach and the muscles at her center started seriously contracting. When her eyes returned to his, she was embarrassed to see that he had been watching her watch him. "I'm…ah, I'm going to get a shower," she murmured, moving in the direction of the bathroom.

"You want some company?" he suggested casually.

"No!" She tossed him a sensuous look over her shoulder. "We'd never get out of this room." Then she disappeared behind the bathroom door.

"Yeah, you're probably right." He let out the breath he'd been holding while she'd surveyed his body. He needed to focus on the events to come. As much as he would have loved to stay in that bed with her for the next couple of days, hell, the next couple of years, he had more pressing matters to deal with.

He'd come to Jamaica to save his mother, and it was time he got down to business. He had plenty of time to woo Leah after he took care of the situation at hand. He quickly prayed for his mother's safety.

An hour and two cups of coffee later, Terrell and Leah sat on the couch in Agent Tobias' room. Pictures were spread across the coffee table, and the other agents and Tobias discussed locations and strategy for moving in.

"There's no picture of Donald." Leah noticed instantly and looked to Terrell.

He flipped through the pictures, shrugged, then turned his attention back to the agents. "So this is all about some weed?" Terrell interrupted the conversation, tired of the way the agents talked only about the drug dealers and the smuggling ring. He was concerned about his mother. That was his sole reason for being here.

"The operation started because of the large amounts of marijuana being transported between the islands and the United States," Tobias tried to explain to him. "We know the key players, we know how they've been smuggling the drugs, and we know who's been moving it in the States. Now it's time for us to put an end to it."

"And my mother, where does she stand in your grand plan to put an end to this drug ring?" He sat with his legs spread, his elbows resting on his thighs, his hands clasped to keep from fidgeting.

"Once we bring the ring down, your mother will be safe," Tobias advised.

"How do you know if she's safe now, right at this very moment?"

"I told you we had men in their hotel. They've kept close tabs on your mother and Donald throughout the night. She seems to be fine."

"Does she appear to be a captive?" Leah asked.

"No, as a matter of fact, she doesn't. She actually was left alone for the greater portion of the day yesterday until Donald returned later that evening. We don't think she knows what's going on, and it's apparent to us that she is not in any danger at present."

Leah placed a hand on Terrell's shoulder. "She's okay. She's not in any danger right now. Just let them get their game plan together and then we'll go and get her."

"But what if..." Terrell turned to her, anguish clear in his features.

"No, we are not going to think about what if. She is fine now and she will remain fine until the FBI makes the necessary arrests. Then we'll go in and get her. It's simple, you just have to remember that she's safe now."

As awful as he felt, as nervous as he was, her words calmed him. The steady feel of her hand on his shoulder soothed him and the fact that she had referred to them as 'we' elated him. "Alright, when do we go in?"

They rode in a white mini van with Agent Tobias, Agent Blum and two other men who tinkered with expensive looking equipment on the back seat. Agent Tobias explained that Donald's room was bugged, and someone was always listening for his next move. Leah looked out the window as they pulled up in front of another resort.

A three-story pale pink building stood draped by palm trees and bathed in sunlight. Off to the side were smaller houses that resembled the huts built on Gilligan's Island. People came in and out of the front doors, scantily dressed women, men in sandals, children with their buckets and shovels heading for the beach. Leah paid particular attention to a young couple that walked hand in hand. There were two children, a girl and a boy, neither of whom was older than about ten, who straggled behind them.

Once the woman looked back and said something to the children, which made them walk faster and smile with glee. Leah smiled as she pressed her forehead against the window. They were a family, and they were happy. That's what she wanted, she realized with a start. She wanted a family and the happiness that came with it. And she wanted it with Terrell.

Her mind drifted to the Ortega wedding, and all she had to do to get ready for the affair next week. Melinda was probably handling most of it now, but there were things she needed to take care of herself. So why was she here in Jamaica instead of at home doing her job? Because she was in love, she thought with trepidation.

She felt a hand jostling her shoulder, "Hmmmm?" Tearing herself from the window and the path her thoughts had taken, she turned to see Terrell staring at her intently.

"I asked if you were okay?"

"I'm fine. Are you alright with what's about to happen?" The agents had told them they had all the evidence they needed to move in and make some preliminary arrests, removing some of the key players and, eventually, toppling the ring. It would also allow Terrell to walk in and get his mother without putting himself or anyone else in danger.

"I'm cool, I just want her to be safe." His hand moved from her shoulder to her lap to entwine his fingers with hers. "I want all three of us to go back home and get on with our lives. And put Donald and this whole mess behind us."

Leah wanted the same thing, but something told her it wouldn't be just the three of them.

It didn't take long for the agents to enter the hotel and round up five men, some of whom Leah recognized from the pictures back at the hotel. But Donald wasn't one of them. She could feel Terrell tensing beside her and knew that he'd noticed the same thing.

"Where is he?" he asked.

"Just wait, maybe they're not finished. Just stay calm," she told him, but she felt unsteady, as if things hadn't gone the way they'd planned after all.

"He was in there, I know he was. I heard him through those head-phones. I heard him talking to my mother. I know he's in there." Terrell was getting antsy, and Leah wondered what he was about to do.

When the side door to the van slid open and Agent Tobias stepped in, she looked at him and prayed he'd have an answer that would keep Terrell from going off.

"Good news," he said sliding into the back seat of the van. "We got our guys."

"Where's Donald?" Terrell questioned.

"He's in the hotel."

"Why didn't you bring him out?"

"Why should we?"

"I don't understand, I thought you went in to make arrests," Leah questioned.

In the distance they heard a siren. Leah looked out the window to see an ambulance approaching. Terrell never bothered to take his eyes off Tobias.

"He was one of them. He was with the guy that night when those men were shot in the alley. Why didn't you arrest him?" Terrell yelled.

"Terrell, there's a lot that you don't understand," Tobias began.

"Then maybe you should explain it to me."

"It's not my place. You can go on into the hotel. Your mother is in room 417."

"I want to know what the hell is going on!" Terrell roared.

With a steadying hand to his shoulder, Leah looked away from the agent. "Terrell, why don't we just go in and make sure your mother's okay." She tried to nudge him out of the van.

"No, I want him to tell me what's going on. Why isn't Donald being arrested? Why is he still in there with my mother?"

"Let's just go in and find out for ourselves." Leah leaned over him and pressed the button that opened the side door.

By the time they stepped out of the van two ambulances had pulled in front of the hotel, and paramedics ran through the revolving doors.

People streamed out of the hotel in a state of panic as Jamaican authorities tried to hold the assembling crowd back.

Terrell's heart skipped a beat when he saw the ambulances parked in front of the hotel, and he started across the street. Leah trailed behind him, praying Rosie was all right. Agent Blum stood at the front door and signaled to the officers to let Terrell and Leah in.

"Take that service elevator to the fourth floor. Room 417," he told them.

Terrell was quiet on the elevator. Leah moved next to him, taking his hand in hers. She didn't say anything, and neither did he. When they exited on the fourth floor, they walked down the hall, both filled with apprehension, afraid of what they would find in room 417.

The door was open, and agents and Jamaican police were going in and out, their voices booming through the narrow hallway. The first stretcher was wheeled out of the room just as Leah and Terrell approached the door. The body was covered completely and she felt Terrell's hand slipping from hers. She gripped it tighter, to console him for the loss or convince him that it wasn't Rosie, she wasn't sure which.

When the stretcher was past them and they could make their way through the door, Terrell entered first, relief washing over him as he spotted his mother sitting on the edge of the bed on the far side of the room.

"Mama." He went to her, falling to his knees on the floor beside her as she embraced him. "I was so worried," he whispered while he held her close.

"Terrell? What are you doing here, baby?" Rosie asked before looking up to see Leah standing behind her son. "How did you two get here?"

"We took a cruise," Leah said, and thought how stupid she must have sounded. In the midst of all this commotion and confusion she had made it sound as if they were on a pleasant vacation.

"I thought you were…I thought…that stretcher." He couldn't bring himself to say it.

"Oh no, baby. I'm fine," Rosie said, figuring out what her son had been trying to say. "That was Cable."

"Who is Cable?" he asked, vaguely remembering the name. And where is Donald?" Terrell rose from his knees to sit on the bed beside his mother.

Tears sprang to Rosie's eyes as she pointed across the room. Just outside the patio door stood another stretcher with paramedics surrounding it.

"What happened?" Leah whispered, looking at the men dressed in dark pants and red jackets frantically working on the body.

"I don't know what's going on." Rosie shook her head from side to side. "Me and Donald were in here, about to go out and do some sight-seeing, when Cable came barging in hollering about Donald being a snitch and lying to him." Tears streamed down Rosie's cheeks, and Terrell hugged her closer to him.

"They yelled at each other, and then Cable pulled the gun out and shot him. He just shot him. I couldn't move. I couldn't stop him," she sobbed. "Donald fell out there on the balcony and then Cable turned to me. He was going to…to shoot me too, but then these other men came through the door yelling that they were the FBI, and when Cable kept pointing the gun at me they shot him 'cause he wouldn't put the gun down. He just kept saying how I had messed everything up, how I made Donald change. I had turned him into a snitch."

"Shhh, Mama it's alright, everything's gonna be alright now." Terrell tried to console her, but wasn't sure what to think of this turn of events himself.

The paramedics came into the room, rolling the stretcher toward the door. Rosie stood and prepared to follow them, but a bulky man stopped her. "Ma'am, I'm going to need you to stay here for now. They're going to take him to the hospital, but we need to ask you some questions first. Then you can go and be with him."

"No, I'm going with him now! I don't have any answers to your questions, so you might as well save them. I don't know anything except that man came in here and shot him, that's all I know. Now I gotta go be with him. He needs me." She tried to push past the man.

Terrell rose, pulled on her arms and begged for her to listen. "Mama, come on, sit down. You've been through an ordeal, just sit down and get yourself together."

"No, Terrell, I've waited too long for happiness, and I won't let him go. I won't let him leave me like…" Her voice trailed off.

"Like Daddy left you," Terrell finished, his heart aching for her, for all that she had lost and for the undeniable fact that he dreaded. She loved Donald.

"I have to go with him, you have to understand." Rosie was pleading with the agent who looked from Leah to Terrell in question. Terrell walked out onto the balcony and Leah looked away, unable to speak. Agent Blum came into the room then and went to Rosie.

"Ms. Pierce, you can ride to the hospital with me." Taking her by the arm, he led Rosie to the door. "Combs, you can question her later," he told the bulky man who stood in the middle of the floor with a stunned expression on his face.

Leah, who had watched the whole scene from an outsider's point of view, wondered how she was going to console Terrell. How was she going to make him see that he'd been wrong about Donald? He had never liked the idea of his mother re-marrying and, the moment he'd come up with a valid reason, he'd grabbed hold and clung to it for dear life because for him, that's what it was.

Donald was a threat—he was taking his mother away from him, just like that car accident had taken his father. And Rosie loved Donald, just as she had loved his father. Would he understand that he needed to let his mother go to find her own happiness? Would he understand that if he didn't, he'd lose her forever?

Leah joined him on the balcony. His back was to her and his hands gripped the banister. She was a little leery of touching him, but then discarded her own anxiety and went to him, wrapping her arms around his waist.

"I guess I was wrong," he said with a shrug of his shoulders. "Dammit, how could I have been so stupid?" He pounded his fists on the railing. "What do I do now?"

With her cheek against his back, she wished she didn't have to say the words she knew he didn't want to hear. "You have to let her go, Terrell. She loves him."

"I know she does," he admitted quietly.

"She still loves you, Terrell. You're her son. But she needs Donald, she needs the man who will become her husband. She loves him."

Terrell took a deep breath, understanding now, more than ever, how it felt to love someone so completely. Leah's warmth was pressed against his back as she soothed him, and he knew he never wanted to lose her. That's what his mother felt for Donald. That was the love she had for this man, and, as much as it pained him to accept it, he wouldn't deny her that feeling, not for anything in the world.

He turned, taking Leah into his arms. "I guess you have a wedding to plan."

Leah smiled up at him, burying her head in his chest. "Yeah, I guess I do. But first we should go to the hospital. Your mother shouldn't be alone."

"You're right. I owe her and her fiancé an apology."

They didn't break their embrace as they moved through the agents still cluttering the room toward the elevator. "You're a good man, Terrell Pierce," she told him once they were in the elevator alone.

"Really? You think so?" He feigned ignorance.

Leah smiled. "I know so. You made a mistake, and now you're going to admit it. Not many people are good with admitting their mistakes."

He brushed his knuckles over the smooth skin of her cheek. "Just let me know when you're ready to admit that your four-step plan was a mistake and that you believe in our relationship. Then I'll believe I'm a good man."

She thought about his words even as they stepped off the elevator and moved toward the lobby door. Once they stepped outside into the bright sunshine, she stopped, held both his hands and looked into his eyes. "I believe in you. And because I do I now see the error of my own thinking."

Terrell grinned. "You couldn't just say, 'I was wrong and you were right'?"

"No, because you'd let that go to your head."

Tobias had left a car to take them to the hospital so they climbed in and rode hand in hand to see Ms. Rosie and Donald.

At the hospital Rosie sat in the small waiting room alone. So much had happened today she didn't know whether she was coming or going. Terrell was here. Leah was here. Donald had been shot. Her heart was still pounding in her chest. Waves of mild relief washed over her when she saw her son approaching.

She stood, and Terrell instantly hugged her tightly. "Mama, I owe you such an apology," he began immediately.

Over his shoulder Rosie saw Leah look away, but not before noticing the feelings in the young lady's eyes as she'd looked at her son. "I'd say you owe me an explanation first," Rosie told him, then motioned for him to take a seat next to her.

"I'll just go and see if I can find us some drinks," Leah said hastily. This was a private moment between mother and son. Besides, it was hot as all get out in this tiny building, and she wanted to find some sort of relief.

"No." Terrell reached for her hand, pulled her to sit on the other side of him. "You said you couldn't let me do this alone. Don't leave me now."

He was right, she had told him that, but she hadn't really thought he'd want her to hear what he said to his mother. Still, she found herself sitting down, placing a hand on his knee and offering him a consoling smile.

The exchange was not lost on Rosie.

"It's like this, Mama. When you told me you were getting married I wasn't overjoyed," Terrell began.

"That's an understatement," Rosie huffed.

"I couldn't readily accept that another man was going to take Daddy's place and so, even though Donald was really cordial with me and tried to assure me that he was good for you, I still resisted."

"Even after I told you he made me happy. You know, Terrell, you were always such a good boy, but there were times when you tried my patience with your stubbornness," Rosie interrupted again.

Terrell almost smiled—Rosie talked just as much as Leah did. It seemed the two women never wanted to allow him a word. He covered her hands with his. "I know, Mama. Can you let me finish?"

"Well, go ahead, I'm not stopping you," she said with a flustered look.

"I had Donald investigated."

"You did what?" Rosie's voice became so loud that two young ladies at the front desk looked over at them in concern.

Terrell sighed in exasperation. "I had a friend of mine look into Donald's past. I know it was wrong, but at the time I felt obligated to do something. I found out things that I didn't like, and then I followed him."

"We followed him," Leah chimed in.

Rosie's eyes went to her suspiciously. "But you're planning our wedding. How did you get involved?"

Terrell looked at Leah, then back to his mother. "I got her involved. I went to Leah because she was working closely with you and Donald and I wanted her thoughts on your relationship. To her credit, she stood up for you two the entire time."

That wasn't exactly true, Leah thought, but wisely kept her mouth shut.

"At any rate, we ended up at Donald's house in Baltimore with the FBI and then we figured out where you two had gone. I was worried out of my mind that you were in danger, so I came here to save you."

"And I tagged along to save him," Leah added.

Rosie looked at both of them, then gave in and giggled. "The two of you sure are a sight, I'll tell you that much. I didn't need any saving, but Leah, I reckon my son did."

Leah smiled, feeling a bit more comfortable about being included in this conversation. "Actually, he's done his share of saving this time around." She was thinking of how Terrell had gotten that basement door open, but mostly how he'd saved her from a lonely life with her four-step plan.

"Baby, I know all about Donald's past," Rosie said to Terrell. "But that's just what it is, his past. Donald was very up front with me when we started dating. Now, I know to you it must have looked pretty bad, but you should have just come to me. I would have told you everything was alright."

"You're right, Mama. I should have come to you first. Anyway, I wanted to apologize for not supporting you immediately."

Before Rosie could answer him, the doctor came through swinging double doors. "Are you the family here with Donald Douglas?"

Rosie stood first, Terrell standing right behind her and Leah behind him. "Yes, we are," they replied in unison.

The doctor with the shiny bronze skin smiled. "He's going to be just fine. The bullet went straight through his shoulder. There was a lot of bleeding, but we've managed to stop it, and he's resting quietly now. You can go in and see him, but don't stay too long."

Rosie moved first, while Terrell and Leah stayed behind. Then she turned. "Come on you two, you owe Donald an apology as well."

Terrell groaned and Leah poked him in the ribs. "You're a good man, remember."

With his hand on the small of her back he let her go through the doors ahead of him, then leaned down to whisper in her ear, "And as soon as we get back to the hotel you're going to show me how good."

CHAPTER FIFTEEN

"Can you believe Donald was actually working with the FBI?" Leah asked when they finally made it back to their hotel.

They'd spent the bulk of the afternoon at the hospital with Rosie, then had finally convinced her to go back to her room and get some rest before returning to their own rooms. Tobias had already come down and talked to them, apologizing for not being able to tell them everything.

"Nah, I'm still trying to digest that one. But I guess it makes sense. That's why the FBI was so concerned with his disappearance. They thought his cover had been blown. I'm just glad Cable was the one who did the shooting in the alley, and not Donald." Terrell watched as Leah fell on the bed, toeing each of her shoes off.

"Cable was a monster. I'm glad Donald was able to convince him to leave us alone." She dropped an arm over her forehead and closed her tired eyes. Today had been so eventful that now all she wanted to do was get a good meal and fall asleep, but only after she had a cool shower and some fresh clothes.

Terrell sat on the bed beside her. "I'm glad Donald thought to lock us in his basement."

She turned toward his voice and glared at him. "What? You like being drugged and locked up? You are so weird."

"No, that's not what I liked about it. I liked having that time to be alone with you."

Leah gave him a slow, tired smile. "I kind of liked sharing bologna and cheese rolls with you too. Speaking of which—"

"Uh oh, here it comes. You're hungry, aren't you?" Terrell joked.

"Well, I haven't eaten all day. I've been on this island for two days now and haven't once had a traditional Jamaican meal. You'd think somebody would take me to dinner or something."

Grabbing her by the waist, he rolled her over, aligning himself with her on the bed. "Calm down, I have every intention of taking you out to dinner and to see the island. That's why I booked the room for a few more days."

"A few more days?"

"Yeah, I don't want to wait to come back here with you. I want us to take a few days together now, to enjoy it. We still have a lot to talk about."

He was making lazy circles on her back, the motion clouding her mind. "You want to stay a few more days? I have a wedding next week," she said sadly.

He understood the need to get back to work, even though SISCO had assured him things with his project were going along smoothly. "Then I'll make a deal with you. We stay one more night on the island. Then when we return to Baltimore, we spend all our remaining nights together."

Her heart pattered quickly at his words. Was he suggesting they move in together? "I have my own place and you have yours. We'll have to compromise." Leah wasn't ready for that step. Even though she readily admitted how good it felt to be with him, to wake up with him, she wasn't about to jump that quickly.

He was only mildly disappointed. He hadn't really expected her to go for the idea of living together that easily. But she hadn't outright shot it down either. She was still game to spend their nights together. He was getting close. "Three nights at your house and four at mine. How does that sound?" His hand moved to her butt, cupping the voluptuous mound.

"It sounds one-sided. Weeknights at my house and weekends at yours," she countered.

"That's not even, but I'll take it." He'd take anything she was willing to give him at this moment.

A few hours later they managed to go down to the hotel restaurant for dinner. "Let's go for a walk," Terrell suggested.

Reggae music played in the background as they walked along the cliffs headed for the beach.

"I love the sunsets here," Leah said after they'd walked a bit in silence.

"They're extraordinary," Terrell agreed with her.

When they came to the beach, they slipped their shoes off and let the warm sand sift through their toes. Holding hands, they walked along the water's edge watching as the sky turned a deep red and the fiery sun sank into the stunningly blue-green water.

"Remember I told you I wanted all or nothing?" Terrell asked her.

Leaning her head against his shoulder she sighed. "I remember."

"I meant it." He stopped abruptly, turning her to face him. There was a light breeze and the gold sarong she'd tied around her waist moved with it, showing so much of her leg it was almost indecent. "I don't want to go backwards or forwards with your four-step plan. I want to be with you, all the time, for always. I love you, Leah."

The moment could not have been more perfect. The sky glowed brilliantly with the sun's descent, the water was crystal clear at their feet, the cliffs were alluring, the little huts, charming. And the man. The man was all she'd ever dreamed of—funny how now 'all or nothing' didn't seem quite so elusive to her. "I love you, too, Terrell. And I completely understand what you want."

He sensed a 'but' coming so he put a finger to her lips. "Don't deny it, Leah. Don't deny us. I won't believe you. We'll be coming back here just as soon as you can plan our wedding."

Leah couldn't speak.

"That's right. I'm marrying you, Leah Graham. And I'm marrying you right here in Negril, where we both finally let go of our past issues and found each other."

"Weddings...in Negril...are...um...expensive," she stammered, unable to believe her own ears.

"I told you I'd give you everything I had, and I meant it." He cupped her face in his hands, pulled her closer. "Just say that as soon as my mother's wedding is over you'll start planning ours, and I'll take care of everything else."

"I…I don't know what to say."

For once she was speechless, and Terrell found he liked her talkative better. He kissed her lips lightly, nipped her bottom lip. "Say, 'I love you, Terrell and I'd like nothing more than to marry you here on this gorgeous island.' "

Her hands went around his waist as he tried to deepen the kiss, and she pulled back. "I can't say all that with you kissing me."

"Oh, sorry." Terrell smiled and pulled back so she could speak.

Leah cleared her throat. "I love you so much, Terrell. Marrying you on this beautiful island would be the best decision I've made thus far in my life."

Terrell let out a whooping laugh as he picked her up, spinning her around until she screamed for him to let her down. "I'm going to make you so happy."

"You already have."

And as they lay entwined in their bed that night, she realized she was truly very happy and thought how nothing could spoil this for them, absolutely nothing.

They were all packed and ready to leave. Terrell was paying their hotel bill, and Leah was enjoying the scenery one last time. She'd already picked up all the brochures in the gift shop she could squeeze into her overnight bag to look at on the flight home. She definitely wanted the ceremony outside, with the light breeze and the swaying palm trees as their backdrop.

She was getting married. Butterflies danced happily in her stomach at the thought. *Just wait 'til Nikki hears this.*

She was so deep in thought that she almost missed the tall figure standing outside the hotel. He wore dark glasses and a baseball cap. His jeans were worn at the knees and his long- sleeved shirt uncharacteristic for the Jamaican heat.

He was looking at her. Of course she couldn't see his eyes, but she could feel they were on her. But the moment she turned toward him, the moment she caught him staring, he disappeared behind the trees, making her wonder if he'd ever really been there at all.

"You ready, baby?" Terrell came up behind her, tucking the receipt into his back pocket.

"Ah, yeah. I'm ready." Leah looked back in the direction where she thought she'd seen the man. He'd seemed vaguely familiar. Then she shook her head. Probably just some tourist that wasn't looking at her at all. With all this beautiful scenery, why would he have been looking at her anyway?

The Ortega wedding went off without a hitch. Leah and Melinda were busy packing up the decorations and chit chatting about the day's events when her cell phone rang.

Immediately recognizing the number, she pressed the talk button. "Hey, baby."

Melinda knew from Leah's greeting, the tone of her voice and the smile on her face who that was and quickly left her alone.

"Hey, sweetness. Listen, I'm gonna be at the office a little later than I thought. We ran into a few problems with the new program," Terrell told her.

She tried to mask her disappointment. "So you're not meeting me at my place?"

"Oh no, I'll be there. I just wanted to let you know I'd be a little later than I originally promised."

"Oh? Okay, that's fine."

"So how did things go?" he asked.

"Just fine," she answered and pulled another tablecloth from the table. "The bride was beautiful, the groom suave and debonair. And the best man got drunk and fell into the punch bowl." She laughed as she recalled the incident. Across the room, Melinda heard her and frowned. She was still sporting the red stain on her white pant suit.

"Damn, I'll bet that went over well."

"Hardly anybody even blinked an eye. I suspect he does this kind of thing often."

"Okay. Well, let me get back to work so I can get to you as soon as possible. I miss you like crazy."

Leah blushed. Terrell was so caring and so attentive that a week after their return from Jamaica she wondered what she'd ever done without him. "I miss you too, baby. You hurry up with your work while I finish up here and I'll be waiting for you at home."

"That sounds like a plan. I love you."

"I love you, too." She disconnected the phone and stood for a moment, remembering the sound of his voice.

"Alright already, snap out of it so we can get out of here," Melinda groaned.

"Oh, yeah, that's a good idea."

Pulling another plastic tablecloth from the table, she stuffed it into the large trash bag she'd been dragging across the floor behind her. Going to the next table, she started the process again, first removing the floating candle centerpiece, then pulling the tablecloth filled with confetti and dirty plates, cups and whatever else the guests had left on them into the bag. The Ortegas hadn't paid the hall for the complete clean-up service, or else she and Melinda would have been gone by now.

She was so wrapped up in her own thoughts that she never heard the man approach her from behind until his hand was on her shoulder. She jumped and turned to stare into dark eyes.

"What are you doing here?" she asked, surprised to see Leon.

He shrugged. "If the mountain won't come to Mohammed…" His voice was as deep and smooth as she'd remembered.

"I apologize for not returning your calls. I guess I've been kind of busy." She really didn't know what to say to him. That was part of the reason she hadn't bothered to call him upon her return. Come to think of it, she hadn't really thought about Leon all that much since she'd told him there was nothing between them.

"Yeah, I figured that."

"How did you know where I was?" she asked while moving on to the next table.

He followed her, taking the trash bag from her hands and holding it open when she needed it. "I stopped by the office yesterday but you were out running errands. Melinda told me about the wedding today."

"Oh? She didn't mention it to me."

"I told her not to."

"Why?"

"I wanted to surprise you." He chanced a smile at her. "I see I did."

"Yeah, you did." And the moment she had a chance she was going to tell Melinda how she didn't like secrets or surprises where Leon was concerned.

"You look tired. Are you almost finished here?"

They were approaching the head table, the last one she needed to break down before she could load up the truck and take all the stuff back to her office.

"Just about."

"Can Melinda finish up so I can take you home? You really look like you could use some rest."

"Well, you sure are full of compliments after not seeing me for a while." She grinned. "Do I look that bad?" She stared down at her suit. It was wrinkled, and she'd spilled something down the front of her jacket at some point during the festivities. She'd discarded her shoes the moment the last guest exited the hall, and she noted a horrific run in her stockings.

"No, you're still beautiful." His words were quiet and stunned Leah into silence.

Did he ever say that before? She didn't remember; she only remembered hearing Terrell say it. "Liar." She smiled wistfully.

He reached for her hand. "Come on, let me take you home."

Leah slowly pulled her hand out of his. "I have my car," she told him.

"Then I'll follow you back to your apartment."

Leon was persistent, she knew this already. And she was tired. The last thing she felt like dealing with was him. Besides, Terrell was coming over. "I don't think that's such a good idea."

"Why not?" he looked at her quizzically.

"I'm really tired, Leon." She hoped that was enough to get rid of him, but soon found it wasn't.

"I know." He touched one of her braids. "This is new. I like it though."

"Leon—"

"That's right, you're tired. You're always really tired after a wedding's complete. That's why you should let me take you home and rub your back or your feet. I know how that relaxes you."

"No, thank you. I don't really need a foot massage tonight. What I need is to go home and go to bed."

"Leah, I really think we need to talk."

Okay, now he was working on her nerves. She'd tried to politely refuse his offer, but now she'd have to be a bit more stern. "What do we need to talk about? I thought we said enough the last time I saw you."

"You said what you had to say, but you didn't really give me much room to tell you how I felt."

He was right, she hadn't. And even though right now she could really care less, she felt that she at least owed him that much. "You're right. You can follow me home." She looked to Melinda. "Can you handle the rest of this?" She gestured towards the head table.

"Sure, you go on and go. You look tired."

"Gee, thanks." Leah rolled her eyes.

Leon motioned towards the door. "Shall we?"

"I guess so, since it seems I look so bad I'd better hurry out of sight. Just let me go to the bathroom first." That horrific hole in her stockings was bugging the hell out of her. The nylons quickly made it to the trash can, and then she was on her way.

Leon walked her to her car, and she waited until she saw his truck in her rearview mirror before she pulled out of her parking spot. He followed her through the dwindling traffic and parked behind her in the parking lot of her building. On the ride over she'd planned to make this short and sweet. She'd give Leon a chance to have his say, then she'd say goodnight and grab a quick shower before Terrell arrived.

"Where's your key?" he asked when they were at the door.

"Oh?" She checked her pants pocket, the small bag she carried with all her miscellaneous stuff in it, then fumbled through her purse until she felt the metal against her fingers and pulled out the crowded key ring.

"Are all these keys necessary?" He took the noisy contraption into his hand.

Leah hunched her shoulders. "I don't know, I guess so."

Leon pushed the door open and stood to the side while she entered the apartment. She flicked on the light in the living room and plopped down in the chair and closed her eyes. "Whew! This has been a long day."

She could hear Leon moving around, and wondered if he'd noticed that she'd purposely taken the chair meant for one person, leaving him no opportunity to sit next to her. She opened her eyes when she felt him lifting her legs to rest on his thighs. He'd taken a seat on the edge of her coffee table, and was now removing her shoes.

His strong hands carefully massaged each foot. Leah moaned with pleasure. She had been running non-stop since returning from her trip. Between the wedding and spending time with Terrell she was beat. Leon was right. She probably did look like she was dead on her feet.

"Better?" he asked.

She'd been so focused on the soothing effects of the foot massage that she'd almost forgotten the person ministering to her wasn't Terrell. Abruptly, she pulled her feet down. "Much. Now you had something you wanted to say to me."

"I've missed you in the last couple of weeks. You haven't returned my calls and I haven't seen you around." Leon looked at her earnestly.

Leah hated that she didn't share his feelings, hated that before their time tonight was concluded she'd have to tell him she was seeing someone else. "I know. A lot's been going on." That was an understatement.

"So I was wondering if you'd like to get away. Just to get some rest. We could take a trip or something?" he asked hopefully.

"Ah, Leon, I, um, I don't think that's such a good idea. You see, I'm kind of seeing someone right now."

For a moment he looked startled. Then his dark eyes settled on her with a piercing glare.

"I see. So that's why you couldn't go any further with me?"

"Yes. I mean, no." Leah took a deep breath and decided to simply spit it out. "The feelings I had for you, or I should say, the feelings I didn't have for you, had nothing to do with my current relationship. Things just weren't meant to be between us. But I'd like to be friends."

His lips melted into a smile that didn't quite reach his eyes. "I'll always be your friend, Leah. That was never in question. And I respect your honesty. I'm just sorry we don't see eye to eye." Leon stood and reached for her hands.

Putting her hands in his, Leah stood as well. That hadn't been as bad as she'd thought. Leon really seemed like a good guy, and she prayed he'd find a woman who could appreciate him. For long moments he held her hands tightly, rubbing his thumbs over her skin as his eyes studied her intently. The strange look in his eyes made her want to pull free.

Then as if reading her mind, he released her hands, smiled and held his arms out. "Can I at least get a goodnight hug, friend?"

"Of course you can." She smiled nervously and went into his embrace.

"I hope he knows what a wonderful woman he's got," Leon said as he held her.

"He does," Terrell said from the doorway.

Leah instantly turned towards the voice and maneuvered her way out of Leon's arms.

"Terrell? I thought you'd be a while longer," she said, crossing the room to where he stood. A quick kiss on the lips and she was grasping Terrell's arm and pulling him further into the living room. "Terrell Pierce, this is Leon Reynolds. Leon, this is Terrell."

"It's nice to meet you, Terrell," Leon said extending his hand.

Terrell eyed the man suspiciously, then extended his hand as well. "Likewise," he said in a guarded tone.

"I was just leaving." Leon began to move toward the door. "Leah, you make sure you get some rest."

"Oh, I will. I have only four weeks until the next wedding, but I'm giving Melinda most of those responsibilities," Leah said as she walked Leon to the door.

"I'll always love you," Leon whispered. Then noticing that Terrell was watching them closely, added, "Take care of yourself."

That uneasy feeling she'd felt before when they were alone resurfaced, but she forced a smile and said, "I will. And you do the same."

She closed the door behind Leon and turned to go back into the living room. She knew Terrell was angry, she'd seen it in his eyes. She needed to assure him he had nothing to worry about.

"How many visits do you need in one night?" Terrell asked the moment she was in front of him.

"He showed up at the reception right after I talked to you. He said he needed to talk. That was all, Terrell. We talked."

"You and I are talking right now and I'm not touching you. So how come Leon couldn't do the same?" He hated seeing her in another man's arms, hated that he'd known instinctively who the other man was.

Leah took a step closer to him, placed her hands on his shoulders. "I can remedy that," she said in a sultry voice.

He tried to resist any reaction to her touch. "I don't want him here again, Leah. You and I are engaged. I don't want another man alone with you in your apartment."

She removed his glasses, set them down on the table beside them. "That's fine, baby. He won't come here again. Now, can't we find something else to talk about besides Leon?"

She pushed him onto the couch, straddled him and began to unbutton his shirt. Terrell's hand stopped her motions. "I'm serious, Leah. It's just me and you now. I'm not into sharing."

Because she knew he was thinking about when he'd walked in on Tanya, she held on to her anger. She could imagine that if she'd walked in on her boyfriend in bed with another woman, that doubt would linger in her mind for a while too. "Listen to me, because this is going to be the last time that I tell you this."

Terrell looked at her intently.

"I don't cheat. When and if I decide to be with someone else, I'll be sure to let you know. Don't bring what she did to you into my house again."

Terrell sighed with the realization of what he'd done. He had thought of Tanya and her little escapade in their bed—the bed he'd since thrown out. He'd seen Leah in another man's arms and felt the sting of betrayal without even giving her the opportunity to explain. Moving his hands to rest on her hips, he gently massaged her. "I'm sorry." He let his head fall to her chest, kissing her breast through her blouse. "I guess I did do that. It'll never happen again."

Leah sucked in a breath as he lightly bit her nipple. "It had better not."

With lightning quick motions Terrell ripped her blouse open. Buttons fell onto the cushions around them as he freed her breasts from her bra, taking the soft mounds into his mouth. "I just can't stand the thought of somebody else touching you, loving you," he whispered between his frantic nipping.

Normally she would have been pissed at the blatant disregard for her clothing but his touch was so electrifying Leah could do nothing but arch her back and hold on to his shoulders for leverage. "You don't have to worry, baby, I'm all yours."

With those words Terrell pushed her skirt up past her hips, was delighted that she had no panty hose on, and slipped her panties to the side to sink his fingers into her warmth. "Say it again, baby," he requested.

"I'm all yours, Terrell."

Her hands fidgeted with his belt buckle and his zipper until she held his hot length in her hand.

"In my back pocket," he mumbled.

She reached behind him, found his wallet, even as ragged moans escaped her throat from his hands' loving. Finding the condom, she ripped the package open and sheathed him.

Terrell grabbed her waist, lifted her slightly, then settled her onto his rigid erection. "Say it again," he told her as he drove into her with one hot thrust.

"I'm...all...yours," she managed once he was completely inside of her. "And you," she looked down into his eyes and began to move her hips, "are all mine."

Terrell quickly picked up her rhythm and moaned. "Most definitely."

"I finished the seating cards. They're in the box alongside the master. The caterer was gone for the day, but I left a message for them to call us first thing tomorrow morning." Melinda stood in the doorway to Leah's office.

They'd been working non-stop for the past two days, making sure everything was ready for the Morgan wedding. With three and a half weeks left to go, the countdown was on. And Leah still had to find the time to go through Ms. Rosie's R.S.V.P.'s and begin her seating chart. Her business was booming and despite the long, exhausting hours, she loved it.

"That's great. Now tomorrow we can get those bows done and make sure we have all the tulle we'll need," Leah told her. The Perfect Day offered more than just planning services. More often than not, Leah threw in her own personal touches, such as decorating the hall or the site for the actual wedding. She loved creating and a wedding day was the perfect canvas to whet her appetite, especially now that she entertained thoughts of her own special day. "You can go ahead and leave. I know you're tired."

Melinda leaned against the doorjam. "That's an understatement if ever I've heard one. But you've done way more than I have. Aren't you leaving too?"

Leah twisted her wrist, looked at her watch. "Yeah, I'm meeting Terrell for dinner, so I'll leave in about twenty minutes. I just want to get these invoices taken care of so we can get paid."

Melinda laughed. "I hear that. Well, I'll turn out the lights up here and turn the sign so you won't get any walk-ins."

"Thanks and have a good evening. I want you bright-eyed and bushy-tailed in the morning."

Melinda sucked her teeth like a child, then gave a fake moan. "I'll bring the coffee and donuts."

"Make that plenty of donuts!" Leah added as Melinda disappeared to the front of the office.

Leah worked for another twenty minutes before shutting down her computer and beginning to gather the things on her desk. She was at her file cabinet, inserting copies of the invoices, when she heard something from the lobby.

Her fingers stilled on the manilla folder as she concentrated on hearing it again. When she didn't, she chalked her overactive imagination up to fatigue and kept on moving. She'd switched the light out in her office and was moving toward the front of the building when she noticed Melinda's computer was left on. "Girl, you know how much gas and electric are charging us," she mumbled and went to the work station to shut it down. As she got closer, the screen instantly blinked from Melinda's tropical screen saver to all black. This startled Leah because she had yet to touch anything. Frowning, she leaned over the keyboard, prepared to hit the keys to shut it down. Before she could do so, the corners of the screen turned red, actually seemed to seep red, in thick flowing rivulets resembling, she thought with trepidation, blood.

Leah jerked her hands back as if she'd been burned, then chastised herself for being foolish. "Probably some new screen saver that girl has downloaded from the Internet," she said to herself, then hit the buttons quickly and watched as the machine shut off completely. She was just about to get her purse and head for the door when she heard footsteps, then the door open and shut.

By the time she turned in the direction the steps had come from, the front door had slammed closed, and the 'Open' sign was swinging erratically on its silver chain.

Her heart hammered in her chest as she realized someone had been in the office with her all this time. She picked up the phone, prepared to dial 911, but there was no dial tone. She pressed the button repeatedly but still received no tone. Fear clawed at her. Leah reached inside her purse, pulled out her cell phone just before the last lights left on in the office began to flicker.

"Dammit!" She gritted her teeth and her fingers trembled as she tried to dial. Deciding she could make the call from outside, she lifted her purse from Melinda's desk and made her way to the door, wrenching it open and stepping out into the balmy spring evening. She turned for a moment, stared back at the door to her office, then gave it up. *What's the point in locking it? Whoever wanted to get in has already been in.*

With that thought she moved quickly across the street to where she'd parked her car. Stopping midway in the street she gasped, dropping her purse and her phone. Her tires were flat, thick pieces of rubber flapped from the rim. All her windows were broken, leaving glass all around the vehicle. She didn't need to walk to the other side to see that the view would be the same, yet she felt her feet moving. Her trembling hands reached for her throat as the sight overwhelmed her.

"What the hell is going on?" she said aloud.

In the distance she heard the screech of tires and prayed that whoever had done this, whoever had just left her shop, wasn't coming back for her.

It was then that she realized how much danger she could be in. Instinctively she looked down at her hands, wondering where her phone was, then remembered dropping it. Running into the street, Leah retrieved her purse and her phone. Her fingers moved with lighting fast efficiency as she first dialed 911, gave them her location, then called Terrell. Lowering herself to the curb she tried like hell to keep tears at bay, yet she felt the warm trickles down her cheeks. *Who could have done this?*

CHAPTER SIXTEEN

"Leah?" Terrell called out to her as he made his way through the uniformed police officers.

"You have to step back, sir," one of the officers informed him.

Terrell glared at the man and pushed past him.

"Sir, I said you have to stay back," the officer yelled, grabbing Terrell's arm.

"She's my fiancée. I'm not going anywhere but to her," he said through clenched teeth.

"Terrell?" Leah heard him. Through all the talking and questions swarming around her, she'd heard his voice—because she'd been waiting for him to come. She stood, her legs shaky. The jacket one of the officers had thrown around her shoulders because she'd been shivering uncontrollably fell to the ground.

Terrell pulled away from the officer, took the few steps required to close the space between them, and folded her in his arms. Her whole body shook as she sobbed. He rubbed her hair, whispered softly in her ear. "It's alright, baby. I'm here now. Everything's going to be alright."

"Sir, we need to ask her a few more questions," another officer said, tapping Terrell on the shoulder.

"Baby, you need to tell the police exactly what happened, and then I'll take you home." He wiped her tear-streaked face with the back of his hands. "Can you do that for me?"

Leah nodded, never before feeling as comforted as she did in his arms. Terrell kept his arms tightly around her shoulders as they leaned against a patrol car to answer the officer's questions.

"Have you been involved in any altercations or incidents in the last few weeks? Anything that would prompt an attack like this?" This officer was a woman, a calm-faced blond who talked slowly and softly.

"Ah…" Leah tried to think.

Terrell filled the officer in, rubbing Leah's shoulders all the while. "We were both involved in an FBI operation. Agents Tobias and Blum were heading up a drug sting and we sort of accidentally fell into it."

This statement got the attention of another officer, the man Terrell had run up against while trying to get to Leah.

"You interfered with a federal drug investigation?"

"That's not what I said." Terrell gave the officer an angry look. "I said we accidentally got involved in the investigation. That was about two weeks ago, and the culprits were arrested in Jamaica."

"Is it possible that this could be retaliation for your interference?" the female officer asked.

Terrell thought then of Cable, but remembered the man had been killed in Negril. But the operation couldn't have been run by only five men. He remembered all the photos Tobias had had on the wall in his office. "I guess that's a possibility." A very real possibility that he didn't want to dismiss. "But why her? Why not me or Donald, the FBI's informant?"

"Sometimes it's easier to go after a more vulnerable subject." The male officer nodded to Leah. "A female is generally frightened faster than a male. They may be using her to get to the informant. What's your connection to the informant, ma'am?"

Leah had been listening to them, praying that what they were considering wasn't true. She'd thought they were finished with the drug dealers and all that came with them. Now it appeared that wasn't quite true. "Um, I'm planning a wedding for Donald Douglas and Rosie Pierce."

"Ms. Pierce is my mother, that's how we became involved," Terrell added.

"I'm going to need to get in touch with this Agent Tobias to get a complete story. In the meantime, we'll write out a report and see if we can get any leads," the male officer stated.

"Is that all?" Terrell asked incredulously.

Before her partner could say another word, the female officer intervened. "That's all that can be done right now," she said more to Leah than

Terrell. "I would suggest you not being alone for the next few days. The scare tactic is usually just the first step. And if they know where you work, it's likely they know where you live. Be very mindful of your surroundings and call the station if you see anybody suspicious lurking around."

Leah's mind instantly went to the man she'd seen before they'd left Negril. Could he have followed them from Jamaica?

"We'll be sure to do that," Terrell said tightly, thinking he'd be calling Seth the moment he had Leah safely at his apartment. He wanted to know who had done this and where he could find him. The authorities would most likely take their time finding him, Terrell wouldn't.

Terrell led Leah to his car, put her in the passenger seat, and buckled her up. Kissing her forehead he whispered, "I won't let anybody hurt you, trust me."

Leah nodded. She did trust him.

At his condo Leah sat on the soft leather of Terrell's couch. She'd been here a couple of times since they'd been back so the surroundings were familiar. Her body ached from fatigue and the stress of the evening's events. Terrell had left her alone and disappeared into the bedroom. She hadn't a clue what he was doing and was just about to get up and go find something to eat when he entered the living room.

"Whoa, where do you think you're going?" he asked, quickly coming to her side.

"I'm hungry. Somebody was supposed to take me to dinner, and here it is after nine o'clock and I still haven't eaten."

Terrell grinned. She was talking about food. That meant she was feeling better. "I'm going to feed you, woman, just relax. I've got something else for you first."

"What—" She was about to ask him what could be more important than food at this moment but he scooped her up and started in the direction of the bathroom.

His whirlpool tub was brimming with bubbles and when she inhaled she smiled. "Since when did you start buying vanilla bubble bath?"

Terrell stood her up, keeping her tightly in his embrace, and kissed her lightly on the lips. "Since I smelled it on a beautiful woman."

Leah lowered her head to hide her blush, but his finger to her chin had her again looking into his intense gaze. "I am going to get to the bottom of this, Leah. I don't want you worrying about it. Do you understand?"

"Terrell, I can take care of myself."

He'd known she'd argue. "Mmm hmm, I know you can take care of yourself, baby. But it's my job to protect you. Can't you just let me do that? Please?"

She could have told him she'd mastered tae kwon do and had managed to fight off three very big, very obtrusive brothers in her lifetime, but thought it best she keep quiet. Men had to feel superior. Besides, she kind of liked that he wanted to protect her. "Okay. But I'm not changing my lifestyle for this jerk. I'm going to keep on with my same routine and…"

Terrell silenced her with another kiss. "You're going to do exactly as I tell you until this is over." His hands were on the buttons of her blouse, then on her bare shoulders as he slid the material down and off her arms.

"Terrell?"

"Shhh. We're not talking about this anymore tonight." He was unbuttoning her pants, pushing them, and her underwear, down her long legs. Her shoes had been discarded in the living room so that she now only wore her bra and with one deft movement he'd unhooked that and watched as it joined the rest of her clothes on his bathroom floor. "You're going to enjoy this nice bath that I've prepared for you." He scooped her up again and then gently lowered her into the tub.

"I'm going to fix you dinner while you relax." He handed her a sponge. "Then we're going to eat and go to bed."

"But—"

Terrell held a finger to her lips, scooped a handful of bubbles into his other hand and smeared them on her nose. "No, buts. Do as I say." He moved away from the tub when a dangerously sexy gleam came into her eyes. As much as he'd like to share a bath with her, he still had a few phone calls to make.

"You have to go to sleep," she said to his retreating back, thoughts of seeking her revenge for the highhanded way he was handling her going through her mind.

He disregarded her threat. "Yes, and you'll sleep silently beside me." He tossed her a grin. "Oh and both Nikki and your mother called your cell phone while you were sleeping on the couch. I gave them a quick rundown and told them you'd be staying with me until we got things sorted out." Before she had a chance to speak Terrell made his escape.

Leah growled, threw the sponge he'd given her at the closing door. She wasn't about to stay with him until this was over. She had her own apartment and her own business and she planned on visiting both of them first thing tomorrow morning. She loved Terrell, but he wasn't about to start controlling her life.

"So do you think it's them?" Terrell paced the floor in his mother's living room. Seth hadn't come up with any leads as to who'd broken into Leah's office and vandalized her car. It had been two days, and no other incidents had occurred, but he needed to know she would be safe. Leah wanted to return to her own apartment. She wanted to get her car out of the shop. Terrell took a deep breath—he'd never realized taking care of a woman could be so hard. Maybe because he'd never counted on such an independent woman winning his heart.

"It's just not their style, Terrell," Donald told him honestly. After the incident in Jamaica, he'd moved in with Rosie. The wedding was only six weeks away and there was no real reason why they couldn't live under the same roof. "If they wanted to get to me they would come right after me, point blank. They'd knock on the door and shoot me dead as a doornail, then board the first plane back to the islands. No, I really don't think it's them."

Terrell dropped into a chair, letting his head fall back, and groaned. "Then I don't know where else to turn. Who would want to scare her and why?"

"What about that woman you broke up with a while back?" Rosie queried. She'd been thinking on this since she'd gotten the call from Terrell about Leah's incident. Women were vengeful creatures, and slashed tires were right up their alley.

"Tanya?" Terrell hadn't given Tanya a thought in weeks. Could she be doing this?

"Maybe it was just a random incident," Donald proposed. "You know, some kids getting their jollies off. "

"That's a thought. But I can't seem to shake the feeling that there's something we're missing here." As he talked his cell phone rang.

"Hello?"

"Hi," Leah spoke in a cheerful voice.

"Hey, baby. What's up? You ready to leave work so soon?" Terrell looked at his watch. It was barely past six. Leah had told him this morning that she and Melinda were going to work until seven.

"Yes. That's what I was calling to tell you. At lunchtime Melinda drove me over to pick up my car. So you don't have to pick me up tonight."

Terrell was quiet.

"Hello? Terrell?"

"I'm here," he said through clenched teeth. They'd been through this over and over again, until Terrell had finally given in. He couldn't keep her under lock and key, it just wasn't fair to her. She needed to resume her regular life. He understood all that, but understanding didn't make him feel any better about it. "So I'll just meet you at home. Do you want me to stop and pick something up for dinner?"

"I made a big pot of spaghetti," Rosie chimed in to his conversation. "Tell her to come on over and we'll all have dinner together."

"Mama made spaghetti. She wants you to come over for dinner."

"That sounds good. But first I want to stop at my place and change."

Terrell was quiet again.

"Terrell, we talked about this already. I'll be fine. I doubt very seriously that this lunatic is going to be waiting at my apartment for me. I mean, I haven't even been there in two days. He probably doesn't know where I am."

"Leah, I just don't like it."

"It will be fine. Just chill. I'm leaving the office now. I'll call you once I get to my place, then I'll call you when I leave. Will that make you feel better?"

"No. But I guess I don't really have a choice."

"Don't be that way, baby."

Terrell sighed heavily, closing his eyes and trying to cut off the bad feelings he had going on inside. "Fine. I'll see you in a little bit."

"Okay. I'll call you back. Bye."

Terrell disconnected the phone and rubbed his temples. Rosie stood and went to him. "She'll be okay, Terrell. All this is going to work itself out in time. Now keep Donald company while I go and fix a salad."

Terrell didn't feel like keeping anybody company. He felt like getting in his car and meeting Leah at her apartment, but he knew that would only irritate her.

Donald started talking as Terrell stared out the window. "Funny thing about women. We always want to protect them, but most of the time they do a damn good job of taking care of themselves."

"And what are we supposed to do about that?" Terrell asked with a grim attitude.

Donald chewed on that question a moment, rubbed his sore shoulder, then answered, "Sit back and relax until we're needed again, I reckon."

Leah put the key in and pushed the door open, expecting that feeling of welcome and comfort after being away for a few days. She didn't feel a bit of it as she walked in and closed the door behind her. Maybe because she was paying so much attention to her surroundings she couldn't really enjoy the fact that she was home. She found herself looking around as if she'd never been in that apartment before in her life.

Abruptly she stopped in the middle of her living room and took a deep breath. This was ridiculous; she wasn't this type of woman. She would not let the unknown frighten her. She moved to her answering machine and pushed the play button to listen to her messages. While the tape rewound, she undid her blouse and walked toward her bedroom to change. She'd throw on some jeans and a shirt, then gather all her laundry together before leaving for Ms. Rosie's. Tomorrow was Saturday, and she could head to the laundromat early and get the bothersome chore over with.

Humming a tune she'd just heard on the radio, she walked through the dark bedroom, letting her memory guide her around until she was near the nightstand, where she leaned over and switched on the lamp. Pulling her shirt from her slacks, she turned to go to her closet and stopped dead in her tracks.

A scream died in her throat as her eyes fell to her bed. There in the center, laid out perfectly as if she were preparing to wear it, was a black negligee, one she'd never seen before. Over the pillows and down on the floor rose petals in an array of colors were strewn all over. At the end of the bed was a brass cart, two glasses and a bottle of champagne chilling in an ice bucket.

She brought her fist to her mouth to keep from yelling out loud. Staggering backwards, away from the frightening display, she backed into the nightstand, knocking the lamp to the floor. Tears welled up in her eyes and her entire body trembled.

"Somebody was in my house," she whispered, then looked around to see if that person were still there. With her heart hammering in her chest, she bolted from the room and picked up the phone.

She didn't remember the numbers she'd pressed, didn't even hear him speak until he yelled.

"Leah? Is something wrong?" Terrell had recognized her number on his phone as it rang, and now he didn't hear anything. Dread filled him and he cursed himself for being stupid enough to leave alone.

She'd been ready to tell him what was going on, ready to tell him that somebody had been in her house when she saw it.

The statue.

It sat regally in the center of her coffee table, surrounded by the same rose petals that were in her bedroom.

She moved closer to the table, closer to the African statue that Leon had given to her and picked it up. It was heavy, had always been extremely heavy, and dark, the ebony stone foreboding and dismal to her thinking. She rubbed her hand over the flattened head and felt a chill run straight down her spine.

"Terrell, you have to come quick," was all she could manage before the phone and the statue slipped from her hands.

Terrell drove as if owned the road, his Mercedes soaring through the night streets like a sleek silver bullet. He had barely put the car in park before slamming the door and heading towards Leah's building. The elevator moved too slow, so he ran the three flights up and then down the hall to her apartment. Using his key to let himself in, he looked frantically into the living room and found her slumped on the floor.

"Baby? Are you okay? Tell me what happened." He was on his knees beside her, checking her arms, her legs, her face, everywhere for any injuries. She hadn't said what was going on when she was on the phone, and each time he'd tried to call her back he'd gotten her voice mail. The last fifteen minutes had been torture, as thoughts of what could possibly be happening taunted him.

"He said the statue was from the Asante tribes in Ghana. It's called an Akuba," she said in a voice so small he could barely hear her.

Terrell looked down at the statue lying beside her leg. Leah stared into space as he picked it up, held the heavy stone in his hand. "Is this what you're talking about? Where did you get it?" He didn't know what the hell was going on, but apparently this figurine had something to do with it.

"It's a fertility figure. It embodies the concept of beauty. He said it reminded him of me." That, she remembered, was the only time he'd ever called her beautiful.

"Okay, baby, I don't get where you're going with this. Who said it reminded him of you? Where did you get this?" Terrell shook the statue in front of her face, trying to solicit a straight answer. A sick feeling swirled in the pit of his stomach.

Leah turned then, as if she'd just noticed Terrell was at her side. "It was on top of the television when we came back from Jamaica."

Terrell put the piece down and took her hands in his. "Leah, tell me what's going on."

Leah shook her head vehemently. "I never keep it on the television because it's so heavy, and I didn't want it sitting on top of my DVD player. Then tonight," her gaze went beyond him to the rose petals on the coffee table, "tonight it was on the coffee table. I don't like it there either, because it's too tall and blocks the television. I keep it over there," she pointed, "on the bookcase."

Terrell followed her gaze and her words. "So how did it get on the coffee table?" He asked the question but already knew the answer. "Who gave you this, Leah?"

She began to shake her head again. "He was here. He was in the bedroom, too. He came here when I was with you. Both times that I was away with you, he came here." Her bottom lip started to quiver. "He touched my things and he walked around my house when I wasn't here."

Terrell pulled her to him, cradled her head and rubbed her back. He knew who she was talking about, knew who had been in her house when she was with him. He knew because he'd shook his hand right in this very living room.

CHAPTER SEVENTEEN

As much of her clothes and personal items that Terrell could fit into the back of his car, he did.

She would not be returning to this apartment, and that was final.

Leah hadn't even bothered to put up a fight. She didn't want to be here—didn't want to think of lying in that bed when he'd so obviously been in her bedroom.

They'd eaten at Ms. Rosie's, as planned, after talking to the police again. Leah gave them a description of Leon, his address and his usual hangouts, even though she still hadn't fully accepted it was him.

Now she was back at Terrell's, sitting cross-legged on his new bed, waiting for him to finish with his phone call. She'd calmed down over the past few hours, even though she occasionally berated herself for not realizing sooner that Leon was unstable.

Her only defense—and it was a logical one—was that most insane people look just like the ordinary ones, making it almost impossible to tell that they've a screw or two loose until it's too late.

Never in a million years would she have believed that a successful entrepreneur, an attractive, educated man, could be an obsessive stalker. All the dates she'd been on with him, all the time they'd spent alone, and the thought had simply never crossed her mind.

The negligee obviously meant sex—which she and Leon had never had. But if he still wanted to have sex with her, would he want to harm her as well? She was getting a headache trying to figure it out.

"Hey, you're too pretty for these worry lines." Terrell smoothed her forehead.

"You remembered I was here." She smiled and leaned into his open arms.

"Don't be smart, I told you I had a few calls to make. But now I'm all yours." He ran a hand up her bare leg.

Leah sighed, let her head rest on his shoulder. "What's going to happen now?"

"I'm going to take care of you, just like I said I would. Don't worry."

"My hero." She smiled up at him.

"Of course, all beautiful ladies have to have a hero." His hand on her leg inched its way up to her thigh.

"Mmmm," she murmured when his fingers slipped beneath the rim of her panties. "An adventuresome hero."

Terrell shrugged, continued on his voyage. "If you say so," he whispered just before his fingers found her warm, pliant flesh.

"Oooohhhh, I definitely say so."

Making love with Terrell had been the sedative she needed. Their hot shower and subsequent round two, the ultimate nightcap. Then they'd fallen asleep under the fluffy new comforter she'd helped him pick out. Now in the dark room and huge bed she reached for him, found his warm body and cuddled closer.

Then she heard it.

A whisper of movement. She froze.

Terrell was a light sleeper and, with a half-naked woman beside him, practically an insomniac. He'd heard the same thing she had, and moved beneath the covers to pull her closer.

"Shhh. Don't move," he whispered in her ear.

Leah nodded to let him know she understood.

Then before either of them could speak, the lights came on.

"Isn't this cozy?" a smooth baritone cooed.

Leah couldn't help it. She turned on her back and looked to the end of the bed where he stood.

"You get off watching other people have sex?" Terrell asked, sitting up in the bed, keeping Leah close to his side. His chest was bare, but beneath the covers he wore lounging pants.

"No. But you will," Leon responded blithely.

He was dressed in all black, his eyes cold and hard.

"Why are you here?" Leah asked, finally letting go of her doubts. Leon was in Terrell's bedroom. The bedroom where Terrell had just thoroughly loved her—had he really watched?

"You know why I'm here. I had to bring you this." Leon held up the statue, the one both Leah and Terrell knew they'd left in her apartment.

"That's the ugliest thing I've ever seen. If you gave me a gift like that I'd break up with you, too," Terrell said as he prepared to get out of the bed. From what he could see, Leon didn't have a weapon. His eyes were dazed when he looked at Leah, his obsession clear. If he could just get him away from Leah, out of this room, he could handle him.

Leon frowned at Leah, then turned an angry glare to Terrell. "Don't be so smug. I'm here to take what's mine. And to get rid of what stands between us."

Tired of the war of words, Terrell climbed out of bed. "Why don't we just go into the other room and settle this like men?"

Leon was looking at Leah again. "I had the perfect evening all planned for us. I've been waiting for you to come back home. But he wouldn't let you, would he?" He gripped the statue tighter. "That's okay, I'll take care of him."

Terrell was only a step or two away when Leon turned, threw the statue on the bed and pulled a knife from the waistband of his black jeans.

Leah gasped. "Leon, this is ridiculous. What can you possibly gain from doing this? Think about your business, your brother who's been working so hard for its success. You don't want to throw all that away."

"You don't understand." Leon looked at Leah. "I want you, Leah. It's that simple. I want you as my wife, as the mother of my kids."

His voice sounded calm, his words rational to any unsuspecting person, yet Terrell knew the man was teetering very close to the edge. "That's not going to happen." Terrell charged him, knocking the taller man to the ground.

Leah wanted to scream as the two men rolled around the floor struggling over the knife. But she refused to be like a pitiful movie heroine, crying and yelling on the bed while her man fought for his life *and* hers. She kicked the covers off and slid toward the nightstand, grabbing the telephone and quickly dialing 911. She didn't take too much time explaining, only said there was someone in her house with a knife before she threw the phone onto the bed and leaped to the floor.

At the bottom of the bed she saw that Leon was on top of Terrell, the blade raised in one hand, his other hand choking Terrell. Terrell struggled to tear the hand away from his throat and also keep the knife at bay. Leah didn't hesitate. She jumped on Leon's back, grabbing the arm holding the knife, using all her might to try to pull him back.

When she couldn't budge him, she bent in closer, bit into his shoulder and heard him growl in pain. Then he turned to her, leaving Terrell writhing and trying to catch his breath.

After throwing Leah backwards, Leon came after her. He grabbed her throat and pushed her up against the wall. The contact was so forceful that a picture that had been hanging came crashing down. "You're mine! We're meant to be. You'll have my children and we'll be happy. Understand?" he yelled at her.

Leah couldn't breathe, and her vision was blurring. With each word he spoke his grip on her throat tightened. Her hands flailed wildly, trying to pull away the hand that robbed her of oxygen.

"He interfered. He showed up and threatened what we had. When I get rid of him, we'll be happy."

On the floor, Terrell sucked in air. He heard Leon's voice but didn't hear Leah's. She had to be hurt, nothing kept her quiet for long. Grabbing at the bed, he hoisted himself up and spotted them near the door. Looking for some sort of weapon, he grabbed the statue and rushed forward.

"I love you, Leah. Don't you understand?" Leon moaned pitifully, resting his forehead against Leah's.

"You can't have her!" Terrell yelled, crashing the statue against the back of Leon's head.

Leon's glazed eyes stared at Leah blankly for a second before he slumped over.

Terrell caught Leah and cradled her in his arms, moving them away from Leon's limp body. "It's okay, baby. It's over. Come on, let's get you out of here." He'd come back and take care of Leon once and for all when he knew Leah was safe.

They staggered into the living room, and Terrell placed Leah on a chair, then checked for wounds.

Weeping and her chest heaving spasmodically, she managed to say, "I'm okay." She swiped at his hands. "You, you're bleeding." She touched a hand to his chest where blood stood out on the honey-toned skin.

Terrell hadn't even realized he'd been cut. "I'm fine. Just let me get to the phone."

"I already called the police," she said.

In the distance they heard sirens. Terrell went to the balcony to see if they were coming in this direction and discovered Seth's limp form in a corner. He'd called Seth before he and Leah retired for the night and asked him to keep watch because Terrell had suspected Leon might make a move. Now he realized why Seth hadn't signaled him of Leon's arrival.

Leah heard a noise in the bedroom and stood dazedly, looking toward the room. He couldn't be... When she heard more noise, she looked around for something else to use as a weapon but Leon was upon her too quickly.

"I'm going to kill him, and then I'll have you all to myself!" he roared as his open palm came crashing down against her cheek.

Leah staggered back, but refused to fall. She turned her head, albeit painfully, back in his direction. "I'll never love you, and you'll never touch me," she spat at him.

"Oh, I'll touch you." He reached out, grabbed one of her unbound breasts in his hand and squeezed until she yelped with pain. Then he grabbed her by the waist, pulled her to him, and ground his lips down on hers until Leah tasted blood. "And I'm going to have you. I'm going to have all of you." With another slap he sent her sprawling onto the sofa, then took long strides towards the balcony.

"Oh no, Terrell," Leah whispered as she saw the direction Leon went. "Terrell!" she finally screamed.

Terrell had been trying to revive Seth. From what he could see, there were no open wounds. Maybe Leon had drugged him or something. When he heard Leah scream, he stood, quickly turned around and caught Leon's first blow in his face. Dazed and caught off guard, he fell into the railing. Leon immediately pounced, punching Terrell repeatedly.

With a surge of strength, Terrell pushed away from the railing, managed to swing and knock Leon through the glass balcony door. When he would have jumped on him to finish the job, Leon lifted a foot and caught Terrell in the stomach.

Terrell stumbled back again and Leon rose, tackling him, moving them out onto the balcony once more.

Leah got off the couch, remembered the knife, and went to the bedroom to find it. When she came back she saw the two men struggling on the balcony and heard the police banging at the door. They'd have to let themselves in, she decided instantly as she ran onto the balcony to help Terrell.

With adrenaline pumping madly through her veins, she raised the knife and brought it down into Leon's shoulder. He yowled but still choked Terrell.

Terrell's eyes were now rolling back. Frantic that Terrell was dying, Leah pulled the knife out of Leon's shoulder and thrust it into his back, this time twisting it until his yelling increased and she felt him backing up. Releasing the knife, leaving it stuck in his back, she moved away.

At that exact moment the police broke down the door, barging in two at a time. Yelling was all around her.

Leon turned to face her, his features contorted with pain, his once dangerously handsome face now streaked with sweat and blood. Eyes she remembered gazing into hers were now tinged with insanity and misery.

"I loved you, Leah," he gasped and took another step towards her.

Tears ran freely down her face as she realized what she'd done, what'd he'd wanted to do to her and Terrell. He reached for her. She couldn't move, only shook her head from side to side. "No. No. I love Terrell."

"Then you die with him!" Leon yelled and charged at her.

For the second time in her thirty years, Leah jumped at the sound of gunshots. She watched as bullets struck Leon's broad body—he jerked this way and that until finally collapsing.

The smell of blood and gunpowder permeated the room, and Leah felt everything around her begin to spin. Then darkness closed in on her like a big heavy blanket, and she let herself be wrapped in it tightly, completely.

"No. Don't touch her. Get away from her, all of you," Terrell yelled as he picked her up, and carried her back to his bedroom and laid her limp body down.

Seth and a few of the officers followed him into the room. "The paramedics are on their way," his friend told him.

"Just leave us alone. Come and get me when they arrive." Terrell spoke in a broken voice as his shaking fingers brushed wild strands of hair from Leah's face.

Seth did as he was told, motioning for the other officers to exit the room as well.

When he knew they were alone, Terrell lowered his head to her ear. "Come on, baby, wake up. Wake up and talk to me. It's all over now, I just need you to wake up."

It seemed so far away, his voice calling her name as if she were in a dark tunnel. But somewhere ahead, somewhere far ahead, was a light and in that light was Terrell's voice. She moaned with the pain but moved her legs anyway. She had to get to him. She had to get to Terrell. He was calling her, he wanted her, he loved her.

Her head moved side to side on the pillow, even as her lips trembled and tears ran down her face.

The paramedics barged into the room the second her eyes opened and she screamed, "Terrell!"

"I'm here, baby. I'm right here."

Her eyes focused on his and she smiled through her tears.

"I'm not leaving you, sweetie. Everything's okay now," he soothed as the paramedics moved toward the bed to get a closer look at her.

With a shaky hand Leah fingered the broken glasses that hung awkwardly on his face. "There was something somebody said about relationships starting under high pressure situations. I wonder what that was?" she asked in a creaky voice.

Terrell grinned. "That they last forever and ever."

EPILOGUE

Nine months later.

The sun had just begun its descent, and the sky was a fiery ensemble of red and orange. Beneath the rose-encrusted archway and with the gentle tropical breeze blowing all around them, Terrell and Leah took their vows.

It was so much more than Leah could have ever dreamed. She'd worn the Cinderella dress, just as her ten-year-old mind had planned, while her prince stood beside her garbed in all white as well. His gentle eyes caressed her with all the love and adoration he had for her. His glasses—still slipping down his nose—glistened in the fading Jamaican sun.

To her right were her best friend and her mother, wearing island peach dresses and tropical flowers tucked into their hair. To his right were his mother and Donald, looking on with that gleam only newly-weds can share.

"I knew the moment I bumped into you that you were the one for me. And while it's been a rocky road getting to this place, I'm glad we journeyed it together. You needed somebody to love you and I needed somebody to love. As opposite as we may seem on the outside, our hearts now beat as one. Every breath I take is for you. You fill me so completely I don't know where you begin and I end," Terrell recited.

Leah valiantly fought back tears when it came her turn. "Terrell, I never presumed this would happen to me. I was resolved to being alone for the rest of my life. Then I met you and no matter how much I tried to keep the door to my heart closed you kept right on knocking until finally I opened it and stood ready to receive all you had to offer me. I cannot begin to tell you how much you mean to me. All I can say is that I will love, honor and cherish you for all the days of my life."

LOVE ME CAREFULLY

As his lips touched hers, the retreating sun kissed the rim of the turquoise sea shimmering around them. When his arms completely enfolded her, their kiss and the minister's words joining them forever, the tropical breeze picked up slightly, swirling around them like an invisible cocoon.

Their guests clapped, the waves crashed against the rocks at the bottom of the cliff, and they stared into each other's eyes, no further words needed, none spoken.

ABOUT THE AUTHOR

Artist C. Arthur was born and raised in Baltimore, Maryland, where she currently resides with her husband and three children. An active imagination and a love for reading encouraged her to begin writing in high school, and she hasn't stopped since.

Working in the legal field for almost thirteen years now, she's seen lots of horrific things and longs for the safe haven reading a romance novel brings. Being named one of three finalists in the 2004 Emma Awards and receiving an additional two nominations in 2005 have been the highlight in her writing career. Coupled with reader enthusiasm, this has motivated her ambition to higher heights.

Her debut novel, *Object of His Desire*, was written almost six years ago when a picture of an Italian villa sparked the idea of an African-American/Italian hero. Determined to bring a new edge to romance, she continues to develop intriguing plots, racy characters and fresh dialogue—thus keeping the readers on their toes!

With her family's continued encouragement—especially that of her hubby and kids—she diligently moves from one novel to the next, hoping to introduce new, entertaining and intriguing characters.

Artist loves to hear from her readers and can be reached via email at **acarthur22@yahoo.com.**

2006 Publication Schedule

January

A Lover's Legacy
Veronica Parker
1-58571-167-5
$9.95

Love Lasts Forever
Dominiqua Douglas
1-58571-187-X
$9.95

Under the Cherry
  Moon
Christal Jordan-Mims
1-58571-169-1
$12.95

February

Second Chances at Love
Cheris Hodges
1-58571-188-8
$9.95

Enchanted Desire
Wanda Y. Thomas
1-58571-176-4
$9.95

Caught Up
Deatri King Bey
1-58571-178-0
$12.95

March

I'm Gonna Make You
  Love Me
Gwyneth Bolton
1-58571-181-0
$9.95

Through the Fire
Seressia Glass
1-58571-173-X
$9.95

Notes When Summer
  Ends
Beverly Lauderdale
1-58571-180-2
$12.95

April

Sin and Surrender
J.M. Jeffries
1-58571-189-6
$9.95

Unearthing Passions
Elaine Sims
1-58571-184-5
$9.95

Between Tears
Pamela Ridley
1-58571-179-9
$12.95

May

Misty Blue
Dyanne Davis
1-58571-186-1
$9.95

Ironic
Pamela Leigh Starr
1-58571-168-3
$9.95

Cricket's Serenade
Carolita Blythe
1-58571-183-7
$12.95

June

Cupid
Barbara Keaton
1-58571-174-8
$9.95

Havana Sunrise
Kymberly Hunt
1-58571-182-9
$9.95

2006 Publication Schedule (continued)

July

Love Me Carefully	No Ordinary Love	Rehoboth Road
A. C. Arthur	Angela Weaver	Anita Ballard-Jones
1-58571-177-2	1-58571-198-5	1-58571-196-9
$9.95	$9.95	$12.95

August

Scent of Rain	Love in High Gear	Rise of the Phoenix
Annetta P. Lee	Charlotte Roy	Kenneth Whetstone
158571-199-3	158571-185-3	1-58571-197-7
$9.95	$9.95	$12.95

September

The Business of Love	Rock Star	A Dead Man Speaks
Cheris Hodges	Rosyln Hardy Holcomb	Lisa Jones Johnson
1-58571-193-4	1-58571-200-0	1-58571-203-5
$9.95	$9.95	$12.95

October

Rivers of the Soul-Part 1	A Dangerous Woman	Sinful Intentions
Leslie Esdaile	J.M. Jeffries	Crystal Rhodes
1-58571-223-X	1-58571-195-0	1-58571-201-9
$9.95	$9.95	$12.95

November

Only You	Ebony Eyes	Still Waters Run Deep – Part 2
Crystal Hubbard	Kei Swanson	Leslie Esdaile
1-58571-208-6	1-58571-194-2	1-58571-224-8
$9.95	$9.95	$9.95

December

Let's Get It On	Nights Over Egypt	A Pefect Place to Pray
Dyanne Davis	Barbara Keaton	I.L. Goodwin
1-58571-210-8	1-58571-192-6	1-58571-202-7
$9.95	$9.95	$12.95

LOVE ME CAREFULLY

Other Genesis Press, Inc. Titles

A Dangerous Deception	J.M. Jeffries	$8.95
A Dangerous Love	J.M. Jeffries	$8.95
A Dangerous Obsession	J.M. Jeffries	$8.95
A Drummer's Beat to Mend	Kei Swanson	$9.95
A Happy Life	Charlotte Harris	$9.95
A Heart's Awakening	Veronica Parker	$9.95
A Lark on the Wing	Phyliss Hamilton	$9.95
A Love of Her Own	Cheris F. Hodges	$9.95
A Love to Cherish	Beverly Clark	$8.95
A Risk of Rain	Dar Tomlinson	$8.95
A Twist of Fate	Beverly Clark	$8.95
A Will to Love	Angie Daniels	$9.95
Acquisitions	Kimberley White	$8.95
Across	Carol Payne	$12.95
After the Vows	Leslie Esdaile	$10.95
(Summer Anthology)	T.T. Henderson	
	Jacqueline Thomas	
Again My Love	Kayla Perrin	$10.95
Against the Wind	Gwynne Forster	$8.95
All I Ask	Barbara Keaton	$8.95
Ambrosia	T.T. Henderson	$8.95
An Unfinished Love Affair	Barbara Keaton	$8.95
And Then Came You	Dorothy Elizabeth Love	$8.95
Angel's Paradise	Janice Angelique	$9.95
At Last	Lisa G. Riley	$8.95
Best of Friends	Natalie Dunbar	$8.95
Beyond the Rapture	Beverly Clark	$9.95
Blaze	Barbara Keaton	$9.95
Blood Lust	J. M. Jeffries	$9.95
Bodyguard	Andrea Jackson	$9.95
Boss of Me	Diana Nyad	$8.95
Bound by Love	Beverly Clark	$8.95
Breeze	Robin Hampton Allen	$10.95

Other Genesis Press, Inc. Titles (continued)

Broken	Dar Tomlinson	$24.95
By Design	Barbara Keaton	$8.95
Cajun Heat	Charlene Berry	$8.95
Careless Whispers	Rochelle Alers	$8.95
Cats & Other Tales	Marilyn Wagner	$8.95
Caught in a Trap	Andre Michelle	$8.95
Caught Up In the Rapture	Lisa G. Riley	$9.95
Cautious Heart	Cheris F Hodges	$8.95
Chances	Pamela Leigh Starr	$8.95
Cherish the Flame	Beverly Clark	$8.95
Class Reunion	Irma Jenkins/John Brown	$12.95
Code Name: Diva	J.M. Jeffries	$9.95
Conquering Dr. Wexler's Heart	Kimberley White	$9.95
Crossing Paths, Tempting Memories	Dorothy Elizabeth Love	$9.95
Cypress Whisperings	Phyllis Hamilton	$8.95
Dark Embrace	Crystal Wilson Harris	$8.95
Dark Storm Rising	Chinelu Moore	$10.95
Daughter of the Wind	Joan Xian	$8.95
Deadly Sacrifice	Jack Kean	$22.95
Designer Passion	Dar Tomlinson	$8.95
Dreamtective	Liz Swados	$5.95
Ebony Butterfly II	Delilah Dawson	$14.95
Echoes of Yesterday	Beverly Clark	$9.95
Eden's Garden	Elizabeth Rose	$8.95
Everlastin' Love	Gay G. Gunn	$8.95
Everlasting Moments	Dorothy Elizabeth Love	$8.95
Everything and More	Sinclair Lebeau	$8.95
Everything but Love	Natalie Dunbar	$8.95
Eve's Prescription	Edwina Martin Arnold	$8.95
Falling	Natalie Dunbar	$9.95
Fate	Pamela Leigh Starr	$8.95
Finding Isabella	A.J. Garrotto	$8.95

Other Genesis Press, Inc. Titles (continued)

Forbidden Quest	Dar Tomlinson	$10.95
Forever Love	Wanda Thomas	$8.95
From the Ashes	Kathleen Suzanne	$8.95
	Jeanne Sumerix	
Gentle Yearning	Rochelle Alers	$10.95
Glory of Love	Sinclair LeBeau	$10.95
Go Gentle into that Good Night	Malcom Boyd	$12.95
Goldengroove	Mary Beth Craft	$16.95
Groove, Bang, and Jive	Steve Cannon	$8.99
Hand in Glove	Andrea Jackson	$9.95
Hard to Love	Kimberley White	$9.95
Hart & Soul	Angie Daniels	$8.95
Heartbeat	Stephanie Bedwell-Grime	$8.95
Hearts Remember	M. Loui Quezada	$8.95
Hidden Memories	Robin Allen	$10.95
Higher Ground	Leah Latimer	$19.95
Hitler, the War, and the Pope	Ronald Rychiak	$26.95
How to Write a Romance	Kathryn Falk	$18.95
I Married a Reclining Chair	Lisa M. Fuhs	$8.95
Indigo After Dark Vol. I	Nia Dixon/Angelique	$10.95
Indigo After Dark Vol. II	Dolores Bundy/Cole Riley	$10.95
Indigo After Dark Vol. III	Montana Blue/Coco Morena	$10.95
Indigo After Dark Vol. IV	Cassandra Colt/	$14.95
	Diana Richeaux	
Indigo After Dark Vol. V	Delilah Dawson	$14.95
Icie	Pamela Leigh Starr	$8.95
I'll Be Your Shelter	Giselle Carmichael	$8.95
I'll Paint a Sun	A.J. Garrotto	$9.95
Illusions	Pamela Leigh Starr	$8.95
Indiscretions	Donna Hill	$8.95
Intentional Mistakes	Michele Sudler	$9.95
Interlude	Donna Hill	$8.95
Intimate Intentions	Angie Daniels	$8.95

Other Genesis Press, Inc. Titles (continued)

Jolie's Surrender	Edwina Martin-Arnold	$8.95
Kiss or Keep	Debra Phillips	$8.95
Lace	Giselle Carmichael	$9.95
Last Train to Memphis	Elsa Cook	$12.95
Lasting Valor	Ken Olsen	$24.95
Let Us Prey	Hunter Lundy	$25.95
Life Is Never As It Seems	J.J. Michael	$12.95
Lighter Shade of Brown	Vicki Andrews	$8.95
Love Always	Mildred E. Riley	$10.95
Love Doesn't Come Easy	Charlyne Dickerson	$8.95
Love Unveiled	Gloria Greene	$10.95
Love's Deception	Charlene Berry	$10.95
Love's Destiny	M. Loui Quezada	$8.95
Mae's Promise	Melody Walcott	$8.95
Magnolia Sunset	Giselle Carmichael	$8.95
Matters of Life and Death	Lesego Malepe, Ph.D.	$15.95
Meant to Be	Jeanne Sumerix	$8.95
Midnight Clear	Leslie Esdaile	$10.95
(Anthology)	Gwynne Forster	
	Carmen Green	
	Monica Jackson	
Midnight Magic	Gwynne Forster	$8.95
Midnight Peril	Vicki Andrews	$10.95
Misconceptions	Pamela Leigh Starr	$9.95
Montgomery's Children	Richard Perry	$14.95
My Buffalo Soldier	Barbara B. K. Reeves	$8.95
Naked Soul	Gwynne Forster	$8.95
Next to Last Chance	Louisa Dixon	$24.95
No Apologies	Seressia Glass	$8.95
No Commitment Required	Seressia Glass	$8.95
No Regrets	Mildred E. Riley	$8.95
Nowhere to Run	Gay G. Gunn	$10.95
O Bed! O Breakfast!	Rob Kuehnle	$14.95

Other Genesis Press, Inc. Titles (continued)

Object of His Desire	A. C. Arthur	$8.95
Office Policy	A. C. Arthur	$9.95
Once in a Blue Moon	Dorianne Cole	$9.95
One Day at a Time	Bella McFarland	$8.95
Outside Chance	Louisa Dixon	$24.95
Passion	T.T. Henderson	$10.95
Passion's Blood	Cherif Fortin	$22.95
Passion's Journey	Wanda Thomas	$8.95
Past Promises	Jahmel West	$8.95
Path of Fire	T.T. Henderson	$8.95
Path of Thorns	Annetta P. Lee	$9.95
Peace Be Still	Colette Haywood	$12.95
Picture Perfect	Reon Carter	$8.95
Playing for Keeps	Stephanie Salinas	$8.95
Pride & Joi	Gay G. Gunn	$15.95
Pride & Joi	Gay G. Gunn	$8.95
Promises to Keep	Alicia Wiggins	$8.95
Quiet Storm	Donna Hill	$10.95
Reckless Surrender	Rochelle Alers	$6.95
Red Polka Dot in a World of Plaid	Varian Johnson	$12.95
Reluctant Captive	Joyce Jackson	$8.95
Rendezvous with Fate	Jeanne Sumerix	$8.95
Revelations	Cheris F. Hodges	$8.95
Rivers of the Soul	Leslie Esdaile	$8.95
Rocky Mountain Romance	Kathleen Suzanne	$8.95
Rooms of the Heart	Donna Hill	$8.95
Rough on Rats and Tough on Cats	Chris Parker	$12.95
Secret Library Vol. 1	Nina Sheridan	$18.95
Secret Library Vol. 2	Cassandra Colt	$8.95
Shades of Brown	Denise Becker	$8.95
Shades of Desire	Monica White	$8.95

Other Genesis Press, Inc. Titles (continued)

Shadows in the Moonlight	Jeanne Sumerix	$8.95
Sin	Crystal Rhodes	$8.95
So Amazing	Sinclair LeBeau	$8.95
Somebody's Someone	Sinclair LeBeau	$8.95
Someone to Love	Alicia Wiggins	$8.95
Song in the Park	Martin Brant	$15.95
Soul Eyes	Wayne L. Wilson	$12.95
Soul to Soul	Donna Hill	$8.95
Southern Comfort	J.M. Jeffries	$8.95
Still the Storm	Sharon Robinson	$8.95
Still Waters Run Deep	Leslie Esdaile	$8.95
Stories to Excite You	Anna Forrest/Divine	$14.95
Subtle Secrets	Wanda Y. Thomas	$8.95
Suddenly You	Crystal Hubbard	$9.95
Sweet Repercussions	Kimberley White	$9.95
Sweet Tomorrows	Kimberly White	$8.95
Taken by You	Dorothy Elizabeth Love	$9.95
Tattooed Tears	T. T. Henderson	$8.95
The Color Line	Lizzette Grayson Carter	$9.95
The Color of Trouble	Dyanne Davis	$8.95
The Disappearance of Allison Jones	Kayla Perrin	$5.95
The Honey Dipper's Legacy	Pannell-Allen	$14.95
The Joker's Love Tune	Sidney Rickman	$15.95
The Little Pretender	Barbara Cartland	$10.95
The Love We Had	Natalie Dunbar	$8.95
The Man Who Could Fly	Bob & Milana Beamon	$18.95
The Missing Link	Charlyne Dickerson	$8.95
The Price of Love	Sinclair LeBeau	$8.95
The Smoking Life	Ilene Barth	$29.95
The Words of the Pitcher	Kei Swanson	$8.95
Three Wishes	Seressia Glass	$8.95
Ties That Bind	Kathleen Suzanne	$8.95
Tiger Woods	Libby Hughes	$5.95

Other Genesis Press, Inc. Titles (continued)

Time is of the Essence	Angie Daniels	$9.95
Timeless Devotion	Bella McFarland	$9.95
Tomorrow's Promise	Leslie Esdaile	$8.95
Truly Inseparable	Wanda Y. Thomas	$8.95
Unbreak My Heart	Dar Tomlinson	$8.95
Uncommon Prayer	Kenneth Swanson	$9.95
Unconditional	A. C. Arthur	$9.95
Unconditional Love	Alicia Wiggins	$8.95
Until Death Do Us Part	Susan Paul	$8.95
Vows of Passion	Bella McFarland	$9.95
Wedding Gown	Dyanne Davis	$8.95
What's Under Benjamin's Bed	Sandra Schaffer	$8.95
When Dreams Float	Dorothy Elizabeth Love	$8.95
Whispers in the Night	Dorothy Elizabeth Love	$8.95
Whispers in the Sand	LaFlorya Gauthier	$10.95
Wild Ravens	Altonya Washington	$9.95
Yesterday Is Gone	Beverly Clark	$10.95
Yesterday's Dreams, Tomorrow's Promises	Reon Laudat	$8.95
Your Precious Love	Sinclair LeBeau	$8.95

Order Form

Mail to: Genesis Press, Inc.
P.O. Box 101
Columbus, MS 39703

Name _____
Address _____
City/State _____ Zip _____
Telephone _____

Ship to (if different from above)
Name _____
Address _____
City/State _____ Zip _____
Telephone _____

Credit Card Information
Credit Card # _____ ☐ Visa   ☐ Mastercard
Expiration Date (mm/yy) _____ ☐ AmEx   ☐ Discover

Qty.	Author	Title	Price	Total

Use this order	Total for books	_____
form, or call	**Shipping and handling:** $5 first two books, $1 each additional book	_____
1-888-INDIGO-1	Total S & H	_____
	Total amount enclosed	_____

Mississippi residents add 7% sales tax